# DARK MATTERS

## A CLASS 5 NOVEL

MICHELLE DIENER

Copyright © 2019 by Michelle Diener

All rights reserved.

No part of this book may be reproduced in any form or by any electronic or mechanical means, including information storage and retrieval systems, without written permission from the author, except for the use of brief quotations in a book review.

This is a work of fiction and all names, people, places and incidents are either used fictitiously or are a product of the author's imagination.

 Created with Vellum

*To every reader who wrote to ask me if I would please write another book in the Class 5 series, this one is for you.*

# ABOUT DARK MATTERS

*DARK MATTERS . . . taking matters into her own hands*

**A time bomb, waiting to go off . . .**

Lucy Harris is on the run, not sure where she can turn to for help, or if help is even available. But even as her abductors chase her down, she realizes they don't just want to recapture her, they want to erase her.

When your very existence puts a planet at the risk of war, there's no choice but to do everything in your power to stay out of your enemies hands.

**A predator . . . waiting for the chance to pounce**

The powerful AI battleship, Bane, is accompanying the United Council envoy to Tecra to mete out the punishment the Tecrans have earned for breaking UC law. He revels in the power he's about to have over his old masters. But his mission isn't only to rain down retribution on the people who kept him chained for years, he's also looking for a human woman his fellow Class 5 mentioned in the final seconds of his life. Paxe admitted to taking Lucy Harris from Earth, and Bane has been looking for her ever since.

*A warrior conflicted . . .*

Commander Dray Helvan thinks the Grih made a mistake in not pushing for war with the Tecran, but he's had to accept the compromise, that he and the other envoys from the United Council will go to Tecra and dismantle its military from the top down. His mission is not one of his choosing, but when he and his team arrive, he's handed a very different job. While he distrusts Bane on principle, when the thinking system tells him there's a woman running for her life on the planet below, he will do whatever he has to to see her safe. And if that means war for Tecra, well, then it means war.

# CHAPTER 1

THE DOOR SWUNG OPEN, the sound of it jerking Lucy from a light sleep.

A light bloomed and then was dropped with a soft curse. In the twist and tumble of its fall, she caught a glimpse of Dr. Farnn, pressed against the wall, a strange dark splatter pattern across the pale green of her shirt.

The dropped light hit the ground and rolled a little, illuminating Dr. Farnn's feet, and then the doctor slid down and sat on the floor.

Lucy swung her legs over the side of her bed, heart hammering in her chest. "What is it?" Her voice was a whisper.

Dr. Farnn lifted a hand for quiet, looked toward the door, and Lucy thought she heard someone scream down the passageway.

The sound galvanized the doctor. She pushed herself back up to standing, her breath coming in pants. "You need to go."

Lucy shoved her feet into the thin shoes beside her bed. "Go where?"

There was nowhere for her *to* go. That had been made clear to her.

"Hurry." Dr. Farnn bent to retrieve the light.

"Why? What's happened?" She was right next to the doctor now, and she saw what she'd thought was a pattern on Farnn's shirt was blood spatter. Dr. Farnn was covered in blood.

Lucy stared at her in shock.

A tiny cry escaped the doctor's throat, her beak-like mouth opening and then snapping shut, and she pointed the light in Lucy's eyes. "Move."

Lucy blinked, blinded, the scent of blood, the stink of sweat, enveloping her.

"No! Wait!"

She stopped, felt the rough pull as Dr. Farnn grabbed the necklace she'd been given more than six weeks ago, and tried to snap its chain.

It didn't break easily, but after another yank, Lucy felt it slither across her skin and then the ting of sound as it landed on the floor.

"Why?" She had always wondered about the gift.

"Tracker." Farnn didn't even try to sound apologetic. "It was either that or embed it in you. In fact, they think we *did* embed it." She drew in a deep breath. "We have to go. Now."

The door swung open.

"Here's my pass, this will get you out." Dr. Farnn shoved the slim card at her.

Lucy looked at it in the dim light of the corridor but didn't take it, even though only yesterday she'd have grabbed it with both hands if it had been offered to her. "First tell me what's going on."

"There's no time to explain." Farnn looked down the passage. "Cantin and Rool are holding them up, they've blocked the door into this section. We have seconds." Her big eyes gleamed in the reflected light from her tiny flashlight. She was shaking, Lucy realized, and shivered herself. "You need to run and hide. If they find you, they'll kill you."

"Kill me?" Her voice rose and Farnn winced. "Who's *they*?"

"Shh." Farnn tilted her head, listening for a moment. "They

sent you here, asked us to work with you, and now they think if they make you disappear, make all of us disappear, that'll clean up the mess they've made."

She grabbed Lucy's arm and pulled her down toward the far end of the facility.

Lucy heard a crash in the opposite direction and Farnn switched off her light. In the brief moment before it winked out, Lucy caught a glimpse of the doctor's face before they were plunged into darkness—she was terrified.

They ran in silence for less than a minute and then Farnn stopped and touched her shoulder, pointed to a door lit with a thin strip of floor lighting.

Before she could say anything, there was a thud of boots running toward them. "My hover is the one with the red wing." Farnn shoved the pass into Lucy's hand, pushed her toward the door and ran on.

Lucy stumbled forward, shouldered through the door, and found herself in a garage full of small hovers.

She forced herself to move, even though she wanted to stand and gawk.

There! Three down from the door. A silver hover with a red wing on the side.

She ran to it, pulled herself in.

She was a little shorter than the Tecran, but not by much. She had never been in a real hover, but she had flown a virtual one almost every day for the last three weeks, racing the doctors and scientists in the game they all seemed to enjoy.

Had they known this moment was coming? Had they been preparing her for this?

She shook her head, slid Farnn's pass into a slot that seemed designed for it, and started up the hover.

As far as she could see, the controls seemed the same as the game. Rool had told her when he'd first introduced her to the game that playing it was just like driving the real thing.

She maneuvered through the parked hovers in her way, and then drove straight for the closed door that was surely the exit, and when she got close enough it started to open. She eased back on the throttle, trying to make as little noise as possible, drifting forward as the hinged door swung up. Just when there was enough space to fit through, she heard a sound behind her and glanced back.

Four Tecran—strangers to her—burst through the door from the corridor, weapons in their hands.

She faced forward again, panic making her heart leap in her chest, and punched the accelerator.

She shot out into a cold, foggy night, the acceleration forcing her back in her seat.

The road from the garage was short, ending abruptly in a T junction and stretching left and right. She heard shouting behind her and she was about to choose a direction, her hands uncertain on the controls, when something hot sliced past her cheek on the left, then another close to her hip on the right, forcing her to continue on straight, over the rough ground beyond the road's end.

She caught the sudden flash of rock and bush below the hover, and then she was suddenly airborne, a bank of fog blocking any view of what lay ahead.

The hover dropped.

She screamed, the sound wrenched from her as she went into free fall.

The wind snatched the scream from her mouth, making her breathless, and then suddenly she was through the fog bank, below it, and the hover's lights, as well as lights that came from somewhere to the right, showed her just what was happening.

She was falling down the side of a cliff toward the sea below.

She couldn't scream again, the sound frozen in her throat as she dropped, as she realized the height of the fall. She blinked watery eyes to make out the rough waves surging below her.

Self-preservation suddenly kicked in.

She knew what to do!

Knew from the racing game she'd played at the facility that the hover needed the ground to be at least five meters below it to fly.

She had to strap in—snap out of her confusion and fear, and strap the fuck in.

She fumbled for the buttons, and the straps shot out, securing her in the seat, and then, with the foam of the waves close enough to blow up to catch on her slippers, she turned the hover hard right, swinging her body to tip it ninety degrees onto its side.

Gravity pulled at her, almost wrenching her hands from the controls, and foam flecked her hair and her cheeks. Suddenly she was driving sideways, using the cliff face as the ground to hold up her hover.

Rool and Ziller had shown her this trick right at the start of her introduction to the game and they'd laughed when she'd used it to win against some of the other scientists.

She felt the hover stabilize, speed up, and she punched the accelerator as hard as she could.

Behind her, she heard a massive boom, and red and orange light filtered through the fog above her.

The facility.

She almost lost her grip, almost plowed into the cliff face she was skimming, and the jerk of the hover jolted her back.

She'd wished herself free of that place many times, and she'd had an uncomfortable relationship with the scientists and doctors who had kept her there.

But tonight it seemed they'd sacrificed themselves to get her free. Although free from what was still something she didn't understand.

# CHAPTER 2

BANE EAVESDROPPED in on the first full meeting of the heads of the United Council team headed for Tecra. They were sitting around a large table in a conference room on the sleek spaceship *Urna,* and they were not a cohesive group.

They had spent the first few days of the journey talking to their own people, organizing their staff and getting to know one another.

This meeting was the first time the leaders were gathered together and he found the interplay of diplomacy and strategy fascinating.

Some were pleased by Bane's presence, as he paced beside the *Urna* in convoy with them, while others feared or despised him. The conversation, instead of being about the trouble ahead of them all in Tecra, circled back around to the need for him to accompany the *Urna,* and the resentment from some of the group that the Grih had gotten their way, that their request for Bane to participate in this mission had been granted.

He could tell some of the team guessed he might be spying on them from the way they responded to criticisms about him. The Grih, in particular, refused to comment. A few Bukari, as well.

There were leadership teams consisting of three representatives each from four of the five member groups of the United Council.

The Tecran had only been allowed one person, more in the capacity of liaison than decision-maker.

They'd lost the right to be a full stakeholder when they'd threatened to destabilize everything the United Council had worked for since the Thinking System Wars.

A war, Bane knew, fought against those just like himself.

That he occupied the moral high ground, and the Tecran were the villains, in this diplomatic nightmare that teetered on the brink of a new war, was thanks to Rose McKenzie and her advice when she'd set him free.

He had followed it against his instincts, and she hadn't steered him wrong.

He was theoretically the biggest threat, and yet, here he was, a legitimate party to the mission.

He was the trusted one, or mostly trusted. The Tecran were the ones to be punished.

After everything the Tecran had done to him, it satisfied something deep inside him.

His original plan of killing every Tecran in his reach would have been but a moment's worth of pleasure. Seeing them punished, and their power stripped from them, was much, much more satisfying.

And because he'd declared himself a neutral party when he'd been freed, because he hadn't aligned himself with the Grih as his brothers Sazo, Eazi and Oris had done, he was the one chosen to oversee this UC mandated power-stripping.

A neutral party.

If he had a mouth, it would be curved in a smile.

Everything about this was sweet.

So, so sweet.

The only thing sweeter would be if he could take at least one thing of significance from them, destroy it in front of their eyes so they understood the depths of his hatred.

He thought of Fa'allen, their capital city and a place he'd hovered over many times in his long servitude to the Tecran military, and wondered what they would do if he destroyed their most revered monument, the statue of Karn.

The tone of the conversation at the meeting had changed, he noticed, and at last the UC team stopped squabbling about him, and moved on to the human women the Tecran had abducted.

That led his thoughts down darker, more sinister paths.

Did he tell the UC team that there might be another woman from Earth still unaccounted for? A woman called Lucy Harris.

She'd definitely been taken.

Whether she was alive or not, he didn't know.

She might be on Tecra right now, hidden somewhere in the sprawling capital of Fa'allen.

If he told the UC leadership team about her, they would raise it with the Tecran. Then the secret would be out, and if she was still alive, the Tecran would have every incentive to kill her.

So he would have to bide his time.

Earth women had his respect.

Between Rose, and the other two women who'd been taken from their home, Fiona and Imogen, they had done nothing but help him and his brothers.

If he could find this last one and save her, he would, although logically Bane couldn't see why the Tecran would have kept her alive. Certainly not since three weeks ago when the UC had demanded full oversight of the Tecran military for the next five years.

As soon as the *Urna's* team and their hundreds of observers landed on Tecra and took over the controls of the Tecran military, it would be that much harder for the Tecran to hide anything.

Not impossible, but harder.

The woman *had* been taken, though. Whether she was alive or not, she had been taken. And the Tecran hadn't said a thing about it. Hadn't come clean and admitted it during the hearings that had recently concluded at UC headquarters.

Before Paxe, the fifth Class 5, had been destroyed, he'd sent Oris a confession. That he'd been responsible for taking a woman from Earth, only days before Oris himself had done the same thing.

And when she was onboard, he'd tried to kill her.

Which had been the start of Paxe's troubles. He'd shown his hand too early to his Tecran masters. Alerted them to his growing rebellion.

They'd worked out he was trying to harm her and transferred the woman to another ship to get her away from him.

Bane suspected she'd been light-jumped across the galaxy to Tecra.

Paxe had tried to keep track of her—with an eye to killing her if he got the chance.

That had never happened, and then Paxe had met Imogen, and realized he'd been wrong to try and hurt the woman he'd had in his hold. He'd been too embarrassed to tell Imogen what he'd tried to do, but moments before he died, he'd sent the information to Oris.

Bane guessed the Tecran thought Paxe had taken that secret with him when he'd been ripped to pieces. Or hoped he had. Hoped very hard.

Oris had shared what Paxe had told him with Sazo, Bane and Eazi. So far all four of them had kept it to themselves, carefully looking for any hint she'd survived, searching for information wherever they could find it.

If the information was out there, they would get it eventually.

Sazo had found a few strange reports from a research facility on the outskirts of Fa'allen that seemed promising, so Bane would start there, would get into the facility's systems when they arrived in Tecra in a day's time, and try to find her.

And in case he did track her down, he would have to decide who on the UC leadership team to trust, because he couldn't physically go down to Tecra and get her out himself. The three Grih, the military head of the Fitalian team, and one of the Bukari were currently at the top of his list, but he would choose carefully.

He would do nothing to endanger the woman more than she already was. And he would save her, if he could.

If it wasn't already too late.

And if they did have her, he would bring down the punishment they so richly deserved.

# CHAPTER 3

DRAY HELVAN LEFT the *Urna's* conference room alone—the first to make his escape.

He had an excuse, but it was just that, an excuse. He chose to prioritize the request sent to his comm unit from Grih Battle Center over the small talk that had broken out at the end of the meeting.

Sometimes, that's when the real business got done, during the informal chats after meetings, when people were less on their guard and every word they said wasn't being weighed.

Although Dray had a very strong feeling that every word of the small talk *was* being weighed and judged. He glanced to his left, out of the long transparent side of the ship, to look at Bane. The Class 5 was easily keeping pace with the *Urna*—in fact, they were probably slowing him down.

Something about Bane, the shape of him, or rather, the ship he inhabited—like a prickle ball from Dray's home planet of Xal—skewed Dray's thoughts. He felt a strange push and pull in his head.

He'd been raised on the notion of how dangerous thinking systems were, yet there was a fundamental Grihan connection to the Class 5s that drew him. They had been built according to the designs of the long-dead Xalian scientist, Fayir. Dray's fellow Xalian had certainly caused a lot of trouble hundreds of years after his death, but there was no going back to the way things had been.

The light jump, as the saying went, was already in motion.

Thinking systems were once again part of the UC's reality.

And that didn't sit well with some of the UC leadership team. Especially those who weren't Grihan, and didn't have the same relationship the Grih had with them.

"Dray."

The call came from behind him, and he just resisted making a face. He hadn't gotten away as cleanly as he'd thought.

"Yes, Ambassador." He turned smartly.

His fellow team leader was from the Grihan planet of Nastra, and she wore the flowing robes the Nastrans favored, the bright orange contrasting pleasantly with her warm brown skin and light brown hair tipped with gold.

"I told you, call me Yolandi, or I'll be forced to go back to calling you Commander."

Dray nodded, but said nothing. He preferred Battle Center's habit of referring to people by rank, but he would have to adjust. This wasn't Battle Center.

Yolandi sighed. "I don't know what you're thinking."

His lips quirked. "That I need to get out of my Battle Center habits. For years, my only family has been my colleagues in Battle Center, and I think I've become a little stuck in my ways. I'm not used to civilian life."

She tilted her head up to look at him, her eyes full of sympathy. He wanted to tell her he didn't need it. The friends and colleagues he trained and fought with, his created family, were more than enough for him.

"Titles aren't very helpful with the three of us, because we're all equal members." Yolandi worried her bottom lip. "But if Zutobi also prefers that—"

Dray shook his head. "She doesn't. It's good for me to change things up."

"Well, I think we'll be getting a lot of that where we're going." Yolandi smiled.

Dray grunted. That was an understatement, but diplomats like Yolandi seemed good at understatement.

Zutobi, from the Grihan planet Calianthra, was the administrator of the group, he was the soldier, Yolandi was the diplomat, and when they arrived on Tecra, they would be the most resented, perhaps the most in danger, of everyone on the UC team.

No planet liked to be dictated to, and the Tecran weren't just being dictated to. They were going to have to welcome invaders into their home, and let those invaders take the reins of control for five years. They would have to let the UC uncover every dark and dirty secret their military had hidden, not just from their fellow members of the United Council, but also their own people.

He could imagine there were plenty of Tecran with the same problem of push and pull in their brain that he had about the Class 5s.

They had been lied to by their own military, but would still resent being in the position of having strangers tell them what to do.

It would be a delicate balancing wire to walk.

Yolandi was going to be better than himself or Zutobi at that.

In fact, Zutobi was refreshingly direct in her speech, and seemed serenely unperturbed by the insult or outrage she caused by giving the facts.

He had enjoyed watching her cut through some of the crap in the meeting, and then watching Yolandi follow behind her administering first aid—metaphorically speaking—to sooth the burns.

"You were called away to the comms station?" Yolandi asked.

"Yes." He glanced behind her, saw some of the other UC leadership team were leaving the conference room as well. "You wanted to talk to me?"

"I'll walk with you." Yolandi smiled, not answering.

Dray started moving and she fell in with him. When they were far enough away from the rest of the leadership team, she cleared her throat delicately.

"I wanted to talk to you without being overheard."

Dray glanced over at Bane again, flying so close to the *Urna* that Dray could see the individual spikes that covered the outside of Bane's Class 5.

Yolandi must have caught the direction of his gaze.

"Hmm. Well, not overheard by the other members of the team. I can't do anything about Bane."

"Some would like to."

She sent him an amused sidelong look. "Quite a few, by the earful I got."

Dray shrugged. There was nothing to be done. Bane was here, at the Grih's request, and no one could send him back.

Any whining was just a waste of time.

"It's about one of those conversations I had concerning Bane that I want to talk to you about." Yolandi's voice dropped, so Dray had to lean closer to hear her. "The Fitalian ambassador on the team, Pilto, put in a request that we ask Bane to hang back a bit when we get to Tecra and stay out of sight of the planet. He seems to think Bane orbiting overhead like a third moon will be seen as an aggressive tactic. Some sort of intimidation."

Dray just lifted his brows.

Yolandi blew out a breath. "And that's just what he is, isn't he? The big stick to our . . . smaller stick." Her lips pressed together.

She was right that there was no sweetener involved in this mission. No possible way the Tecran could see their arrival as anything other than a punishment.

Except . . . "The sweetener is they get to stay in the UC, and not be at war with the rest of us."

"Not taking something away that they already have isn't a very compelling sweetener." Yolandi sighed. "You think Bane will refuse?"

"I refuse to ask him. Bane looming over Tecra is exactly the kind of power move we need to make it clear we aren't messing around and we have the means to enforce the agreement they signed if we have to. It'll save all kinds of stupid power plays."

"What should I say to Pilto?"

Technically, none of the Grih had any special access to Bane, and Dray hadn't been designated as the liaison between the Grih and the thinking system, but he understood why Yolandi had approached him. He was from Battle Center, and almost every interaction Bane and his fellow thinking systems had had with the Grih had been through the military.

"Tell him no. And if he wants to argue the point, he can come and speak to me."

Yolandi sighed and nodded. "I'll avoid him as long as possible and then send him your way if he persists. Thank you, Dray."

She gave a small wave and turned off toward the staterooms the main leaders had been given to sleep in, and Dray carried on to the comms station.

There was a faint ping in his earpiece, and he lifted a hand to accept the incoming communication.

"I'm in full agreement."

Dray was so surprised by the comm he almost missed the second ping indicating the comm had been dropped.

He didn't recognize the voice, but he had a feeling he had just heard from Bane.

He stopped, turned to look out of the clear wall toward the Class 5. A light on the deadly prickle ball winked back at him.

# CHAPTER 4

THE SOUND of two hovers passed by, their powerful engines a hum in the thick fog, their speed almost a crawl.

Lucy curled tighter around herself, pushing back into the cold, damp corner of the garage she had found as a hiding place.

They were hunting her.

Or perhaps covering all their bases, because she still hoped they thought she'd gone into the sea.

The interesting thing was that they were very quiet in their hunting.

They weren't storming doors and striding around.

They were creeping.

They were hiding the fact that they were hunting at all.

That would give her an advantage if they caught her in a public place. They wanted to avoid attention, and she'd take any help she could get.

The sound of the engines faded and she slowly stood up and waited another ten minutes but they didn't return. Finally she shuffled through the garage, looking through the hovers parked there for anything that could help her.

She'd parked Farnn's at the far end of the slightly shabby

space. She didn't know what her plans were, but she wanted to keep the hover somewhere she could come back to if she needed it.

In one of the hovers near the door, a much older and more battered model than Farnn's, there was a cloak, a medieval looking garment with a fastening that clipped under her chin. She had noticed a few hanging in the staff lounge in the facility as she'd been marched past the door.

The cloaks were obviously the fashion in Tecra.

She pulled it on, and began shivering even harder as the warmth enveloped her.

The hem hit the tops of her feet, and she became aware that she could barely feel her feet now, the thin slippers she'd been given to wear in the facility useless against the cold, hard floor.

She worked her way through the rest of the hovers, wondering why they were all open, with no roof or way to enclose them like a car.

It must be something to do with the Tecrans' love of open skies.

They were obviously close evolutionary cousins to birds, or at least bird-like creatures, and she guessed they liked to feel the wind on their faces.

She, on the other hand, would be happy to stay out of the wind, find a warm place to curl up in, and sleep.

By the time she'd reached the last hover, she'd found a scarf and a small blanket made of something very soft, but nothing more.

She looked over the garage, aware that her movements were sluggish, that she was swaying on her feet.

There was nowhere to lie down, and the thought of lowering herself back to the icy floor sent a shiver through her.

She shuffled back out the small side door she'd found open, and took a better look at the building attached to it.

There was no sound except for the suck and surge of the waves far below at the foot of the cliff, and the fog wrapped around her, icy and suffocating. She would have to step carefully. She knew the edge of the cliff wasn't far away, but the fog obscured everything.

It also completely shrouded the building to her right, but a few small lights were strong enough to penetrate, their glow diffused by the swirling cloud.

Lucy moved cautiously toward them, and found they were on either side of a set of stairs.

She climbed up them, finding the staircase strangely deep and narrow.

She stumbled a few times, and at the top found a large set of doors, which would not open.

Above the doors was a carving, something that looked art deco in style to her eye, which she couldn't make out well, but seemed to be a hooded hawk, wearing a cloak much like the one she had stolen from the garage.

She had the blanket she'd found clutched to her chest, but she knew she would need to find somewhere to sit and wrap her feet in it before she lost feeling in them altogether.

There was a narrow walkway leading around the building, to the left and the right, with no railing. Lacking any other option, Lucy followed it right, keeping close to the wall to make sure she didn't fall off.

The fog seemed to thicken, and as she made her way around the side of the building the sound of the waves grew louder.

If she did fall, she guessed it would be to the bottom of the cliff.

The walkway ended abruptly in a small door set in a wall that seemed to stretch up forever.

She stared at it, trying to think what to do, and then turned her head as lights seemed to bloom to her right.

She blinked, sure she must be hallucinating, but after a

moment, she realized the fog had cleared, giving her a view down the length of the cliffs.

In the distance she saw tall buildings, lights blazing from them as they rose up out of the cliffs. Further along she could see a city of sorts, where the buildings stood two or three rows deep.

Just as suddenly as the fog had parted, it closed in again, leaving her with nothing but a vague glow in the distance.

She shook her head, concentrated on what was in front of her again, and pushed at the door.

It swung open, and in what little ambient light she had, she made out some kind of storage shed.

She was out of options, so she stepped inside, crouching down in the doorway to feel for something to prop the door open with.

The idea of it enclosing her in complete darkness was too much.

Eventually she found something long and thin to keep the door open a little.

She sank down on the floor near the door, leaning up against the wall. Cool, damp air blew over her through the thin crack. It chilled her face, but she wound the scarf up to cover her mouth and nose and the fresh air helped dissipate the smell of dust and mold. She sneezed, pulled the cloak around her, wrapped her feet in the blanket, and closed her eyes.

THE TECRAN MET the *Urna* with a full envoy a day's journey from Tecra. The five massive Levron battleships coming toward the UC ship were the most powerful the Tecran had in their arsenal now that the Class 5s were no longer theirs.

If it was meant to be intimidating, Dray thought, it was successful.

A hush came over the crew as soon as the envoy was picked up by the *Urna's* systems, and a fair crowd had gathered in the large communal area of the ship to watch them arrive.

"Do you think this is all the Levrons the Tecran have left after the battles we had with them?" Zutobi leaned closer to Dray, her voice soft.

Dray lifted his shoulders. "Maybe." Five were not enough to police the massive Tecran space boundaries. "I don't know if I hope it is, or not. They can't keep their people safe with so few."

"Word is, they poured every resource they had into building the Class 5s. They cut back on Levron production. They don't have any in construction to replace those we destroyed when they attacked us." Zutobi leaned forward to get a better look. "What flight configuration is that?"

Dray scanned the five ships moving toward them, three in the front, two in the back.

To him, it looked like an attack configuration. And that's probably what the Tecran were going for.

They had to be feeling more than a little sensitive about having their military and government run by strangers for the next five years.

They couldn't help flexing a little muscle, perhaps.

They would be very much aware that every battleship in the United Coalition would descend on Tecra if anything happened to the UC teams coming to take the reins.

Although it would be cold comfort to him and everyone else onboard the *Urna* to know their deaths would be avenged.

Suddenly Bane, who'd been lurking beside the *Urna* like a large wrecking ball, moved forward, and faster almost than the eye could track, flew up and over the Tecran envoy and settled into place behind them.

There were audible gasps among the crowd.

"The weapons on the back two Levron are hot, and being

shielded to disguise the fact." The words in Dray's ear surprised him enough that he jerked.

Bane.

He drew in a breath. "I'll pass that on."

His murmured response had Zutobi glancing at him with a frown.

He began moving through the throng, looking for the head of the UC leadership team.

Around him, he could hear the tension in people's voices as they speculated about what was happening.

There was no one here who didn't understand they stood on the very knife edge of violence.

"Wait before you do anything." He spoke conversationally, hoping Bane was still listening, but tension coiled in his gut. He didn't know how to exert any control over a thinking system. They had no Earth women with them, and he wondered now whether that had been a mistake.

Someone like Rose McKenzie would know what to do. More to the point, Bane would at least consider what she had to say.

He caught sight of Filavantri Dimitara, the head of their delegation, as the crowd swirled around her. She was Bukarian, chosen to lead the council team because she had been one of the first councilors to see firsthand what the Tecran had done with the Earth women and the thinking systems they'd built into the Class 5 battleships.

It had been decided that the Grih couldn't lead this delegation. Shots had been fired between them and the Tecran, and no one believed they'd be objective. But the Bukari had a reputation for evenhandedness, even if Dimitara was considered too attached to the Earth woman, Rose McKenzie, and perhaps less objective about the Tecran because of it.

The Tecran had tried to block her appointment on those grounds, but they just didn't have enough standing in the UC after everything that had happened, and Dimitara had been voted in unanimously by the other members.

"Ambassador." Dray interrupted the conversation Dimitara was having with one of the Fitalian members of their leadership group, Pilto. The one who'd requested that Bane hang back when they approached the Tecran.

He knew he had a suspicious mind, but Dray found himself looking at Pilto a little more carefully given the current circumstances.

"That thing is causing exactly the kind of chaos and ill will I suspected he would." Pilto flung a hand out toward the Tecran envoy. "Look at that."

"You don't think the Tecran were doing the same, coming at us in attack mode with five Levron?" Dimitara's question settled something in Dray's chest.

Their leader was no idiot.

He'd planned to draw Dimitara aside, but given the fuss Pilto had made, and the mutterings of agreement around him, he decided it would be useful for everyone to understand the benefits Bane brought with him.

"I have information that the rear two Levron are coming in with weapons hot, and they're shielding it."

Dimitara had turned when he'd addressed her by her title, but now she gave him her full attention. "How do you know this?"

Like Pilto, Dray gestured toward the envoy, and Bane.

Dimitara drew in a sharp breath. "He told you directly?"

Dray nodded.

The Fitalian ambassador's gaze moved between Dray and Bane, his eyes getting even wider than they were usually. "I thought he was neutral, not aligned with the Grih."

Dimitara turned on him, eyes flashing. "The Tecran are approaching us with their weapons hot and shielded, Bane has moved into a protective position to help us, and your take on the situation is jealousy that the information was passed on through the Grih?" The disbelief and disappointment in her tone had the effect of making the ambassador shuffle back a few steps.

When he had nothing to say, Dimitara dismissed him by turning her back on him and scanning the crowd. "Vauk!" Her call to the only Tecran representative on the team was loud enough to silence those around them.

The Tecran woman moved toward them reluctantly, aware of the avid eyes on her. She had been standing to one side, watching the Levron approach, and Dray could see the snap of temper in her eyes at being waved over.

"Why are some of those Levron coming in with weapons hot?" Dimitara didn't mince words.

Vauk blinked. "I'm sure that's not the case—"

"They're shielding, but that doesn't fool us. It certainly didn't fool Bane. Please explain." Dray noticed his words registered with most of the team members standing in earshot, and they all drew closer, faces serious.

"I—" Vauk tapped at her ear, and then turned away, murmuring in Tecran.

"I can hear chatter between the Tecran battleships." Bane's voice was soft in Dray's ear. "Some members of the military decided to try and launch an ambush. They weren't planning on shooting at the *Urna*, just me. This wasn't known to the political leaders who are present in the front three ships."

"Apologies for any distress caused," Vauk turned back to them, her face twisted in a false smile. "This is just standard practice when our Levron travel in convoy. No offense or harm was meant."

"No harm other than to Bane," Dray said.

Vauk blinked again.

"We know your military were planning to fire on him." Dray made sure he could be heard by everyone.

There were plenty here who resented Bane, and were more sympathetic to the Tecran than they deserved. He wanted all the Tecran's tricks out in the open, so no one was fooled.

"How dare you say that?" Vauk drew herself up. "What proof do you have—"

One side of the *Urna's* transparent wall became opaque, and then a visual comms of three Tecran generals discussing their strategy to shoot Bane played out across it.

There was dead silence when it finished.

"I've relayed the same clip to the Tecran politicians onboard the Levron and back home on Tecra." Bane's voice was dry, but Dray thought he heard the edge of glee in his tone. "As well as to UC headquarters."

Everyone's gaze swung to Vauk.

"I . . . didn't know! I'm not in the generals' confidence." She took a step back, turned on her heel and ran out of the viewing area.

"My guess is she's off to resign." Zutobi had moved in next to Dray again. She was watching the Tecran woman disappear down the passageway.

"The Tecran won't accept it. They can't lose her now, because the UC would need to appoint a new liaison, and that would take a few weeks. They won't want to have no eyes or ears in the leadership team that long."

Zutobi nodded at his words. "Then she's in for an unhappy time."

"Look, they're leaving." One of the Garmman delegates pointed toward their Tecran escort.

Sure enough, the two at the back had broken away from the other three, dropped down out of sight, and then Dray felt the faint buzz against his skin that told him they'd both light-jumped away.

He turned at the sound of voices, saw Dimitara was following a comms officer out of the viewing area toward the comms station.

Most likely, the Tecran wanted to smooth things over with her.

But they were already at a significant disadvantage with the UC leadership team now.

They had shown themselves to be a nation divided.

Bane drifted up and then over the remaining three Levron. He stayed directly above them for a long beat, and then lazily rolled back to his place next to the *Urna*.

As the crowd watched him, Dray thought he could sense awe, rather than fear, this time around.

# CHAPTER 5

A SHAFT of light woke her.

Lucy opened her eyes on a shiver.

She had spent a restless night, waking often, cold to her bones from the hard, icy floor and the sharp wind blowing through the door. Sometime around dawn she must have fallen into a deeper, exhausted sleep, because the Tecran sun had risen high enough to hit her in the face.

She closed her eyes and let warm orange light bloom behind her eyelids as she tried to absorb every bit of its meager heat.

The wind seemed to change, to find a newer, sharper cut, and she shivered again and stood.

She moved cautiously, stiff and achy from being curled up all night, and saw for the first time what was in the room she'd taken shelter in.

It looked like climbing gear, but higher tech than anything she'd seen on Earth. There were grapple hooks attached to what looked like crossbows hanging from hooks on the wall, along with loops of rope and strange gloves with small hooks on the palms and fingers.

She opened the door a little wider, and stepped out, cautiously pressing up against the high wall of the building as she eyed the narrow walkway and the sheer drop beyond it.

Now it was light, she could see for the first time that there was a small platform right near the storage room she'd hidden in that protruded out over the clifftop.

This must be where the Tecran suited up before climbing down the cliffs.

She shuddered, and brushed at the dust on the cloak she wore. She didn't do well with heights, although she had to admit the view was amazing.

The fog had completely dissipated and she could see everything. The sparkle off the water, the black rock of the cliffs, the green of the grass on the plateau and the astonishing, breathtaking buildings that grew out of the cliffs.

In what she guessed was the middle of the city, a massive statue rose up, set a little back from the cliff, with no buildings in front of it. It faced the sea, arms held out with palms cupped.

It stood head and shoulders higher than any of the buildings around it.

It represented a hawklike figure, hooded, and something about the positioning of its arms and hands made her think it was waiting for benediction as it gleamed silver in the morning light.

She'd seen something like it somewhere before, and then she remembered the small figure above the doors of the building she'd glimpsed last night. A tiny imitation of the real thing.

She stared at it in amazement for a long moment before the wind gusted a little harder and forced a cough from her.

She was still in her pajamas, and her feet, now she'd stepped out of the blanket she'd wrapped them in, were already freezing.

Before she went anywhere, she would have to find a solution to her footwear problem.

She pulled the door wider, letting in as much light as possible, and looked over what was inside the tiny space.

She found what looked like a soft shoe, and after a few minutes of searching, found its match.

She stepped back out to look at them properly, and decided even though they looked too big, she didn't have much choice but to wear them.

She sat down and pulled them on over her thin slippers and then yelped in fright when they tightened around her feet. After a moment of panic, she felt them loosen a little, so they fit her perfectly.

She stretched out both feet to look at them more carefully, and had to admit they were warm, but they looked strange, with tiny hooks all over them.

The Tecran must be mad if their idea of fun was hanging from a cliff with nothing but shoes and gloves with little hooks holding them up.

At least the soles were thick, and when she stood, she bounced a few times, enjoying the cushioning.

The wind shifted again, and she went still as she heard the murmur of voices.

The door behind her banged shut, and she winced as the voices cut off suddenly.

She dithered, torn between whether to hide in the tiny storeroom, knowing she'd be trapped if she went back in there, or stay where she was.

Suddenly, two Tecran stepped around the corner of the building, and came to a startled halt at the sight of her.

They didn't stick close to the wall as she had, and after a moment's hesitation, one of them, the man, began walking toward her right on the edge of the drop-off.

It seemed like he was coming at her fast.

Panic seized her, and she opened the door of her hidey-hole, leaned in, and grabbed one of the crossbow devices.

When she turned back, the Tecran was much closer, and his

face was slack with astonishment, the feather-like protrusions around his face standing up like a surprised owl.

Her scarf had slipped down around her neck, the hood of her cloak was off her head, and she realized he could not mistake her for a fellow Tecran. Her hair, the thing about her that seemed to most fascinate the Tecran scientists she'd come to know at the facility, was dancing around her head in the breeze.

She held the crossbow tightly to her chest, the grapple dangling awkwardly from the front of it.

"Be calm, we won't hurt you." He spoke slowly, as if he didn't expect her to understand him. His gaze kept moving from her face to her hair and back.

A woman came up behind him, her own expression wide-eyed with surprise, her beak-like mouth open. It occurred to Lucy that their very alien features no longer had much impact on her. It was all she'd seen for so long.

The woman blinked. "She's one of the ones they said . . ."

She trailed off, and the two exchanged a panicked look.

"What does 'I'm one of the ones' mean?" Lucy stared at them. They knew something about her?

They flinched in surprise when she spoke.

"You speak Tecran?" The woman's voice was soft with shock.

"I've been here for months." Lucy lifted her shoulders.

Again, the two shared a look.

"Can you tell me how you seem to know something about me?" Lucy clutched the crossbow a little tighter as they both shuffled back a few steps.

"The explosion. Last night." The woman ignored her, spoke to her companion as if she'd just realized something.

"Yes." He drew the word out. "That was a military facility." The man turned wary eyes back on Lucy. "This is not something I want to be mixed up in—"

The woman hesitated, then gave a nod.

They shuffled back a little more.

"Please, just tell me what you know." Lucy took a step toward them, and it seemed to galvanize the man. He turned, took hold of the woman's shoulders, and turned her as well.

As she gave Lucy one last parting glance, the woman lowered her eyes, as if she was embarrassed at their retreat, then she walked quickly back the way she'd come, the man close on her heels.

A moment later, Lucy was alone again, with nothing but the low moan of the wind and the spectacular view along the cliffs for company.

Those two had recognized her.

Or if not her, specifically, people from Earth. The woman had even made the connection with the facility.

Which meant, if they spoke to anyone, word would get out that she was here. And that would lead those hunting her right to her.

She had to go.

Go now.

She walked along the side of the building, keeping close to the wall again as the wind swirled around her, tugging at her cloak.

The ledge dropped off to the sea far, far below.

When she turned the corner, relieved to have solid ground in front of her, she saw the two people who'd found her talking to another Tecran, both of them gesticulating wildly to the newcomer.

They all went silent at the sight of her, and Lucy realized she was still clutching the crossbow.

She'd shot crossbows, and even longbows, for fun, but what was she going to do? Shoot someone with a grapple hook?

The idea was so ludicrous, she bent slowly and set it down on the ground at her feet.

The wind had kicked up another notch, and it blew her long hair wildly around her. Her cloak streamed behind her, revealing her body in her thin pajamas, and she could see from their expressions she was the strange, alien creature here. Not them.

"Please," she said, hearing the weariness in her own voice, "just tell me what you know about me and I'll be on my way."

"Do you have a credit bank?" the new Tecran asked.

"No." She didn't even know what the system of money was here. She'd been tucked up in the facility the whole time.

"I'll give you mine. It's got enough to last a couple of days on it. Go into the city. You'll find help there. For us . . ." He flicked a look at the other two. "It's a tricky thing. We might be seen as traitors if we help you." He lifted his hands, the fluff on his feathery arms ruffling in the wind.

"I have a credit bank on me." The woman who'd walked away from her dug into a pocket, and the man with her did the same.

They gave them both to the third man, who'd pulled out a colorful rectangle from his own pocket. He leaned forward and set them on the ground, as if scared to get closer.

Like they were afraid to touch her, or get too near her.

She frowned. "Are you frightened of me?"

She would need to know this if she was going into the crowds of the city.

They looked at each other uneasily.

"The scientists and doctors at the facility weren't afraid of me."

The woman closed her eyes. "Don't tell us anything about the facility."

"We aren't afraid," the new man slid both hands into his pockets. "It's just . . ." He eventually shrugged, unable or unwilling to explain.

"Good luck." The man who'd found her originally shuffled back toward the door of the building. "The zipu comes every five minutes and it'll take you all the way to the city. It's only a short walk along the path." He gestured to a meandering path that disappeared between two low, stunted trees. Then he turned and walked into the building.

After a moment of silence, the other two followed him, the woman glancing at her with a frown more than once.

Lucy waited until they had disappeared and then she scooped up the credits they'd left her.

It felt a little humiliating taking the thin, bright rectangles, each a colorful rainbow made of something similar to enamel, but she couldn't be picky. She hadn't eaten or drunk anything since last night, and the Tecran's version of money had to make things easier for her.

She contemplated the path, guessing the zipu they'd referred to was some form of public transport.

Did she take it, or did she use the hover?

She decided to have a look at the zipu first. She might stand out more on the hover.

And she knew where to find it if she wanted it back.

She looked over her shoulder at the closed door of the building, caught a glimpse of the three Tecran watching her through a narrow window, and turned back to the path. She straightened her shoulders and started walking.

# CHAPTER 6

"THAT CONFRONTATION earlier was a little too dramatic for my tastes." Filavantri Dimitara stared at Dray from across her desk, her big, dark brown eyes set in a slender, elongated face.

He didn't move, but Yolandi squirmed a little beside him.

Zutobi just made herself more comfortable in her chair.

All three of the Grihan leadership team members had been called into Dimitara's office after her conversation with the Tecran envoy, and no one needed to be a genius to guess why.

Dimitara sighed. "If only Bane had contacted me instead of you."

"Is his contacting Dray causing problems for you?" Yolandi asked.

Dimitara lifted her shoulders. "Everyone, from the Tecran to the UC team, already think you're too closely aligned with him, and this just reinforces that. Has he contacted you before?"

"Only once."

Everyone looked at him.

"Regarding Pilto, actually. The Fitalian ambassador was trying to get Yolandi to tell Bane to hang back when we met the Tecran envoy. Bane said he wouldn't."

"That's all?" Yolandi asked, eyebrows raised.

"That's all. A few words at most."

"All right." Dimitara blew out a breath. "I'm going to ignore that, then."

Dray folded his arms over his chest. "Given what happened when Bane did meet them, you'd have to wonder why Pilto wanted that. Did he know what was going to happen?"

Dimitara frowned. "What reason did Pilto give for wanting Bane to make himself scarce?"

"He said Bane's presence would be antagonistic, and if he hung back we'd make more progress with the Tecran than if he accompanied us," Yolandi answered.

Dimitara nodded. "That's what Pilto was saying to me just before we realized the back two Levron had their weapons trained on Bane, so I believe that's all there was to his request."

They were all silent a moment.

"Why are we here?" Dray stretched out his legs.

Dimitara lifted both of her slim, four-fingered hands. "The thing is, like Pilto, the Tecran have made a similar request that Bane stay out of sight. They are asking for him to hang back when we arrive at Tecra. They think him looming over the planet will cause panic."

"That wasn't the agreement." Dray had read every word of the contract that gave him and the rest of his colleagues the right to investigate the Tecran military and set up a structure to run Tecra for the next five years.

"I know, but I actually agree with them in this case. The Tecran are suffering a massive loss of face over this takeover. They also have some understanding of why the Class 5s might bear them ill will. Having Bane literally casting a shadow over their planet is going to really inspire fear and resentment, and that's going to make our jobs a lot harder."

"What did they say about the planned ambush on Bane?" Zutobi tapped a finger on Dimitara's desk.

"What you would expect them to have said. Rogue elements. Now under control. Blah, blah, blah." Dimitara's wry smile showed the row of sharp teeth in her mouth.

Sometimes Dray forgot about those teeth. The Bukari looked delicate and unimposing. Until they smiled.

"So now they want Bane to do them a favor? After some of their people were planning to shoot him?" Yolandi was outraged.

Dimitara funneled her fingers through her dark copper hair in frustration. "Yes. And I think that's what the covert action by those military officers was supposed to prevent. Even if they didn't get off a shot, they knew it would make asking Bane to hang back almost impossible."

"Does this make sense to you? Was the military trying to manipulate us all so that I wouldn't agree to hang back?" The quiet whisper in Dray's ear made him go completely still, and then he forced himself to relax.

"Someone in the military whose role in the Class 5 project might be exposed by our doing our jobs when we get down to Tecra, and who knew what the Tecran government envoy was going to ask of Bane, would probably think they couldn't lose, either way, with their plan to shoot at him. Whether they actually damaged him, or just tried to, the Tecran politicians would find it difficult to ask a favor of him afterward." Dray looked at Dimitara as he spoke, answering Bane's question while agreeing with her.

"It would certainly help people like that go undetected if our jobs are made harder because of resentment and lack of cooperation with the general Tecran population." Yolandi gave a decisive nod.

"So, will you speak to Bane?" Dimitara asked, and Dray could see she already looked exhausted, and they were still a day's journey from even reaching Tecra.

"I won't hang back, but I'll pretend to. There are two moons that circle Tecra. I'll land on Gyre, the larger one, and cloak myself." Bane's voice was calm. "I'll stay there unless I think I have to move, for whatever reason."

Dray wondered if Bane had spoken into all their earpieces, but no one reacted. His lips twisted, because this favoritism was going to ostracize him if it became well known.

"Bane says he'll make sure no one can see him." He didn't know why he didn't give Bane's exact location, but he was from Battle Center, and he never gave out information unnecessarily.

Dimitara gasped. "He's listening? Will he talk to me?"

Dray shrugged. "Ask him. I don't have any control over him. I thought he might have given his reply to everyone, but clearly not."

Dimitara grimaced. "Thank you for agreeing to this, Bane. It will help the team's objectives greatly. We appreciate it."

Dray could see Dimitara was hoping for an answer, but none came and she slumped down in her chair.

"I'm grateful he's so willing to be accommodating." She blew out a breath. "That is a huge concession, and it'll give us quite a bit of leverage with the Tecran government."

"You going to tell them right away?" Zutobi asked.

Dimitara shook her head. "I'm going to have a bath, have some dinner in my rooms, and get a good night's sleep. Tomorrow, before we reach the Tecran solar system, is soon enough."

Dray grunted in approval, and Yolandi gave an elegant nod of her head.

"Keep them guessing for a bit. It'll make them even more grateful," Zutobi agreed cheerfully. "And given the work ahead of us from tomorrow, I think I'll follow your example, Ambassador."

She stood, and Yolandi stood with her.

"I just have a few technical issues to discuss with the ambassador," Dray said, and they nodded and left, although he knew they were curious.

"If it's bad news, I don't think I want to hear it." Dimitara rubbed at her temples.

"It's not bad news. I want to know how much resentment there'll be if the rest of the leadership team learn Bane has chosen me as his liaison."

"Oh." Dimitara sat up a little straighter. "Quite a lot of resentment, I'd guess, although it's not as if they weren't expecting him to favor the Grih. He's been living within your space boundaries up 'til now, his three surviving . . . friends are all aligned with the Grih, and the woman who freed him, my friend Rose, is very much part of Grihan life." She lifted her hands and shoulders in a 'what are you going to do' gesture.

"True. But I'd prefer to keep it as quiet as possible, please. It could impact on my role within the team, and I'd rather that not happen."

She nodded. "I won't say anything. If you're happy for me to pretend Bane spoke to me personally, I could do that."

Dray nodded. "That works."

He got up.

"Why do you think he has chosen you as his liaison?" Dimitara asked him as he reached the door.

He turned back. "I'm from Battle Center, so maybe he's just more comfortable with me," he said with a shrug. "After all, Bane was created as a weapon of war."

# CHAPTER 7

LUCY STARED out at the glittering ocean and huddled deeper into her cloak, grateful for the warmth of it, and for the scarf that had the dual benefit of hiding her mouth and nose and keeping her face warm.

The zipu had proved to be a system of fast, individual carriages that ran on a single, humming strip of metal. Each carriage held a maximum of four people and she'd had one to herself most of the way in to the city. She'd gotten out at the first station that had a crowd waiting on its platform, keeping her head down as she wove through what looked like early morning commuters.

The city center didn't look to be far, and she found a path that ran parallel to the cliff edge. The wind was to her back, and she let it push her along.

To her left, buildings rose up as if they were extensions of the cliffs, their lower floors out of sight, below the clifftops. The closer she got to the city center, the more buildings rose up on her right as well, as tall or taller than the buildings that blocked most of their view of the sea, although there were some gaps between the buildings at the front, concessions to those behind them, so that they at least got a glimpse of the ocean beyond.

A third line of buildings and then a fourth appeared, and she guessed from the air the city must look like a long snake that had swallowed something large that was sitting in its middle.

The buildings were tall but they were all different, and each one she passed seemed taller than the next, in a sort of height progression that might have told her when she'd reached the city center—because they got lower again on the other side—if it wasn't for the statue.

It stood dead center, flanked on both sides by buildings that came to its shoulders. Nothing stood directly in front of it, which created an open square surrounded on three sides by the statue and buildings, and the cliff edge as the fourth.

What struck Lucy was the variety in the buildings that rose around her. All were tall and relatively narrow, but none looked the same. Some were made of stone, others of a kind of glass or polished enamel, the designs and patterns worked into them stark and compelling.

She had seen some of the same patterns in the walls and pictures in the facility, and guessed they were intrinsic to Tecran culture.

The closer she got to the statue, the more populated with commuters the path became, and she eventually stepped off it and found a parallel road behind the second row of buildings.

The midmorning sunlight struggled to reach past the buildings on the cliff, and it lent a gloom to the back streets.

She relaxed a little. The shadows suited her.

She still caught a few glances directed her way, but no one approached her, and she kept her stride quick and purposeful, the hood of her cloak pulled low enough to keep her hair and eyes hidden.

She would have been outed as an alien long ago without the

scarf, though. The Tecran's beak-like mouth included nasal openings on the top, and there was no way anyone could mistake her human mouth and nose as anything like theirs.

She kept heading toward the square, even though she didn't know quite what she'd do when she got there. It didn't really matter. Having any goal at all was a relief.

Buildings that clearly housed apartments started to change subtly the closer she got. Little shops appeared at ground level, mostly cafes and grocery stores, and some buildings had what looked like sophisticated vending machines built into them.

The pavements and streets that surrounded the square contained food stands, cafes, and long stone benches. In the open space in front of the statue, the sea sparkled and glittered, blinding Lucy when she looked in that direction.

A raised dais had been erected at the very center of the open space, bordered with large planters full of dark green foliage, and paved with stone edged with bright green moss. Stone steps on one side led up to the top.

Lucy sat on a bench on the right side of the square, facing left, rather than looking out over the sea, and watched people using the vending machines for fifteen minutes before she tried it herself.

She slid in the bank credit and chose a cup of water. When the cup dropped down for her to take, she suppressed a squeak of triumph.

She sat back on her bench and gulped it down, then went back for a cup of grinabo—the hot drink she'd become addicted to at the facility—and a nutrient bar.

When she turned back, her bench had been taken, so she leaned against a wall, sipping her grinabo, and hoped no one would notice her in the shadows.

Most of the Tecran looked like they were on their way to work, but some were wearing uniforms and looked like the Tecran version of the police.

Suddenly nervous, she lifted her scarf a little higher and turned toward a small stall selling something that smelled terrible to her, but which had a snaking queue of patrons. That suited her fine. She joined the end of the line, and shuffled forward as it moved along.

When she looked again, the police were gone.

She could have approached them. Maybe.

So far, the Tecran she'd met outside the facility seemed to know something about her and not want any involvement. Which meant she was a complication, and sometimes, people just wanted complications to go away.

Whatever happened with the police, they would probably hold on to her.

She decided to find out a little more first, before she took a step that would take away her autonomy.

She'd only just gotten it back.

She stepped out of the line and went back to the vending machine for a second cup of grinabo, and found a new bench that was empty.

As soon as she sat down, she noticed the large screen set to one side of the square.

More than one Tecran stood in the central part of the square, looking up at it as they sipped their morning drink and ate whatever they'd bought for breakfast.

Perhaps it was due to the lack of space in the city center, but none of the cafes had places for people to sit and eat.

Lucy noticed more and more people began gathering in front of the screen and wondered if it had to do with the time of day. Maybe public announcements were made at this time every morning?

The screen flickered to life and an image appeared, and she almost spilled her grinabo as she recognized the facility—a fireball against the night sky. Tecran were racing around, dressed in protective suits, and she caught a glimpse of Dr. Farnn being led off to the side.

She was alive!

She couldn't hear clearly what was being said, and so she stood and began to work her way into the crowd until she was close enough.

There was nothing in the report about survivors. The woman doing the voice-over simply said there was an unknown number of deaths and authorities would have to investigate the scene before more was known.

Then the image faded and she saw three Tecran sitting around a small table. They began discussing the imminent arrival of a United Council battleship, and the upcoming takeover by the UC of the Tecran military, and the overseeing of Tecran political structures.

The crowd grew around her, she could no longer see the square, just people on every side. Their attention was on the screen, though, and she didn't think anyone noticed her at all.

The people onscreen began to discuss the implications for Tecran society of having UC interference, and it was clear that none of the three were happy about the outcome.

"We were forced into this, there was no choice about it," one of the men on the panel insisted.

"Well, the choice was being kicked out of the UC, and potentially going to war, or submit to their demands," the woman said. "So we did have a choice, but not a feasible one. My understanding is that the military left us so vulnerable by investing in the Class 5s that once we lost them, even the military thought this UC interference was better than a war we couldn't win."

"At least this way, after five years, we are once again a sovereign nation," the third man said. "Not the loser in a war with the Grih."

"Are we though?" the first man asked. "After five years, can we be sure the UC will walk away?"

"What choice do we have but trust that they will?" the woman said. "We have to hope they keep their word, and to be honest, I haven't known them to lie before."

"They better keep their word," someone in the crowd close to her muttered, and the Tecran around him nodded in agreement.

"It's a silent coup, is what it is," someone spoke a little louder, to Lucy's right.

"That's crazy talk," someone else called back. "Do you think we're innocent in all this? We should be directing our anger at the military for putting us in this situation, not at the UC. All they've done is follow the laws we helped to write. We've been betrayed by our own."

There were mutters of agreement, and Lucy realized the crowd was not at all a unified group. Everyone had strong opinions.

But what were these rules the Tecran military had broken?

Suddenly, up on the screen, was an image of people standing on a stage lit with tiny lights, and behind them were buildings that looked like exquisite works of art. The part that had Lucy really riveted, though, was that none of the people were Tecran. Some looked so human, at first she thought they were, until she noticed their pointed ears, and others were shorter, more stocky, with dark hair and silver eyes.

Then the view of the people on stage became clearer as the lens zoomed in.

She cried out and dropped her cup of grinabo as three women came into focus.

Human women.

She barely noticed the curses around her as hot grinabo splashed the people closest to her in the crowd.

She stumbled forward, pushing people aside to get a better view of the screen, and the wind chose that moment to blow a little harder, swirling through the square and lifting her hood from her head.

There was a gasp from the woman beside her, her gaze on Lucy's long hair.

"She's one of them." The woman pointed at the screen. "One of the Earth women."

Lucy turned and suddenly realized the crowd had moved back. She was standing alone.

She pushed her hood all the way off, pulled down her scarf, and faced them.

"Yes. I am one of them. And I want to understand what I'm doing here. What is going on?"

"Where did you come from?" someone called out.

"I was being kept at that facility that blew up last night. One of the scientists there said the military was trying to clean up their mess."

There were audible gasps.

"Please, tell me what is going on."

She looked around at the alien faces surrounding her, and felt a deep, desperate wish to go home.

The sense of isolation, of otherness, that she'd felt in the first weeks she'd woken up in the facility came crashing back down on her.

She hadn't felt it the last few months, she realized, not because she was suddenly one of them, but because her gaolers had started talking to her, joking with her, even playing with her, and even that small amount of acceptance had made her feel less different.

These Tecran were looking at her with the horror and condescension she'd seen in Farnn and the others' eyes when she'd first interacted with them.

"You are the reason those UC people are coming to take over our military and government." The man who spoke was the same one who'd claimed it was a coup.

"How am I the reason?" she asked.

That shut him up, and he looked down, mumbled something.

"What did you say?" she asked.

"He doesn't have a good answer, because you aren't the reason. The person who took you from your home is the reason." The woman standing next to him spoke with what sounded very much like contempt. "How long have you been here?"

"Three months, I'm told. I wasn't conscious for all of it."

Again, there was silence.

"This is just pure trouble." One of the men in the crowd started moving backward. "No good can come of it, and if the military are cleaning up their mess, I don't want to be in their way."

"That makes you a coward, and the reason they were able to put us in this situation to begin with," the woman who spoke earlier told him.

Everyone shifted uncomfortably, and Lucy realized they were put on the spot with the coward accusation. No one wanted to look like a coward, but some were already looking around to see if there was a military clean up crew on the way.

That thought jolted her.

Someone would be recording this, surely. It was enough of a spectacle, after all.

And she didn't think, even if they wanted to, anyone here could help her if the military came for her.

"Just, please, tell me what I need to know." She caught the woman's eye.

"You aren't the only one they took," the woman said, waving up at the screen. "And they were caught out, and now—"

Someone at the back screamed.

The sound of the cry started a panicked movement by the crowd. People began to edge away, and then to run.

Lucy didn't bother trying to see what had caused the panic. She dove into the crowd, letting it sweep her along and then she slipped down a narrow alleyway.

She crouched down in the shadows, pulling her cloak over her head, and peered around the corner to see what had caused the fuss.

Two hovers were moving across the square, and while a lot of the crowd had dispersed, some of the people were still standing there, watching the hovers approach. Some were holding their wrists in a way that made her think they were recording.

"Who are you? What is your business?" The woman who had at least shared some information with her called out, a challenge in her voice.

"Are you here to 'clean up your mess'?" A man who stood near the woman shouted. "Show your faces. Are you with the military?"

His demand drew some people back, and as they converged on the square, cutting the hovers off, the drivers lifted them higher.

They hung, suspended for a moment, and then something hit Lucy's ears, a pulse of some kind.

It hurt.

She curled over her knees, hands to ears, just barely hearing the screams from the square.

The pain disappeared as fast as it had come, and she raised her head cautiously.

People were picking themselves off the floor, and the screen on the side of the building was blank.

The hovers were gone.

They had killed all the electronic devices with some sort of electro-magnetic pulse, she guessed.

Whoever was hunting her couldn't afford for any comms of her to surface, and they couldn't answer the questions that had been thrown at them, either. They'd run when challenged.

That was good to know.

But if they caught her on the street without the benefit of a crowd around her, they wouldn't hesitate to grab her.

She had no doubt about that.

What she needed was more information. Some way to understand everything that was going on.

The Tecran here were conflicted, that much was certain. It would be difficult to work out enemies from allies, but at least not everyone *was* an enemy.

She rose to her feet, pressing back against the wall. The military knew she was here now.

They could just as easily have left someone in the square to wait for her to show herself again. In fact, they'd have been stupid not to.

She didn't know what to do next.

Where to go or how to find out what she needed to know.

But standing here wasn't going to help her. She needed to move.

The square was almost empty now. Most people had picked themselves up, but they were standing in small groups, talking, and she didn't think they'd be shrugging off the incident and pretending nothing had happened.

More than one of the uniformed officers she'd noticed earlier were now visible, and it looked like they were questioning witnesses.

As she watched them approach a group, she saw a woman step back and walk slowly away. It reminded her of herself earlier, of the nonchalance she'd affected, and so she was still watching when the woman glanced casually down the first narrow alleyway she passed.

Her heart sped up as she waited for the woman to pass another. The woman glanced down that one, too.

Looking for someone.

*Looking for me.*

Lucy turned, and jogged down the alleyway as fast as she could.

## CHAPTER 8

BANE WAS interested that Dray Helvan hadn't shared the details of his plan to stay out of sight of Tecra with the UC ambassador, or even his own Grihan colleagues.

He'd expected Dray to simply repeat what Bane had murmured into his earpiece, but the Grihan officer had editorialized, giving no specifics whatsoever.

Pretending Bane hadn't given him anything more.

It had surprised him so much, Bane had started following him around almost constantly.

His choice of Dray had been random, he'd thought. Any one of the three Grih would have done.

But Dray's parting shot to the ambassador, that Bane was probably more comfortable with a military officer than someone else, rang true, and for the first time, he realized he wasn't as self-aware as he thought he was.

He still had things to learn about himself.

That in itself was mind-altering.

Rose had something she did, putting her fists on either side of her head and opening them and softly saying, 'boom'. Like an explosion.

She said it meant 'mind blown'.

He'd never understood it.

Now he had an inkling.

This was all so . . . interesting.

He liked it.

He also had to get going now—put his plan into action. The Tecran solar system was coming up and he needed to disappear. Needed to uphold the agreement he'd made, although the Tecran thought he'd be out of sight because he'd be sitting at the edge of their system, not out of sight because he'd be shielding himself as he sat on Gyre, the bigger of Tecra's two moons.

He'd be minutes away from the planet there, instead of hours.

"I'll be in touch if something comes up," he said to Dray, watching through the visual comms as the officer went still, holding up the heavy weights he was lifting in the battleship's gym with a grimace. "I'm off to hide now."

Dray set the weights down carefully and wiped his forehead. "You sure you can be that close and stay hidden?"

"Very sure." Bane thought of all the times he'd come and gone from Tecra when he'd been under the control of the Tecran military, and if he'd had a mouth, it would have been turned up in a wry twist.

"You've done it before." Dray's eyes went up to the lens in the gym. His expression was one of sudden understanding. "You're an old hand at it."

"Let's put it this way," Bane allowed amusement to color his tone, "it's not my first time."

"The military knows you can do that." Dray spoke softly. "If they've done it when you were under their control, they probably won't believe you're sitting at the edge of the system."

"Yes." He'd already thought of that. "But if they come looking for me on Gyre, that'll leave a trace in the system. You'll need to look out for it."

Dray nodded slowly. "And if they find you?"

"Dead Tecran tell no tales." Bane kept his voice even.

Dray said nothing, his lips a tight line. And then he nodded. "Agreed."

He'd chosen his ally well, Bane thought, and something that felt like warmth flooded him.

If he did find the Earth woman, he would at least have someone he was beginning to trust as his feet on the ground.

His sidekick, as Rose called herself in relation to Sazo.

He smiled at the thought of Rose. She'd sent him a message this morning, telling him she was thinking of him, and hoped the trip wasn't too hard on him. Too traumatic.

It made him wonder about the anger and tension he'd felt when he'd come into contact with the Tecran envoy. Was that part of the trauma?

He had no one to ask. And he didn't mind the anger. He . . . relished it.

He hadn't been able to express it until Rose had freed him, and for a while after she had, he'd wallowed in it.

Now it was more focused. And he controlled it, not the other way around.

Mostly.

Because he enjoyed doing it, and because Rose told him it had a lot of visual impact, he started to spin his Class 5 in place. It didn't do anything, didn't have any significance, except that he was having fun, but Rose was right in that it seemed to take up a lot of discussion time among the allies that were part of the United Council.

Then he shot up and kept going.

The moment he was out of range, he changed course, shielding himself as he sped toward Tecra, and when he was more or less directly above the moon, he slowly sank downward.

He would land on Gyre a few hours before the Tecran envoy and the *Urna* got here.

His shields were one way. He could pick up signals while his own remained untraceable.

As he dropped lazily through space, he began listening for any comms coming from Tecra.

If an incident was local, most likely he'd only pick it up when he got to Gyre, but he scanned anyway.

If the Earth woman was still alive and on Tecra, the arrival of the UC would hopefully spark some reaction.

If it did, he didn't intend to miss it.

---

"That was quite a show Bane put on." Zutobi leaned back in her chair as Dray joined her and Yolandi at the dining table.

They tended to eat together at dinner every night, talking over things that they thought were important to the mission, but having lunch together was unusual. It was probably one of the last lunches they'd have onboard, though.

"Was it?" Dray slid into his seat and set his plate down. "I was in the gym. I didn't see it."

"Oh." Yolandi looked up in surprise. "You missed something good. It was a show, as Zutobi says."

"An unnecessary one, in my view. All he needed to do was stop and let us pass him, surely?" Zutobi's glance across at him was amused.

Dray let his lips quirk. "But then no one would be talking about it as much."

"No." Zutobi grinned. "He's certainly adept at playing to the crowd."

"Given what the crowd thought of him and his kind until

recently, you can hardly blame him." Yolandi set down her cutlery. "I'm guessing the ambassador is probably pleased with what he did. Maybe she even discussed it with him."

"Maybe." Dray didn't think he'd be so lucky, but he was happy to agree. He hoped Yolandi shared her theory with more than just him and Zutobi.

"Speaking of whom . . ." Zutobi murmured.

Dray turned and saw the ambassador heading for their table, a plate in her hand.

"Mind if I join you?"

"Of course not." Yolandi pulled back the chair next to her. "Please do."

Filavantri Dimitara sat daintily down and held Dray's gaze. "Did you see Bane leave?"

He shook his head. "I was in the gym. I heard it was a sight to see."

She inclined her head. "He has completely disappeared from our scanners. The Tecrans, as well."

"So they're happy now?" Yolandi asked.

"We've given them what they asked for, so I assume so." Dimitara shrugged. "I didn't exactly get a thank you, though."

"How long until we reach Tecra?" Zutobi set her empty plate aside.

"We'll be there in two hours." Dimitara looked less than enthusiastic. "Already I've seen footage from Tecra that shows how deeply they resent our coming."

Dray lifted his shoulders. "If it was my planet, I'd be resentful, too, but they can't pretend they didn't bring it on themselves."

"I think the line is that they didn't know what the military were doing, so they shouldn't be punished." Dimitara started eating the meat on her plate, and Dray caught a flash of those sharp, sharp teeth again.

"We expected that." Yolandi sighed. "They don't want to accept responsibility, but the people of Tecra run the government, and the military is part of that. They can't use the excuse that they didn't know. They should have known. They weren't vigilant enough."

Dray thought of all the checks and balances in place in the Grihan military, and had to agree.

If they hadn't known—and some of them *must* have done—they should have. They needed to accept their punishment and cooperate.

"Well, eat up, then get ready to face what looks to be a hostile welcome," Dimitara said. She had looked worn down for the last few days, but she lifted her head and drew in a breath, and Dray realized she looked fierce. "I received a message from Rose McKenzie this morning. She thanked me for leading this team. And it reminded me all over again what I found in Sazo's Class 5 holding cells. The death and destruction. You're right, Yolandi. They should have known, and I'm damn sure some of them did. So we do not cower, and we do not bend in the face of their unhappiness. They broke the most sacred rule we have, and they need to accept the consequences."

Dimitara's voice rose as she spoke, and Dray realized everyone in the dining hall had heard her. Every eye was on her.

Including the Tecran liaison's, Vauk.

Dray watched her turn away and hurry out.

But there was no place to run.

The UC team was arriving in Tecra, and he had a feeling in his gut that this was going to be a lot less cordial than the councilors representing the five member groups had thought it would be when they created this alternative to war.

He shook off his foreboding and made his way to his rooms to pack. Grihan Battle Center had been a lot more realistic about this mission than the UC. They'd discussed the likelihood of things not going as planned. Dray had a list of possible scenarios and he could and would alert his superiors if any of them looked likely.

They'd be ready if the Tecran realized they really couldn't accept UC rule.

And so would he.

# CHAPTER 9



Lucy shivered against another gust of freezing wind that ripped through the narrow back alleys, but it was even colder closer to the cliffs.

She'd zigzagged her way across the city as the day wore on, taking the narrow alleyways, cutting across from street to street, always moving.

She tested doors as she went, finding them all locked.

She could only hope there wasn't some kind of video surveillance, or the police would be looking for a suspicious person who was trying doors all over the city.

She realized with a start she didn't even know what the city was called, and then shoved the thought aside.

What did it matter right now?

Suddenly, the wind cut off, and she blinked, saw that in keeping close to the wall of the building she was walking past, she'd found a little pocket of protection.

Unable to face the sting of cold on her cheeks again, she huddled in closer, closed her eyes and felt the seep of tears behind her eyelids as her whole body shuddered in relief.

Just a few minutes, she told herself.

Just a few minutes of not moving, of not being cold.

She didn't know when she heard the sound of footsteps, but not soon enough, because they were almost upon her.

She tensed, unable to see who was coming past the curve in the building that was giving her shelter, but suddenly she was looking at the back of a Tecran carrying an armful of parcels.

He didn't slow down or so much as look her way.

She dismissed him, glad for the deep shadows and her cloak. She'd encountered very few people in the back alleys, but those she had passed had barely looked at her.

She was smaller than them and obviously no threat. And the cloak, something she'd found reminiscent of tragic family sagas set on moors or highway robbers in Regency England—although, come to think of it, also Darth Vader—appeared to be standard dress. It wasn't just the outfit on the massive statue in the square, most people wore one when they were walking out of doors and she wasn't going to complain.

It suited her needs perfectly. It hid her face, her hands, and her body.

A curse snapped her out of her thoughts, and she realized she'd been drifting, not paying attention again. The parcel-carrier was swearing softly as he stood at the back door of the building she was leaning against, fiddling with his access card.

It was similar to the one Farnn had given her at the facility, and eventually he got it close enough to the reader to activate the lock. The door clicked and he shouldered it open, dropping a parcel as he staggered through.

She straightened, watching the door swing closed and then stop just short of shutting completely, with the edge of the parcel in the way.

She tried to run, but it was more a stumbling lope.

She got to the top of the stairs, peered through the crack in the door, just in time to see the Tecran turn a corner with the parcels.

She squeezed through the narrow gap, and stood, panting, in a big open space with a spiral staircase winding above her head.

There had to be a closet or storage room she could find to rest in, just for a little while.

Blood hammered in her ears, and she tried to slow her breathing, make it quieter.

If she was caught . . .

She forced her shoulders up and then down. If she was caught, maybe that would be a good thing. She could ask for help.

But there was a deeply cynical part of her that suspected that was a big maybe.

She looked right, the opposite direction to where the Tecran had gone, and started moving.

He'd be back for the parcel. His curse when it had dropped told her he knew it had, but he hadn't been able to set the others down to pick it up.

She heard footsteps behind her, and moved a little faster, hand out against the wall because for some reason she felt light-headed.

She was suddenly in a small alcove which contained a vending machine, a smaller version of the ones she'd used in the square, and felt a sudden lift in her spirits.

Things hadn't gone her way for hours, but it seemed her luck was turning.

Except, there wasn't a room off the alcove. It was a dead end.

She was stuck.

She drew in a breath, cocked her head to listen.

The footsteps had stopped, and then she heard the faint click of the back entrance closing.

She waited, trying to gauge which direction the Tecran would go next, and when she heard the footsteps coming closer, she wheeled around, desperate to find a corner to tuck herself into.

There was nothing.

Out of options, she stepped up to the vending machine and chose grinabo and another energy bar. Tapped her credit bank against the reader.

A big cup dropped down, filled with hot, fragrant liquid, and the bar was set down beside it.

The footsteps came to an abrupt halt behind her, and Lucy took the grinabo carefully.

She wanted to gulp it down, get a little warmth into her, but this might be the only weapon she had.

She turned slowly, grinabo clutched in both hands, and raised her gaze.

The Tecran stood, blocking the way out, his eyes curious. "I thought I heard someone back here."

She didn't want to speak, so she flapped her elbows under the cloak in the way she'd seen the scientists and doctors at the facility do—the Tecran version of a shrug.

"Who are you?"

Her response had shifted his tone from curious to suspicious.

Nothing she said would do anything but complicate the situation, so she kept quiet and took a step closer to him, the steam from the grinabo rising tantalizingly in front of her.

She really didn't want to waste it by throwing it at his face.

"You left your energy bar in the slot," the Tecran said, and startled, she turned to look, hand out to grab it.

As she did, he lunged forward and pushed off the hood of her cloak then stumbled back, his beaky mouth stretched open in surprise and shock.

"I thought you looked strange. The light lay just so on your cheek, and you looked . . . wrong." He swallowed, his neck bobbing, and then he leaned against the wall. "I just didn't know how wrong."

The words angered her.

"If I'm wrong," she hissed at him, "then it's because I shouldn't be here. And you tell me how I got here, why don't you? Because I don't know!"

He slid away from the wall, took a step back out of the alcove.

"You really are one of those Earth women?"

She nodded. Lifted the grinabo for a sip, because it looked like she wouldn't have to throw it after all.

"What should I do?" He looked at her as if she had the answer to that question.

"How about letting me sit somewhere quietly to drink my grinabo, eat my bar, and tell me what is going on?" She spoke pleasantly, evenly, but her face must have given her away because he backed up a little more.

He didn't look happy.

"All right." He drew out the words. "I can do that."

"Thank you." She blinked away sudden tears. "That would be much appreciated."

He looked at her for a long moment. "You're not . . . dangerous, are you?"

She stood shoulder height to him, and she lifted both arms out, a bar in one hand, her grinabo in the other. "What do you think?"

He bobbed his head. "Come with me."

He turned and walked away, and she followed in his wake.

She would finally get to sit out of the wind and drink and eat something.

She actually didn't care what happened after that.

# CHAPTER 10

BANE TOOK HIS TIME, carefully probing one satellite, invading its systems, and then moving on to the next, until he found an opening to reach down to the planet itself.

Because they would expect him to be coming, he infiltrated more carefully than usual.

Once he was sure he'd looked at everything useful, and had created a side door to move through whenever he wanted, he'd be more obvious, give them the attack they must know was coming. If he didn't, they might suspect he'd succeeded in breaking in, and he wanted them complacent, smug in the knowledge they'd kept him out.

The Tecran military had taught him the tricks he'd used when he was very young and new, and even though he had advanced on his own since then, he couldn't shake the feeling that they would be able to predict some of his moves.

So he was careful.

It didn't take long for the first alarm bell to ring.

A facility, just outside Fa'allen, had burned to the ground in the night.

It was being reported that unstable weapons had been

the cause, and given the look of the place, only two stories high on a planet where the only thing more valuable than height was proximity to the edge of the massive cliffs that rose above the ocean, he could believe it was a storage facility.

Except, Sazo had managed to get a hint of something happening at a facility in Fa'allen that he thought might relate to the Earth woman, and had passed the information on to Bane. So near the arrival of the UC team, the timing of the destruction was very, very suspicious.

Bane monitored the *Urna's* approach while he hunted. They'd be here within the hour. He briefly considered sharing what he suspected with Dray, and then decided against it.

He didn't have anything. Yet.

And if the Earth woman had died in the fire that was still burning, there was no one to save.

If she was dead, he would still look for proof she'd been held there, because he would not let them get away with imprisoning her and then murdering her when her existence became inconvenient.

He had to admit to not feeling optimistic.

The Tecran military had been his masters for years, and he did not think they would hesitate to kill her.

But he listened to the chatter about the fire and looked carefully at the visual comms taken.

He focused on one of the survivors, astonished to recognize her.

Dr. Farnn.

She was one of the explorations scientists who'd been assigned to study some of the lifeforms he'd collected for the Tecran while he'd been under their control.

He hadn't distinguished good from bad much in those days, but now he was more aware and awake, he understood that she had been unhappy with the animals' condition, and had never hurt them.

It was very unlikely she'd be working at a weapons storage. She had no role in a place like that.

It didn't mean the Earth woman was there, though.

It didn't rule it out, either.

He carefully scanned the comms, looking for clues to the Earth woman's presence, but there was nothing obvious.

That might be why they burned it down. It would be impossible to hide all trace of her if she had been there.

And then he saw Dr. Farnn jerk her hand away from someone in a black uniform, and openly stride toward the people using their handhelds to film what was happening.

The look on the face of the soldier who'd been trying to steer her away was furious, but instead of going after the doctor, he faded into the background.

Dr. Farnn reached the local security officers who were holding a perimeter, and spoke to one, then he saw her walk along the line to speak to a woman who looked to be in charge. They both moved out of range.

He hunted through the security force database for a match to the security leader. Found her. Captain Rivynn.

He did a search for Dr. Farnn, using the military system.

There was nothing.

It was as if she had ceased to exist.

He felt a rise in . . . excitement? Tension? He wasn't quite sure what to call it, but he knew there should be evidence of the doctor. He had had her onboard his Class 5 in his younger days. She worked for the military.

The erasure of her online presence was extremely significant.

He went back to Rivynn, found her call signature, and gave the polite tap most UC members seemed to expect.

He had noticed Dray Helvan seemed a little grumpier if he

didn't knock first, so to speak. Purely for the purposes of smoothing his way, he had started following the protocol.

"This is Rivynn."

For a moment, Bane floundered, suddenly unsure what voice to use.

"Hello?"

"Sorry, Captain, this is a friend of Dr. Farnn's. I've been so worried about her, and I saw some footage of the fire at the facility yesterday and she was talking to you. Can you give me a way to contact her?" Bane made his voice female, and hesitant.

"Can I have a name?" Rivynn asked.

"It's Dr. Duy." Bane wondered if using that name was a mistake or not. But it would get Farnn's notice.

Duy had been the other scientist who'd come onboard to observe the creatures Bane had collected, and to decide what the Tecran military should do with them.

Last he'd heard, the scientist had been sent to the Tecran's secret desert facility on the planet Balco, but that was gone now. Blown up just like the facility near Fa'allen.

Bane's friend Eazi had been responsible for the Balco explosion, and he had done a thorough job.

No one and nothing inside had survived.

"One moment, Dr. Duy."

Bane saw he'd been placed on mute, and overrode the command.

"Someone on the line for you," Rivynn was saying. "Says her name is Dr. Duy."

He heard Farnn gasp. "Duy? A woman?"

"What's wrong?" Rivynn asked her.

"Duy was a colleague, but he's dead. And he was a man."

"What should I do?" Rivynn's clothes rustled, as if she was moving around.

"Let me talk to them. At the very least to find out what they want." Farnn sounded frightened.

Bane decided that was the logical response to the situation.

There was a buzz as the earpiece was handed over.

"Hello?"

"Hello Dr. Farnn. Forgive the deception, but I didn't want Captain Rivynn to know who I was." Bane used the voice he used the most. The one he used with Rose McKenzie.

"Who are you?" Farnn whispered.

"You were on my ship over a year ago. At the time, I didn't have a name, but I've found one since. I am Bane."

She was absolutely quiet, as if she held her breath.

"I don't intend you any harm, Dr. Farnn. I liked what I saw of you that time you came onboard my Class 5."

"What do you want, then?" Her voice wavered, but Bane had the feeling she knew very well what he was after.

"The Earth woman. Is she still alive?"

"You know about her?" Farnn sounded . . . relieved?

Could that be?

"I tried to help her. I got her out before they came for her. Some of my colleagues . . ." Her voice shook. "Some died helping to get her out."

"Where is she now?"

"I don't know. They may have her or she may have gotten away."

"Have you told Captain Rivynn about this?"

"No." Farnn sighed. "If I do, things will go . . . crazy."

"Things are already crazy, Dr. Farnn." Bane used his driest tone. Because why would the doctor go to so much trouble to help the Earth woman, and then leave her to fend for herself? "Can I confirm her name is Lucy Harris?"

"Yes." Farnn drew in a breath. "How did you know that?"

"The Class 5 who abducted her told one of us about her before he was destroyed."

"He tried to kill her," Farnn said, indignant.

"Yes, he did. He regretted it. That's why he gave us the information. So we could find her. Save her. From your colleagues. Who are also trying to kill her."

Farnn was silent for a beat. "You're right. I got her out to save her from them, but seeing the facility burned, my friends killed, frightened me into silence." She breathed out heavily. "I'll tell Captain Rivynn what I know."

She sounded resigned, as if it might be the end of her, if she did.

"How did she escape?"

"I gave her my hover." She told him the hover tracking number. "That's all I have."

"Not all, Dr. Farnn. You know how long she was kept in that facility. You know what was done to her."

She said nothing in response.

"I would prefer you to be alive to testify to that, so I'm going to get a UC official to come fetch you. Where are you?"

"You don't know?" She sounded startled.

"No." Although given time, he could find out. She was with Captain Rivynn, after all.

"Captain Rivynn has kindly put me up at her home. I'll ask her if she wants me to stay here or move somewhere else. I'll let you know where you can find me."

Bane gave her a comms address for the information. "Don't leave it any longer than necessary, Dr. Farnn. You and I both know how much the military has to lose here."

"Almost as much as I do." Farnn sounded resigned. "I'll be seen as both a traitor and a participant in the crime."

That was probably true, but Bane didn't waste time feeling sorry for her. She had made her decision when she'd first stepped aboard his Class 5 a year ago, seen what the military had collected, and said nothing.

That she eventually had a crisis of conscience didn't excuse what she could have prevented if she'd spoken sooner.

"Lucy is strong," Farnn said. "I liked her from the first interview I had with her, but she's never set foot outside the facility, and she'll stand out wherever she goes."

Bane had assumed as much. Had assumed she'd been kept hidden. They'd never have taken a chance of letting her be seen. So he had better find her before someone realized who they had walking among them.

# CHAPTER 11

HIS NAME WAS GUGI.

At least, that's what Lucy thought he'd said. She'd stumbled after him, into his ground floor apartment.

He seemed somehow apologetic for its location, and then had shrugged at her blank look.

"We like to be up high," he said. "So ground floor is the most affordable."

That explained all the skinny skyscrapers.

She sipped at her grinabo, blinking away the tears the warm air of the apartment caused after the freezing conditions outside.

Her hands were stiff, the one holding the energy bar almost a frozen claw, and she rubbed it against her thigh until she could loosen her fingers and then clumsily opened the wrapper, taking small bites.

"I can get you something, if you want." Gugi sat opposite her, eyes wide, expression both curious and awestruck.

"Maybe some water?" She gulped down the last of her grinabo, and Gugi rose up, walking backward as if he expected her to run at any moment. He came back with the water, hand shaking in excitement.

"Your Tecran is very good."

"Thanks." She took the water, made herself sip it slowly so she didn't feel sick.

Tecran was what she'd heard around her every day. The way she communicated with her captors. So she made sure she understood it very well.

"What are you doing here?" Gugi shifted in his chair.

The heat, the food and drink, combined to make her suddenly sleepy, and she leaned back in her chair and closed her eyes. "I escaped from the facility. The one that was burned down."

The sound he made was so strange, she forced her eyes open.

He was staring at her, beak-like mouth open. "The facility in the news?"

She nodded. "They were trying to kill me. Clean up their mess." She used the same words Dr. Farnn had. Even though she still didn't fully understand what that mess had been.

"They broke the Sentient Beings Agreement, and they reactivated five thinking systems. I think it's more than just a mess." Gugi shifted again in his chair.

"What does that mean?" She was almost too tired to care right now, but she forced herself to sit straighter in her chair. "And who is 'they'?"

He blinked; two long, slow movements of his eyelids. "*They* is the Tecran military. And what it means is they took unknown advanced sentients, you and the others like you, against your will, and caused you harm. That is not allowed for members of the United Council. The Tecran are signatories to the Agreement. The penalties are severe." He stood suddenly. "So severe, a team sent by the UC is landing any moment to take over the running of our military, and oversee our political process for the next five years, as punishment for what they did."

"They were caught." She said it slowly. "But then, what about me?" She sucked in a breath, looked up to where he was looming over her. "That's why they tried to get rid of me. They didn't tell anyone about me. I'm more evidence against them."

He bobbed his head. "You could argue they had already lost everything, but it may be that those who were personally involved in taking you are currently unsullied by the scandal, or less sullied than those who were revealed to be a part of what has already been uncovered. They're probably trying to save their reputations going forward."

"Cleaning up their mess." It made sense. And that meant . . . "Can you get me in touch with the UC team that's about to arrive?"

He looked down at her, his eyes gleaming. "The thing is," he stepped right up beside her chair, forcing her to tip back her head to look at him, "one sure way for me to go up a few levels is to ask how much handing you over would be worth to the military."

It took her a moment to work out what he was saying.

She started to move, to launch out of her chair, but he grabbed her arms, held her in place.

"Sorry, I know you've done nothing to deserve this, but the Tecran will only lose more honor if you're found, and so I'm being patriotic and helping myself at the same time."

He slapped something against the skin of her inner wrist and she looked down at it with horror. "What is that?" Her voice was a broken whisper.

"Something that will help you sleep. It's perfectly harmless."

She looked up at him, saw his focus was on her face, waiting for her to react, and she took stock, realizing she felt . . . fine.

It wasn't doing anything to her.

Her eyes widened in surprise, because he seemed so sure, and then she almost rolled her eyes at herself.

*Play along, stupid.*

She let her eyelids flutter closed, then open, then flutter closed again, and slowly let the tension seep from her body, so she slumped sideways on the chair.

"Good." He stood, letting go of her arms.

She sensed him standing over her for a while, and she kept her breathing even, her body relaxed, even as her heart hammered in her chest.

She wanted the patch off. Even if she wasn't reacting as immediately as he thought she would, it could still be doing her harm.

"How do I do this?" His words made her freeze, and she had to slowly relax again as she heard him moving away, and realized he was pacing, talking to himself. "Not from here. Better start the negotiations somewhere else."

He went silent, and she could just make out his footsteps in another room. When he came back, she had to force herself to stay limp, even though her muscles wanted to twitch. He leaned over her again, ran a finger down her cheek. "Smooth." He sounded surprised, and then she felt a patch being stuck on her other wrist. He gave a grunt of satisfaction as he stepped back.

"That'll hold you." There was a smug satisfaction in his tone.

He walked away, and the door opened and closed.

She stayed still, uncertain if he was gone or not. After a moment, the door opened and closed again, and she felt the shock of adrenaline run through her.

He'd been watching her.

She tried to keep her hands from shaking. A minute ticked by and she cracked her lids a little, saw the room was empty, and stood up, ripping the patches off her wrists and throwing them on the floor.

Dr. Farnn had told her that they'd done plenty of tests on her while she was unconscious, and they'd found her reactions to their drugs very atypical.

She was lucky the patches hadn't killed her, because it could just as easily have gone that way.

She drew in a long, shaky breath, pressed her fingers to her eyes. A sound escaped her throat, and she forced it back down.

Her relationship with the Tecran was complicated.

They'd taken her, but those who had done the taking weren't the ones who interacted with her on a day to day basis at the facility, and the scientists and doctors she spoke with were . . . friendly.

But they hadn't set her free.

The guards at the facility, though . . . She had refused to let them forget they held her prisoner. She had chafed at their rules and broken them every chance she could get.

The Tecran at the apartment building on the cliff had helped her a little, but they hadn't put themselves out to give her a safe place to stay or information that she could use to save herself.

The people in the square . . . they were a mixed bag of allies and enemies.

And now Gugi—he'd done her harm.

She forced herself to shake it off.

She started for the door, and then paused.

Gugi was coming back, but once she was out the door, she'd be in the same position she'd been in before. Alone, cold. Hunted. Maybe it would be wise to see what he had that would be useful to her.

At least now she knew her priority was to contact the UC team coming in. They would hopefully protect her.

She looked around, slowly spinning in a circle.

The room she'd sat in was just one of three in the apartment. There wasn't much in it for her to use, so she stepped into the kitchen, unhooked a bag from the wall and threw in food she recognized from the facility and an insulated mug.

Aware of time slipping by, she moved through to the bedroom and began opening drawers. When she found Gugi's clothes, she quickly stepped out of the thin pajamas she'd been in since the day before and pulled on warmer pants and a shirt. They were too big, but not by much.

She decided to keep the rock climbing shoes. They fit her, and they were waterproof, but she pulled on new socks and added some clean pairs to the bag, then took an insulated jacket which she put on under the cloak.

She was about to leave when she saw the handheld on a desk.

She shoved it into the pack and jogged to the front door, then listened carefully before she cracked it open.

There was no one in the corridor, but she heard voices up ahead and quickly stepped out and moved silently, retracing her steps to the back door.

It opened easily from the inside. She braved the biting wind again, looking in both directions. There was no one around. The afternoon light was almost gone and shadows enveloped the alleyway.

She hunched a little against the cold, turned her face away from it, and disappeared into the darkness.

# CHAPTER 12

THEY STOOD on the knife-edge of war.

Dray took a few steps closer to Filivantri Dimitara, as did a number of others from the UC leadership team, as she faced off against the Tecran Defense Leader.

Suu Ulima had puffed himself up, chest almost bumping into the much smaller Bukarian, but Dimitara held herself with a cool disdain.

"You knew we were coming, your own people agreed to this solution instead of war, so your hostile attitude has no place here." She spoke without giving him the respect of his title, which, by virtue of the UC takeover, had ceased to exist.

"How do you plan to run something you don't understand?" Ulima hissed at her.

"I understand you broke the law. Flagrantly. Again and again. And endangered the whole UC by playing with banned thinking systems. So if I decide to dismantle your military down to the ground, and build it up again from scratch, then I will. I don't have to understand how it works now. You will be the one who needs to understand how it works in the future."

Dimitara's words caused a hush over the crowd. Dray saw people were literally holding their breaths.

Ulima took a step back, shock on his face. "They said you'd run it, not destroy it."

"If I don't get cooperation, if the only way I can work is to start from scratch, that's what I'll do. If you continue to refuse my people access to your systems, refuse to answer questions, we'll find another way. We have our mission from the UC, and we intend to carry it out." Dimitara took a step forward, and the Defense Leader just stopped himself taking another step back. "Do you understand?"

Instead of answering, Ulima spun on his heel and strode out of the room.

A little way off to the side, the Tecran political leaders stood, trying not to wring their hands, but Dray thought they were a little pleased with Ulima's stand, as well.

They didn't want to look like they were capitulating too much to the 'invasion', as he'd heard their arrival referred to a number of times on the comms in the big parliamentary building.

"Well?" Dimitara turned to the politicians. "Do we turn around and get ready for war? Do I call Bane in closer? What's it going to be?"

She let her voice carry over the assembly room, and while some looked defiant, like they would prefer that outcome, a lot more looked uneasy, or downright nervous.

"You must understand it is hard—" One of the politicians stepped forward, again, trying to have it both ways.

"So the word of a Tecran is once again not to be trusted." Dray spoke to Dimitara, cutting off the politician. He made sure his voice could be heard. "First, they break the Sentient Beings Agreement, then they lie to the UC about the Class 5s, and now they break their word on the agreement made to prevent war. I look forward to them being out of the United Council. We need allies we can trust, not dishonorable liars."

There was more than one hiss of outrage at his words, but they had the desired effect.

The tension in the room eased, and some of the Tecran military officers who'd had their hands on the weapons strapped to their thighs moved them to hang at their sides.

That they were armed would have to be rectified. They would have to hand their weapons in. Dray felt the tension ratchet up in his chest, because that would not go down well, but he wasn't prepared to walk around with armed enemies all around him.

"Your words are insulting. We have no intention of going back on our word." The politician who'd been speaking to Dimitara sent him an outraged look.

"Sounded like it to me." The Fitalian ambassador, Pilto, stepped forward, the two members of his team flanking him. One was military, like Dray, the other, Synter, was an administrator-type, like Zutobi. But she had military training, Dray saw now, in the way she stood just as ready to attack as the Fitalian military officer, Chep.

He'd spoken to Chep a few times on the journey to Tecra.

He'd recognized Chep's name from one of the classified reports he'd been given to study for this trip. Chep had been involved in the last big standoff with the Tecran before they'd capitulated and agreed to the UC overseeing their military. Chep and another Fitalian officer had been taken prisoner by Paxe, the Class 5 that had destroyed himself rather than be taken back under the Tecran's control.

The Fitalian military officer had Dray's respect. He'd helped a UC team get out of the situation with Paxe alive, and according to the Grihan officer caught up in the incident, Captain Kalor, Chep and his colleague had had Kalor's back.

As if he sensed eyes on him, Chep glanced across and they exchanged an almost imperceptible nod.

"I'm going to start feeling left out." Juno Cossi sidled up to him. "Making eyes at the Fitalians. I thought the Bukarians were your favorites."

Despite himself, Dray's lips twitched.

Cossi was the Bukarian military officer assigned to the leadership team, but he knew her light banter was a cover for a cool, hard-eyed demeanor he had caught a few glimpses of during the journey to Tecra.

"There aren't supposed to be favorites," he said.

She gave a genuine chuckle. "Sure."

She tilted her head as she kept her eyes on the scene before them, and Dray turned his attention back to it himself.

Pilto's comment had had the effect of backing up Dimitara with a weight that smacked heavily of the United Council old guard.

Pilto was of the era of cooperation with the Tecran, and his word held weight here.

The politicians had genuflected a little when he'd stepped forward, and were now trying to smooth over Defense Leader Ulima's obstructionism.

Chep let himself drift back and Cossi and Dray drifted forward, so they were suddenly standing side by side as if by accident.

"They're going to suggest we go off and settle in, and start fresh tomorrow," Dray said.

"I'd say that's a given," Chep said.

"And I say fuck that," Cossi murmured.

"What does Yuf say?" Chep asked.

Yuf was the Garmman military representative. From what Dray had seen, he seemed more a bodyguard to his ambassador than an actual military attaché.

"He'll say whatever his master tells him to." Cossi made the comment with a neutral voice, but Dray caught the disrespect.

And agreed.

There weren't supposed to be favorites, but there were. And of the five members of the United Council, the Garmman were the closest to the Tecran. They had been more than a little involved in the illegal development of the Class 5s, but that had been proved to be through the cooperation of private actors, not the Garmman government itself.

Luckily for the Garmman.

They were also responsible in large part for the pirate scourge that was the Krik.

So yes. There were favorites, and right now, Dray didn't give a damn about diplomacy. He wanted people on either side of him who he could trust.

"Then let's go break the news we're taking our teams in right now." He spoke quietly, catching Cossi's grin, and the quick bob of the head from Chep.

They moved forward together.

"Ambassador Dimitara, we're going to assemble our teams now and start looking over things at military headquarters, see what we're dealing with." Dray noticed that Chep and Cossi had fallen back a half step, so he was the leader.

Clever of them.

That put the target squarely on his back, but he'd prefer to be the one setting the agenda, so that worked for him.

"Of course. Can you get someone to show them the way?" Dimitara turned to the hand-wringing politician.

The man gave Dray a vicious look. "I'm sure your people are tired, Ambassador. Surely they can start tomorrow?"

Behind him, Dray thought he heard Cossi snigger.

He said nothing in response, just held Dimitara's gaze, and she gave a nod.

"My people are very much rested and up to the task. Thank you for your concern, but it isn't necessary."

"We don't need an escort. I already know where to go." Dray smiled. "We'll see you later."

He gave a half-bow and turned on his heel, and Chep and Cossi strode after him.

He glanced back, looking for Yuf, giving him a chance to join them, but the Garmman military officer was nowhere in sight.

With a shrug, he faced forward and went to do his job.

# CHAPTER 13

WHOEVER WAS LOOKING for her would have a place to start when Gugi got hold of them.

So she needed to mingle, Lucy decided.

Skulking through back alleys was asking for trouble. If they found her there, there would be no witness to what happened to her.

She made her way toward the cliffs and the main buildings. That was surely where the United Council people would be. If she could work out which government building they were headquartered in, she could at least watch for a chance to approach one of them.

She wondered if they would be easy to pick out. She recalled the tall, pointy-eared aliens from the video clip on the screen earlier, and the shorter, stockier aliens, all standing around a stage with three human women. She'd watch for anyone who looked like them.

She guessed her ace in the hole was her appearance. If she worked out who the UC teams were, they would certainly recognize her.

They wouldn't simply dismiss her.

But until then, her appearance would only endanger her.

She had wrapped her scarf around her mouth again and tugged at the hood of her cloak so it hid her face, but it also narrowed her scope of vision, made it difficult to see anyone coming at her from the side.

It was still safer than showing more skin, though.

She reached the main street and stepped into the flowing crowd.

There seemed to be more people around now than there had been earlier, and there was an ugly mood, with people shoving past others and shouts of annoyance as people were jostled.

When she'd been in the square earlier she'd sensed the tension and the discontent, but now the UC team had actually arrived, it had intensified.

She was careful not to bump anyone.

Keeping her head down, she made her way along the length of the street.

A crowd was gathered in the square, but she slowed down before she reached it, sensing violence in the air. She had the feeling things could turn nasty in a blink, and she wasn't sure which side the security forces were on.

Or if there even was a side represented here.

It didn't feel organized or cohesive.

The security officers, whatever their personal feelings, were much more visible than they'd been earlier. They stood in small groups of two or three, scattered through the area, for the most part seemingly relaxed as they chatted with the public.

There were other Tecran who, like her, were hovering, avoiding the decision of whether to join the growing gathering. On the faces of some of them she could read fear, in others, contempt.

Someone gave a shout deep in the crowd, and it decided her. She turned away, but before she could find a group of people to attach herself to for cover, she noticed more than one cafe had now set tables outside, despite the cold. There were enough people sitting at them, watching the unfolding drama in the square, for her not to stand out.

She veered out of the stream of pedestrians, moving carefully between small tables to find one in deep shadow, and sank down.

The tabletop immediately flickered to life, offering a variety of menu options. Nervous that not ordering something would bring her attention she couldn't deal with, she placed an order for grinabo and chose a dish at random.

The credit bank she'd been given that morning worked again, and she relaxed a little, feeling more secure here than she had on the street.

She took a careful glance around, but no one was looking her way, with most of the attention on the gathering crowd in the square.

A few protesters were standing on the benches in the square to address the crowd, and more had made their way up onto the dais in the center of the massive space.

She tuned them out and pulled the handheld she'd stolen from Gugi out of her bag.

It lit up, and she stared at it, perplexed, unsure how to work it.

Before she could try, a server slid a tray in front of her, his attention barely on what he was doing, let alone her, as his gaze fixed on what was happening in front of him.

He walked away, setting a second tray on another table, and then stood, legs apart, arms crossed, watching the growing mayhem.

"How do I find out where the United Council team are right now?" she asked eventually, recalling the scientists often spoke into wrist units at the facility.

She'd never seen any of them with a handheld, had never been offered one of her own, but that was clearly because they didn't want her to understand just how illegal, even in their own system of laws, what they were doing to her was.

She'd spoken in Tecran, but the handheld obviously had trouble understanding her, because suddenly there was a keyboard option, and with a sigh of relief, she began tapping in search terms.

She sipped at the grinabo with one hand as she read the information, although it was a struggle, because she could speak Tecran far better than she could read it.

The food smelled sour, but not disgusting, and she lifted up a spoonful of what looked like black rice and gave it a nibble.

It was okay.

She wasn't hungry enough to chance getting sick, though, so she pushed it away.

She started searching for more information about the Earth women who'd been taken, but nothing came up.

She frowned, wondering why that was when she'd seen that clip of them singing on stage in a magical city, looking both at home and at ease.

A sudden longing swept over her. She wanted to go home.

She'd started to dream in Tecran, and that frightened her.

She tried a few alternative phrases, trying to find the clip, when her screen went blank and then a sentence popped up.

"Who are you?"

She stared at it, feeling winded. As if every bit of breath had been sucked from her lungs.

She wheezed and her hand shook as she reached out a finger to touch the words.

They were in English.

Which was impossible. The Tecran alphabet was nothing like the English alphabet.

The virtual keyboard that came up didn't even have the letters for her to respond in kind.

Carefully, heart thundering, she typed back in Tecran. "Who are *you*?"

There was no immediate answer.

"Seriously, how do you know my language?" Lucy typed. "How are you even communicating with me?"

"Are you Lucy Harris?"

She leaned back in her chair so sharply, the front two legs momentarily lifted off the ground.

"Yes."

There was another delay. Lucy wondered if it was a connectivity issue, or whether the person communicating needed time.

And then, suddenly, her Tecran keyboard was replaced with an English one.

"Where are you?"

"I don't think it's wise for me to say." She lifted her gaze from the screen. The open area in front of the cafe was thick with people now, far more crowded than it had been when she first sat down.

It gave her a start that the situation had changed so much, so quickly, and a little thrill of fear ran down her arms and lifted the hair at the back of her neck.

Things were getting worse.

The security officers weren't chatting in a friendly way anymore.

She watched as one walked around the crowd, hand on the weapon strapped to his thigh.

The shouting in the square was louder now, too, as if there were people competing to have their views heard, and she could no longer see the benches through the press of people.

The screen gave a chirp, and she started, looked back down at it.

The sentence *"Are you there?"* was repeated five times.

"Yes! Sorry. Got distracted." She almost stumbled at typing in

English. It was a QWERTY keyboard. It was impossible, and yet, it was right in front of her. "Please. Are you one of the women they took from Earth?"

Another delay, so long, her knuckles were white where she gripped the sides of the handheld.

"No. I'm a friend of those women, though. I have been looking for you. I am happy to find you alive, Lucy Harris."

Tears burned suddenly in her eyes and she had to swallow down the lump that stuck in her throat. "I'm happy to be found."

Her hands were shaking again.

"My name is Bane. I was also a prisoner of the Tecran once, but an Earth woman the Tecran stole, just like you, called Rose McKenzie, helped me escape. I'm here with the United Council group."

"You're here in Fa'allen?" Hope soared in her chest. She had an ally right here!

"Not quite. The Tecran don't trust me, they think I'm dangerous, and that I'm probably holding a grudge, so they asked me to stay out of sight of Tecra. But I have a friend in the UC team who I can send to you. And I'm not as far off as the Tecran think I am."

Lucy wondered why the Tecran were so afraid of him, and then recalled the argument about thinking systems in the square this morning.

"Are you one of the thinking systems I heard about?"

Another long delay. "Yes."

"Thank you for looking for me. How did you find me?" A sudden chill ran through her. If Bane could do it, what was stopping the military?

"I was curious about your search terms, and then I hopped into some of the portable lenses being carried around the square, and saw you, and thought you might just be an Earth woman under that hood, scarf and cloak."

She tried not to look suspicious as she glanced around again.

"Do you think the Tecran military might be using the same methods?"

"I'd say most definitely. I can't block them too obviously, because right now being invisible in the system is more useful, but I'm going to have something delivered to you in a few minutes, so don't be surprised when a courier approaches you, please."

"What have you ordered for me?" She lifted her gaze, and saw that sure enough, a Tecran was dodging through the crowd with a small package in his hands.

She raised her hand as he came closer and he stopped at her table with a nod and put the package down. She was afraid she would have to look up at him, sign for it, and thus give herself away, but he just turned and walked back the way he'd come.

She opened it, and lifted out an earpiece.

Huh.

Clever.

She put it in her ear.

"That's better." The voice was smooth. Deep.

"Much better," she answered, the words catching a little in her throat. "Nice to meet you, Bane."

"Very nice to meet you, Lucy. Let's get you somewhere safe."

# CHAPTER 14

"HOW DID YOU MANAGE THIS?" Lucy tapped the earpiece.

"I paid three times the price for it, to get it delivered as I specified."

"Thank you."

"There is very little I wouldn't do to get you safe and free."

The words were said so matter-of-factly, but they were everything she hadn't had before.

A sob shuddered through her and she bit down hard on her lip, bent over and covered her face in her hands.

"Lucy? What's wrong."

She struggled to answer, fighting against the constriction of her throat. Eventually she felt composed enough. "Nothing is wrong. I'm reacting to the sudden realization that things are finally going right."

He was quiet, and then made a funny sound she thought might be a laugh. "I understand that."

She smiled at his tone as she looked up and then went still.

Someone was staring at her.

As soon as she noticed him, he started moving forward.

"They found me," she murmured.

"I can't see you now. Those in the crowd are all focused on filming what's happening in the square." Bane's frustration was clear. "What do they look like?"

"One Tecran, tall, in black, wearing a cloak like mine." She stood up, looking around for possible escape routes.

She had chosen the table closest to the shop, as far back from the street as possible while still being outside, but that meant there were two rows of tables between her and the crowd, and as she began to sidle to the right, she saw the Tecran lift his arm and say something into a wrist unit.

Calling for backup.

"Hang on, I've found a way to get eyes on you." Bane's voice was not as calm as it had been.

And suddenly there was a sound of someone shouting overhead, and a hover skimmed over the crowd, the security officer riding it struggling with the controls.

The hover stopped above the tables, between Lucy and the Tecran approaching her.

He stopped moving forward as a number of people turned to look at what was happening.

"You're using the lens on the hover to see what's going on?" Lucy asked.

"Yes. It's had the unexpected benefit of making it difficult for the military to grab you anonymously."

Except, she could see the Tecran military officer weighing up the risks, and realized the moment he decided that grabbing her anyway and running, what with the growing chaos on the street, would be worth it.

He lunged forward, batting chairs out of his path.

Lucy flicked a final look at the solid wall of bodies a few meters away and jumped onto the chair, and then stepped up onto the table.

"Bring the hover lower and toward me." She didn't take her

eyes off the officer as he shoved people sitting at the tables aside. He was nearly on her, a step or two away, and she jumped, grabbing the hover's stabilizer bar, and as her hands closed over it, it shot up into the air.

A hand grabbed her ankle and she wrenched her foot up, lifting her legs by bending them at the knees. His fingers couldn't get a grip and suddenly she was free.

He was shouting in fury and frustration, but she didn't look at his face. The hover was still moving, flying over the crowd, and she gaped at all the people below her. It seemed as if the antagonism was growing, spreading and getting worse as people shoved at each other and the security forces tried to separate them.

There was a sudden flash of light, and her arms wrenched as the hover jerked to the left.

Below, people in the crowd started screaming.

"Someone shot at you," Bane said. "I'm getting you away from here."

The hover sped up, and her arms began to shake with effort.

"You need to set this thing down, I'm going to fall." She hoped he heard her, because she could barely gasp the words.

The crowd was at last behind them, and Bane lowered the hover, but kept it moving, turning a corner so suddenly her arms wrenched again and the pilot above nearly lost his balance.

"Hey!" The pilot looked down at her, and she blinked up at him. "Are you doing this?" He lifted his hands. Then his eyes widened as he finally looked at her face. His mouth fell open.

"No." She could feel her fingers starting to loosen their hold. She was going to fall any moment. "Does it look like I'm doing it?"

The hover dipped as she lost her grip, and her fall was short. She landed in a crouch.

The hover shot back up, heading for the square.

"I don't want the pilot to see which way you go. Run." Bane's words were urgent in her ear.

She started at a shamble, but managed to get up some speed by the time she hit the next corner.

She looked behind her and saw two figures in black chasing her.

"I see them." Bane's voice was like a balm to her, even though this was the most danger she'd been in since the night she'd escaped.

Just having someone on her side made all the difference.

"Go right," he told her.

She turned right, down a narrow alley, and slowed because she couldn't see anything.

"Move faster," Bane ordered.

"I can't see," she whispered back.

"Oh. Put your hand out, touch the wall, and move as fast as you can until you get to the steps. Then go up them."

She did as he asked, the wall smooth under her fingers, but the sound of footsteps at the entrance to the alley made her freeze.

"Keep going."

She started again cautiously, quiet as she could, and then heard the footsteps stop.

She stopped again, straining to hear over the whistle of the wind.

"We see you. We don't mean to hurt you. We just need to get you out of sight for a while." The officer who called to her from the entrance to the alleyway tried to sound sincere.

If she'd been in less danger, she'd have snorted out a laugh.

And why would they think being put 'out of sight' was in any way okay with her?

She began to move again, slow and smooth.

She hadn't realized the steps Bane told her about were so close, and almost cried out in relief when she bumped into them.

She swallowed the sound and started up them.

"You sure she's down there?" A voice called down the alley from the main street.

"I think so." The officer who'd tried to reassure her was a lot closer than he had been. He'd been moving forward faster than she had. He was almost at the bottom of the stairs.

"Door's open, push it." The voice in her ear snapped her out of her panic, and she shoved at the door, but it didn't budge.

She slapped at it, looking for a handle, heard the sound of the officer right behind her, and turned it just as he grabbed her.

She cried out as she fell inside, with him landing on top of her.

Panicked, she kicked back, closing the door so that she only had one Tecran to contend with.

"Lock it," she shouted at Bane, and then twisted, drawing her legs up to her chest and kicking out.

She caught the soldier by surprise, hitting him in the stomach, and it was enough to shove him off her.

He grunted as he fell back, and she scrambled up on her knees, leaning over him as she tried to snatch his weapon from his hand. When she couldn't, she grabbed his arm and banged it against the floor.

The weapon slid away.

He bucked against her. He was taller than she was, but she had muscle and bone density in her favor.

She swung her elbow at his face and whimpered at the pain when it connected, but it *had* connected.

She edged back and felt a surge of satisfaction when she realized he was stunned.

"What's happening?" Bane's question was panicked.

"He's down. But he'll be back up soon."

"Go through that door to your right," Bane said, his voice more monotone again.

She jogged to it and stepped through into a dark stairwell that lit up as soon as the door closed behind her.

"Take the stairs down. It's a pedestrian passageway to the main street, so the tenants don't have to fight the weather in winter. There're a few exits before the square. I'll try to get my friend in the UC to meet you outside one of them."

Lucy nodded, then realized he couldn't see her down here. "Okay. Thanks."

She reached the bottom of the stairs and then leaned against the wall.

"Are you moving?" Bane asked.

"In a minute." She leaned over, hands on knees, and squeezed her eyes shut.

"You don't have a minute, they're breaking through the alleyway door."

The sound of his distress forced her upright, forced her to take a deep breath. She started jogging.

"I'm going to need to rest soon," she whispered. Every muscle in her body hurt, and she could feel a bruise on her hip where the officer had landed on top of her.

"I'll look for somewhere for you," Bane said.

And although he couldn't see her, she lifted her fingers to her lips and blew him a kiss.

# CHAPTER 15

DRAY LOOKED DOWN on the chaos in the square below him, and then glanced at Cossi.

She was leaning against the window, looking down herself.

"They sound as if they're getting louder," Chep spoke from his place at the desk. He looked up from the screen. "Don't they have crowd control here?"

"You need to want to control the crowd, first," Dray said, and watched as the security forces withdrew a little more as the crowd surged.

"What are they protesting, exactly?" Cossi asked. "There are so many different slogans and signs down there, I can't work it out."

"Maybe they don't know themselves. Or they're too divided." Dray frowned.

The streets leading to the square were choked with people, and the square itself had reached capacity. People were chanting and shouting, and the security officers were simply lending their presence, doing nothing constructive to break things up.

A flash that was unmistakably shockgun fire lit up the corner of the square, and panic set in to the crowd.

"Do you see that hover?" Cossi asked, and there was something urgent in her voice.

Dray squinted, and then saw where she was pointing. A security forces hover seemed to have a hanger-on, as if someone in the crowd had grabbed hold.

"The shot seemed to be aimed at whoever is hanging on, and the pilot doesn't look like he's in control. He's been waving his hands for at least a minute." Cossi cupped her hands on either side of her face against the window to get a better look. "The hover's gone round the corner."

"What's this about?" Chep pushed away from the desk and came to stand beside them.

"Not sure, but I think we should go find out."

"You think that's wise?" Cossi waved at the crowd below. "No one on the UC team is exactly a favorite down there by the looks of things."

"Who's the head of security for this part of Fa'allen?"

"I just looked them up." Chep lifted his handheld, and Dray saw he'd created a flowchart of who reported to who.

He gave a nod of appreciation at Chep's efficiency. Tapped his earpiece.

"Captain Subre." He waited longer than he thought was necessary for the connection. "This is Commander Helvan, from the UC leadership team. We're watching what's happening down in Fa'allen Square."

"This was a spontaneous event, Commander." Subre sounded tense and hostile. "This wasn't a planned gathering. From what the first officers on scene could gather, it started after an incident in the square earlier this morning, where some citizens insist they spoke with an Earth woman."

"An Earth woman." Dray kept his voice even, and then flicked the conversation onto the handheld, so Chep and Cossi could listen in.

They had come to immediate attention.

"Do you think that's likely?" He asked after a long silence.

"I don't know what to think." Subre's tone was short.

"Are there any visual comms to confirm?"

"I've been hunting for confirmation since this thing started building up. No luck so far. Some of the people claim there was an electronic pulse that interfered with their handhelds just after the woman was seen."

"And do you know why this possible sighting of an Earth woman is having the effect of a near riot?" Dray looked down and decided he wasn't exaggerating.

"Some say she's a plant. Conveniently arriving the same day you got here, to make us look even worse. Some say she escaped, looking for help from your team. One woman gave a statement that the Earth woman said she was being kept at the military facility that was destroyed yesterday." Subre faltered a bit when he said that, and with sudden understanding, Dray realized Subre considered that at least plausible.

"And the people in the square who talked to her today just let her walk off?" He couldn't see that happening.

"No. According to some witnesses, two hovers came out of nowhere, shots were fired, and she ran away. That's when the pulse wave occurred, as well."

"And it wasn't your people on the hovers?" Dray kept the question light.

"No. More than one person insisted they were military, but there were no insignia, so that isn't necessarily true."

"Why is this the first I'm hearing about this, Captain?" Dray had been in military headquarters for three hours. They'd been given an office at the rear of the building, looking down on the square rather than out across the sea, which he knew from his study of Tecran culture was an insult.

The best offices would be at the top, looking out over the ocean.

A mid-level office at the back was a gesture of disrespect, but it had the benefit of a good view of the growing unrest in the street below.

"I didn't have any proof of the claims, and I would prefer to be sure before bringing something this explosive to our new administrators." Subre's words were stiff.

He obviously didn't like the deal that had been struck between the Tecran and the rest of the UC, and Dray knew in his place, he wouldn't, either. But tough.

That's how it was.

"Has the woman been seen again?"

Subre hesitated. "No."

Cossi lifted her gaze from the handheld to catch his own, and he nodded. Subre was lying.

"You're sure about that?" Dray asked softly.

"Yes. And while I'm happy to talk to you at another time, in case you are unaware, I've got a crowd control problem on my hands, so I'll have to end this now."

"Wait." Dray threw all his authority into his voice. "Who shot at that hover a few minutes ago?"

"Good bye, Commander."

The comms cut off.

"Could there really be an Earth woman here?" Chep asked, skepticism in every word. "Just running around Fa'allen?"

Dray's instinct was no. He forced himself to lift his shoulders. "Unlikely. But obviously some people believe it." He looked back down at the square.

"I'm just glad it wasn't sparked by our arrival," Cossi said.

Dray shook his head. "Or it was, and someone made up an elaborate story to agitate those who weren't already onboard."

Chep made a sound. "That's a good possibility." He looked down at the protests. "They seem to be onboard now."

"I need you down on the street."

The words in Dray's ear were so surprising, he froze.

Bane.

The thinking system sounded the least in control Dray had ever heard him.

"Why?" Out of the corner of his eye, Dray saw Cossi and Chep go still as well, and turn to stare at him.

"There's an Earth woman down there. She needs your help."

"Do you know this, or have you heard the rumor like everyone else?" Dray asked, but he had a sinking feeling Bane did not deal in rumor.

"Her name is Lucy Harris, and she is currently running for her life from Tecran military officers through the tunnels under the city."

"Tell me where." Dray grabbed his jacket and checked his weapon.

Chep and Cossi watched him warily.

"Bane knows where the Earth woman is," he told them. Then he ran out the door.

# CHAPTER 16

THERE WAS no easy way to get through.

Dray stepped out of the back door of military headquarters right onto the square and was immediately shoved by someone in the crowd.

He looked back at Cossi and Chep and wondered if it would be better if Cossi stayed in the building.

Like all Bukarians she was much shorter than him and Chep.

"I can see what you're thinking. The answer is no." She moved to stand beside him, and stumbled as someone pushed her into his side.

The Tecran who'd pushed her fell inexplicably to his knees, gave her a startled look, and then scrambled up and disappeared into the crowd.

"We should have gone out the front entrance and come into the square down one of the side streets," Chep said, looking over the chaos.

Despite the crush, there was something so alien about him, he wasn't so much as touched by the Tecran.

"There's a Tecran military team waiting for you outside the

front entrance," Bane said in Dray's ear. "The Fitalian is correct, it would be faster, but you'd lead them straight to Lucy."

"Can you transmit to Cossi and Chep's earpieces as well?" Dray asked.

"All right."

From their startled looks, Dray guessed he'd included both his colleagues in his answer.

"Now, go right, keep to the edge of the square, and then continue past the first building and take the first street to the left after that." He paused. "Hurry. She's not . . . well."

"What do you mean, not well?" Cossi asked as they started pushing their way through the swaying, shouting masses.

"I mean the few times I've had eyes on her, she keeps stopping and leaning against the wall, and she doesn't look healthy."

"She's injured?" Chep asked.

"She had to fight a military officer a little while ago to get away, and she's favoring her left hip, so I think so."

"Can you talk to her?" Dray asked.

"Yes."

"Ask her what's wrong. It will help us to know her limitations when we find her."

Bane was silent, probably speaking to Lucy Harris, and that was fine with Dray. He needed all his concentration to get through the crowd without being knocked off his feet.

More than one Tecran did fall, but he was relieved to see people stop to help them up. It wasn't a stampede.

Yet.

"You!" The shout came from his left. "You're one of them!"

Dray's hand closed over his shockgun as he turned to face the Tecran pointing at him.

There was a sudden hush as the crowd around him went quiet.

"I'm part of the UC team, if that's what you mean." He kept

his voice at a moderate level, forcing those who wanted to hear him to keep their silence.

"We don't want you here," the Tecran hissed at him, eyes narrowed.

Dray shrugged. "I'm sure you don't. The alternative is war. If you don't like the decision your politicians have made, vote in a different government." He let the impatience he was feeling shine through.

"Why are you here, really?" Someone near the Tecran who'd challenged him called out.

"I was assigned to come here. And you know why we're here. You know." He looked each person in the circle around him in the eye.

"Dray. Let's go." Chep tapped his shoulder. He must have turned back, and worked his way through the crowd.

The sight of the Fitalian, with his slender neck and massive eyes, so very different from the Tecran—from every other group in the UC, Dray had to admit—broke whatever mood had settled over them all, and most turned away, muttering.

Dray sent him a quick look of thanks, and Chep's thin mouth quirked.

"Cossi wanted to do it, but I told her she was too short to have the same impact."

It was hard to read the Fitali's facial expressions, but Dray had the feeling Chep knew it wasn't his height that had diffused the situation, and was amused by it.

He grinned. "I'm surprised you're not limping like the Tecran who shoved her earlier."

"I only maim people I don't like," Cossi said, suddenly on his other side. She smiled, and Dray's gaze caught on those sharp teeth again.

Just as amused as Chep, her smile widened. "I managed to get a comm connection to Ambassador Dimitara. She's . . ." Cossi shook her head, suddenly serious. "She's incandescent that this might be true. That they've been keeping another Earth woman here all this time in secret."

"I assume she's happy for us to follow Bane's lead?" Chep asked as they pushed through the crowd. It seemed as dense on the outskirts of the square as in the center.

Cossi nodded. "She's friends with Rose McKenzie. She was on the Grihan explorer the *Barrist* as a UC liaison when the Grih found Rose. She saw where the Tecran had kept Rose prisoner." Cossi shrugged. "She has strong feelings about it."

"There are two military teams trying to intercept you." Bane's voice was deadly calm. "One moving along the north side of the square, the other coming from the east. You'll walk straight into them if you keep going the way I directed you."

Dray glanced at Chep and Cossi, saw Bane had included them in the warning. They had both gripped the stocks of their shock-guns, strapped, like his own, to their thigh.

"How many in each team?"

"Four in each. They're dressed as civilians, though. I only know who they are because I'm monitoring the chatter in the square," Bane answered.

"So there could be more moving in without talking?" Cossi asked.

There was a moment of silence. "Yes," Bane said. "I didn't think of that."

"We won't be able to spot the ones you've identified in this crowd, let alone those who you haven't." Dray tapped his shock-gun, and it whined as it charged to readiness.

There were two massive screens on each side of the square, and they showed an aerial view of the crowds. Suddenly, the feed changed, and each one showed a different part of the square, with a circle around four Tecran on each screen.

"You doing that?" Chep asked.

"Yes." Bane zoomed in a little more. "Now you can see them."

It took the Tecran standing near the covert military teams a few moments to work out they had been singled out and were on the screens, and they began to point up at the images. Then they turned to look at the people beside them who were circled.

"Move. While they're distracted." Dray sped up, weaving through the crowd, and when he glanced at the screen again, he caught a glimpse of himself moving toward the four officers Bane had warned him about. They were blocked from view by the milling crowds, which suited him just fine.

"You go ahead. Draw them off." He gripped Chep's shoulder. "Following you is all they can do, especially if you stay in the square. Lead them around the perimeter for half an hour or so, and then go back inside headquarters."

"And what'll you do?" Cossi had turned back, so they stood in a huddle, not unlike many others around them.

"I'm going to steal a hooded cloak and find Lucy Harris."

Chep nodded. Then shared a look with Cossi.

They both moved off, striding confidently through the crowd, which parted in their wake and then swallowed them up.

Dray bent, as if to fiddle with his boot. "See any spare cloaks lying around?"

"Give me a few minutes." Bane's tone didn't convey approval for his decision to split from the other two, but Dray decided he'd have made his displeasure known if he hadn't agreed.

Unable to keep crouching down without drawing attention, he rose up, and went still when someone tapped his shoulder.

"You the one who wants a cloak?" The Tecran who asked was young, perhaps just into adulthood. He was holding a cloak out to Dray.

"Yes." Dray took it, confused.

"Good deal." The Tecran looked down at his handheld,

grunted in appreciation, and then with a final glance at Dray, turned and disappeared into the crowd.

"What was that?" Dray pulled the cloak on, lifted the hood, and immediately relaxed a little as he suddenly became just one more body in the square.

"I sent him an offer through his handheld for more money than the cloak was worth."

Dray could hear the dismissive shrug in Bane's voice.

He began to edge out of the crowd, making for the right-hand side of the square. There was chanting near the center, although another group was obviously trying to drown the chanting out with shouts of their own. Most, however, said nothing. Instead, they watched the massive screens, where the debate about the UC's arrival played out with various opinion leaders, and kept an uneasy eye on the more vocal and committed protesters, of all persuasions.

They were invested, but weren't sure of the correct course, Dray realized. They knew they were in the wrong with the UC, but they didn't like having their sovereignty taken from them, even for a set period of time.

It was a hard place to be caught in.

So they stood watch, waiting to be persuaded over to one side or the other.

Most of them balanced on the middle line. He could see it in the way they put some distance between themselves and those who had picked a side and waged a war of opposing views in the center of the square. They huddled together in smallish groups, jostled at times by the sheer number of citizens in the square, but their presence kept things just the right side of nonviolent.

Dray reached the pavement and then eased into a narrow alleyway that had almost no one in it.

"Keep going until the next intersection, then turn left." Bane's voice in his ear was louder now he had a little distance from the shouting and noise.

He turned when he reached the corner, and almost stopped dead when he noticed two Tecran standing close together outside the door of one of the soaring Fa'allen buildings.

He checked his reaction, forcing himself to continue walking, head down, hands in the deep pockets of the cloak.

There was no response from Bane, and Dray realized he couldn't see the Tecran. In this environment he wasn't all knowing, as he'd been when he'd flown side by side with the *Urna*.

He hoped the Tecran didn't ask him anything, as he couldn't risk speaking, particularly as he knew his Tecran was accented. Everyone who'd been assigned to the UC team had to learn fluent Tecran in order to be able to fulfill their duties, but they sounded like the foreigners they were.

The two Tecran were level with him now, a man and a woman, and the way they watched him walk past had alarms ringing in his head.

Unless they were agitators planning on mayhem in the square, these two were part of the military teams running around town looking for Lucy Harris.

Once they were behind him, the back of his neck itched at his vulnerability and when he heard the faint sound of footsteps, he reached beneath his cloak and drew his shockgun out of its holster.

He glanced over his shoulder, saw with a frisson of shock only one of the two were following behind him, the other had disappeared.

He didn't like not knowing where they were.

"You should be coming up to another alley to the right soon. Take it," Bane said.

His voice gave Dray a shock in the tense silence. He was moving fast, and the alleyway came up almost immediately.

He turned down it, his stride confident, and then pressed

himself against the wall when he reached the deepest shadows, waiting, shockgun ready.

The Tecran stepped in after him, and after a few steps, came to a stop.

He was listening, Dray realized. Listening for Dray's footsteps. And couldn't hear them.

Dray heard the whine of a shockgun charging, and found the calm he always reached for before a confrontation.

He should shoot first, ask questions later, but he wasn't running a Grihan incursion. He was as much a diplomat as a fighter here, and he knew the repercussions of shooting a Tecran would be significant. Especially if this Tecran wasn't a member of one of the covert military teams.

"What do you want?" he asked into the dark, and then crouched down silently and took a careful step to the side.

There was a startled silence, and then the flash of shockgun fire above his head.

He returned fire from his crouch, saw in the snap of light that the Tecran was flung backward, landing hard.

He was up and running immediately, but he heard the shout from beyond the alley entrance, and the thunder of boots.

"Ran into a little trouble," he managed to whisper to Bane as he reached the end of the street. It intersected with another lane, running right to left.

"What kind of trouble?" Bane asked.

"Got shot at. Some Tecran are following me."

There was a flash as someone behind him tried to shoot him again.

"I don't know where you are. I need you safe to help Lucy."

Dray turned left, keeping close to the wall and slowing down to make as little noise as possible. His lips quirked. Good to know where he stood with Bane.

He was only useful insofar as he could help Lucy Harris.

He didn't comment on it, though. Someone had turned down the lane after him and silence was essential.

"What's happening?" Bane asked in his ear.

He didn't reply, he needed Bane to be quiet so he could judge where the Tecran stalking him was.

A light suddenly flared, just for a moment, as the Tecran scanned the alley, and Dray flung himself into a roll and came up on the other side of the lane. He crouched low and shot in the direction the light had come from.

His opponent sucked in a breath, but more in surprise than pain, and he heard a whisper—the Tecran talking to his team.

He was about to be outnumbered.

He needed to get away, to lose the Tecran dogging his heels, so he could find Lucy Harris.

He rose silently to his feet and shot at the Tecran again in a single, fluid motion, and then he ran.

# CHAPTER 17

SHE WAS BACK UP at street level.

No matter how useful the tunnel had been, now she was back up in the open air and cold wind, Lucy finally felt she could breathe properly.

There was something about narrow, enclosed spaces that set her heart thumping, her hands shaking.

She'd never been claustrophobic before, so she laid her new issues at the feet of the Tecran. They had done this to her.

The building behind her was designed like a series of waves coming to shore and she was huddled down in the curve of one of them, deep in the pocket of darkness it created.

The sound of someone shuffling past had her going suddenly still, and for a long, terrifying moment, she thought she'd been run to ground.

"Who are you?"

She looked up, eyes wide, to see a Tecran peering around the curve of the next wave at her.

There was something very different about her, and Lucy realized she was young. A teenager, perhaps.

The first young Tecran she'd ever seen.

She'd only dealt with adults before now.

"I'm not sure you should be talking to me," she answered.

With a chuckle, the girl moved around the corner and leaned back against the wall, arms tucked under her cloak. "You sound funny."

"I'm not what you'd call a native speaker." She didn't lower the scarf from around her mouth.

"Your eyes are funny, too." The girl leaned closer.

"What are you doing out here?" Lucy asked her.

"Got separated from my parents in the square," the girl said with a shrug, but Lucy thought she detected a little quiver in her voice. "And I'm locked out. We don't live in Fa'allen. We're only staying here for the UC arrival and I don't have the codes to get into the building." She paused. "Why are your eyes funny?"

With a sigh, Lucy pushed back her hood and pulled down the scarf. "I'm not Tecran."

"I knew it!" The girl crouched down into the deep shadow to get a better look. "Are you with the UC?"

She shook her head.

"Then why are you here?"

"Someone brought me here against my will." She didn't know if it was fair of her to say this to a young Tecran, who'd had no part in her abduction, but it was the truth.

"Someone . . . us?" The girl tilted her head, eyes even bigger than they'd been before.

"Someone in your military, apparently."

"You're an Earth person. You're why we're in so much trouble!"

"So it seems. I only found out about the trouble you're in today."

"How can that be? It's been the non-stop news for *months*." The girl looked at her with surprise.

"I was locked up until yesterday."

"I . . . don't want to believe it." The stark truth in her voice had Lucy leaning back, closing her eyes, and resting her head against the wall.

"I've gotten that a lot since I escaped." She opened her eyes and held the girl's gaze. "My understanding is that most Tecran didn't know what was going on. They don't like having to pay the consequences, because those consequences are harsh, and they weren't personally guilty. Which leaves me, the person who was wronged, with no one to turn to." Well, not no one. She sent a silent apology to Bane, who'd kept quiet since she'd started talking.

It would not be a good idea to advertise that she had his help.

"Pulina?" The call came from the back steps of the building.

"I'm here." The girl rose up and stepped back into the lane, her eyes still on Lucy, her expression conflicted.

Then she turned and ran toward her parents.

She didn't say goodbye, or alert her parents to Lucy's presence, and that was just as well.

She'd thought a few times about approaching someone else, asking for help. Not everyone could be out to get her.

But she was nothing if not a fast learner.

No one she'd met so far had had a simple reaction to her. The complexity around what was happening on Tecra and how they felt about it kept getting in the way. Even the teenagers couldn't square it in their minds.

She heard the murmur of voices, and then a door close.

She shivered, suddenly cold to the core.

"Where is this friend of yours?" she asked Bane. He'd been quiet so long, all through her conversation with Pulina, and when he didn't respond, a hot touch of panic had her rising to her feet. "Bane?"

"I'm here. I don't know where he is." Bane sounded . . . worried. "He isn't answering me, which means he can't without putting himself in danger. I think he's run into one of the military teams out looking for you."

"You can't track him?" She didn't know why she thought he could. In her head he was all-seeing. He could tell where she was because she'd given him a link to the handheld she'd taken from Gugi, but even then, he couldn't actually see her unless she turned on the visual comms setting, he just knew her location.

"You're close to where I was leading him to when he had to take evasive action. I don't think he can be too far away."

She saw a flicker of purple light up ahead, coming from one of the back lanes behind a building.

Shockgun fire.

"I can see something," she whispered. "Someone's firing a shockgun up ahead."

She hesitated as the shockgun fire flickered again.

"Should I go see?"

"No." Bane's hiss made her jerk. "Wait. I'll tell Dray where you are."

She felt like she was climbing out of her skin by the time he spoke again.

"Get ready," he said.

"For what?" She couldn't keep the fear and impatience out of her voice.

"For—"

Someone was suddenly on the street, running.

He was big—bigger than any of the Tecran—and he turned slightly as he ran, shooting at the Tecran following him.

The flare of shockgun fire hit the Tecran full in the chest, and he went down, but Lucy could see he wasn't dead, or even unconscious. He rolled to the side.

He must be wearing some kind of protection.

The figure running toward her turned to face forward and she caught a quick glimpse of him in the reflected light from the windows of the building soaring above them.

He was like the aliens she'd seen this morning on the screen in the square; tall, broad shouldered, and with elf ears.

"Is that your friend?" she whispered.

"Dray Helvan," Bane confirmed. "UC military team leader."

She straightened, stepping out of the dark pool of shadows and into the lane.

She saw the flare of surprise in Dray's eyes, and then his gaze flew past her, up and beyond her shoulder.

She glanced back, shocked at the sight of a hover flying toward her at top speed.

It wasn't silent, but the sound of the wind had risen in the last half hour, and she could barely hear it over the high-pitched whistle. It flew over her head and then Dray's, lowering to the ground between them and the Tecran Dray had shot.

Was it there to shield the Tecran or them? The pilot looked like any other Tecran on the street, not a soldier or a security guard.

The pilot on the hover stared at them both in shock. "What's going on? Who's controlling this?"

"Get off the hover." Dray lifted his shockgun and shot at the Tecran soldier standing behind it again.

The pilot flinched back and then stood, struggling with something at his side as the soldier returned fire. Dray ducked behind the hover, and Lucy realized the pilot was trying to get to a weapon.

She crouched beside Dray, close to the pilot, and just as he pulled the weapon from a holster, she scooted closer and shoved his legs with both hands.

He lost his balance with a cry and fell to the side, his weapon flying off into the darkness.

Dray shot her a quick look of surprise, then shoved the Tecran the rest of the way off, so he landed in the road.

He swung up onto the seat and looked down at the pilot. "Report this to Captain Subre, and tell him the rumors of the Earth woman are true, and he has rogue military units running amok in his city."

He lifted his shockgun one handed and shot at the soldier again, while he put his other hand out to her.

She grasped it, and he swung her up behind him.

As soon as she was on, he rose up, spun around and hit the accelerator.

Lucy hung on, her cheek turned against his broad back.

Purple light flickered behind them, and she winced, waiting for a hit, but Dray wove from side to side, and nothing touched them.

She clutched his waist a little tighter.

"I have to give it to you, Bane," she whispered in English. "When you promise something, you deliver."

CHAPTER 18

DRAY DIDN'T KNOW that he'd mistrusted Bane, exactly. But meeting Lucy Harris in the flesh was more than shocking to him.

They had kept her here, all the while the UC considered the weighty matters before them, the misdeeds and breeches of trust and law by the Tecran military and some of the Tecran government.

The time to step forward and admit they had taken a fourth woman from Earth was four weeks ago at the latest.

They had said nothing.

Now her arms encircled his waist, and she pressed herself into his back as he pushed the hover as fast as it could go, traveling on instinct to the north, out of the city, to the flat, scrubby escarpment that stretched from the top of the cliffs to the low mountains in the distance.

The city lay behind them, a long, thin line of towering structures running east to west, the glow of lights reflecting off the fog creeping in from the sea.

"Where are we going?" Lucy asked him in Tecran, and the sound of the language on her tongue was so strange to him, so wrong, he tensed.

"Do you speak Grihan?" he asked her, and winced at the snap in his voice.

"No," she answered. "Is that what you are? Grihan?"

He hadn't understood how little she knew, and he forced himself to swallow back the fury that had risen up in him at how isolated they must have kept her.

"Yes. I'm part of the Grihan contingent the UC sent out to Tecra."

She waited a moment before he felt her nod against his back, and wondered if his accented Tecran was hard for her to follow.

"Where are we going?" she asked again, and it was so tentatively said he was ashamed of himself for snapping at her and making her worry about how he would respond to her questions.

"I don't know," he answered honestly, forcing the Tecran words out of his mouth. "Bane? Do you have a suggestion?"

"Head west," Bane told him, his tone clipped. "There's a small cluster of houses just outside the city and all of them are currently empty. A lot of Tecran traveled to Fa'allen to be there when the UC arrived."

Dray turned the hover to the left, looping in a wide arc toward the dark coastline.

Lucy said nothing more and he worried that he had stifled the conversation, but the wind had picked up and howled around them, and he decided talking was probably going to be difficult anyway.

It took an hour before they found something that resembled a road, and another half hour before a small huddle of what looked like narrow towers loomed out of the mist.

"Turn here," Bane said in his ear, and Dray turned into a paved lane that led to a garage that was open on both ends, looking out at the escarpment on one side, the sea on the other, although almost nothing was visible now in the thick fog that swirled in blinding patterns in the wind.

He powered the hover down and waited for Lucy to climb off. When she simply sat there, arms still tight around him, he turned to look at her.

She blinked up at him. "Sorry, I can't seem to unclench my hands."

He covered her hands with his own, warming them, and then carefully raised them up so he could get off the hover. When he was down, he put his hands to her waist and lifted her up, set her gently on the ground.

She stood, shivering, as he switched off the engine.

"What is wrong with her?" he asked Bane, using the Grihan dialect from Xal he'd grown up with so she wouldn't understand him.

"I don't know. I can't see her." Bane sounded panicked. "What have you done to her?"

"Nothing." He looked around, feeling a little panicked himself. "Where is the door into the tower?"

"I can't see that, either," Bane told him, voice going icy. "That's why you're there."

With a curse, Dray walked toward the cliff side, and saw a narrow path leading to the right. He followed it, amazed at how close to the edge the path was, and found a door set into the stone face of the building.

He tried the door, but it was locked. "Do you have a way to open this up?"

"I'm looking." Bane's answer was short. "I have found a way into the system, but it's hard to pinpoint the exact house—"

"Open them all then." Dray turned and strode back to the garage.

Lucy was still standing where he'd left her, hunched over in her Tecran cloak.

He scooped her up, and then nearly dropped her as he realized she weighed far more than he'd been expecting.

He had to heave her a little higher in his arms, and pull her tight against his chest. The walk beside the cliff had him in a light sweat by the time he got to the door. He pushed against it, and it opened, and suddenly they were in a warm, sheltered space.

It smelled slightly strange; the meaty, gamey scent he'd noticed on some of the Tecran he'd come into contact with.

"Where are we?" She was shaking even worse now they were in the warmth of the house and she barely got the words out between chattering teeth.

Bane must have answered her, because she nodded and hunched over, crossing her arms over her chest.

"What do you need?" He didn't bother to hide the panic in his voice.

"Cold." She rubbed her arms with shaking hands. "Is there a hot shower?"

And then he got it, and he felt a hard, sharp sense of disgust for himself.

He wasn't with a colleague. She didn't have a uniform like his, with temperature regulation. She'd traveled in freezing temperatures with nothing but his own body to protect her from the wind.

And she hadn't said a word.

"Let's find one." He scooped her up again, bracing himself against her weight this time, and headed up the staircase that curved to his left.

The first level contained a cozy lounge and a kitchen, the second level a bathroom and a bedroom.

He set her down and ran the shower. When steam started billowing, she edged past him, dropping her cloak, and stepped into the hot water with her clothes on.

"Can you find me something else to wear?"

He nodded, backing out and closing the door behind him.

And then turned and leaned back against it, fists clenched, and called himself every insult he could think of.

Getting her out of danger in Fa'allen had been his first priority, and he'd managed that with Bane's help, but after that, his failure to find out what equipment she had, and whether she could cope with the cold—

With a grunt of disgust, he pushed away from the door and began going through the closet set into the curved wall. He chose items that looked like they'd fit and put them on the bed.

He opened the bathroom door a little way and heard the sound of the water still running.

"I've put some things out for you. There's more in the cupboard if you don't like them. I'll be looking around the rest of the house." As soon as the words were out, he realized he'd spoken in Grihan.

There was a moment of silence, and he was about to repeat it in Tecran when Bane spoke in his ear.

"I've translated that for her." The censure in Bane's tone was clear, and Dray bowed his head, just as annoyed with himself as Bane.

"Thank you." Lucy's words were choked. The beauty of her voice was clogged, and he knew there was something wrong, but when he waited a beat for her to say more, nothing was forthcoming.

He closed the door and left, climbing up the next flight of stairs to find an identical bedroom and bathroom above, and then, on the top floor, a comfortable, plush room with an even more massive window than the rooms below, although the fog pressed up against it, leaving smudges of frost in its wake.

"How is she?" Bane asked, his voice overloud in air muffled by fog.

"I think she'll be better once she's warm. I'll make some grinabo for her, and something for her to eat."

"That's all it was?" Bane sounded dubious.

"I think so. If the Grih get too cold, they can die. I think Earth people are similar."

"Don't let her die," Bane said, and there was a warning in his tone that chilled Dray.

"I won't."

"No one will like the results if she does." There was a promise in Bane's voice that made Dray wonder what he was talking about.

He decided he didn't want to find out.

"Can you connect me to Ambassador Dimitara?"

"She has been asking about you," Bane conceded. "Quite vociferously. Just give me a moment."

There was silence, and Dray left the top floor and ran lightly down the stairs. He stopped for a moment on Lucy's floor but he heard her moving around and that settled him a little, allowing him to continue down to the kitchen.

"Dray?" Dimitara's voice was sharp.

"I'm here." He started pulling out mugs and bowls, taking some ready-made dishes out of the cooling unit and opening cupboards to find the grinabo maker.

"Where is here?"

"It might be better not to say, just in case someone is listening." He guessed Bane would have good shielding, but Dimitara was sitting in a Tecran office, with hostile Tecran all around her. He'd take nothing for granted.

She was silent, then drew in a breath. "True. You're safe?"

"We are." He didn't mention Lucy, but Dimitara's gasp told him she understood what he meant by 'we'.

"Good." He heard a rustle, as if she was shifting in her chair. "That's very good. Things are less well here. The mass protests in the square haven't turned violent, but they show no signs of dissipating."

"What are you going to do about it?"

She sighed. "It's a tricky one. The people are neither military nor government. They technically come under the government laws, but there is a right to gather. That was set into the UC rules after that bad business with the light guns thirty years ago."

"So you're going to let it play out?" He didn't think that ignoring the protesters was a good idea either.

"No. I'm going out to talk to them." Dimitara sounded resigned.

"Take Cossi and Chep with you. Let them set up a secure perimeter."

"Chep and Cossi have already suggested that. They let some people follow them around the square for nearly an hour and then came to find me to report." She didn't sound happy. "I thought it would be bad when we got here, but my imagination was obviously not up to the task."

"I'm surprised it isn't worse," Dray admitted. "I know how the Grih would react, and I honestly don't know if we'd be this restrained. What is the government saying?"

He heard her chair squeak, as if she was leaning back in it. "They're panicked. They don't want to harm any of the protesters, but they also want to clear the square. And the shots fired in the square and in the side streets didn't go unnoticed." She paused. "I'm guessing that was you?"

"I was responsible for some of the shots in the side streets. I don't know who fired in the square."

"The military were firing at Lucy," Bane said, and from the startled silence on Dimitara's end he guessed Bane had included her in the transmission.

"They were trying to kill her?" Dimitara's voice suddenly grew, as if three of her were talking at once.

"I think they planned to stun her so they could grab her and kill her elsewhere. I'm sure they'd have left her body where no one would find it. They would not have wanted a dead Earth woman to be found in the square."

"Who's doing this?" Dimitara asked. "It can't be the whole of the military. It's surely a smaller group."

"Speak to someone called Dr. Farnn," Bane said. "She's one of the few survivors of that fire at a military facility a few days ago. She was one of Lucy Harris's doctors there, and Lucy said she's the one who helped her escape. She'll have a good idea of who had something to lose by Lucy being found."

"Do you know where she is?" Dimitara asked.

"I'll send you the details, Ambassador." Bane hesitated. "I would suggest you put Dr. Farnn somewhere very safe, like the *Urna*. I don't think the military will be happy that she's still walking around free."

"And you, Dray? What's your plan?" Dimitara asked.

"We have to come back to the city. I need you to send a team to get us."

She hesitated.

"You won't send a team?" He didn't hide his outrage.

"No, I want to send a team. I'm just worried they'll be followed."

Dray gave a snort. "So what if they are? What are they going to do? Shoot down a UC team?"

Her silence spoke volumes.

And, yes, maybe they were crazy enough to do just that. "Even if they do, we can shoot back. And there can't be more crazy military officers caught up in this cover up than we can handle." He would relish shooting a few of them. It was sounding like a better idea all the time.

"If they shoot to kill? Or if one of them gets seriously hurt? How will that play out in the current mood on Tecra?" Dimitara asked quietly. "Do I care all that much about them getting hurt? No. I'm so angry about this, I want to call Bane back and get him to blitz the whole planet, but I'm here to make this agreement work. And so far, it really does look like a small group is causing this. That's not fair to the rest of the Tecran. And how much more damage will I do if I agree to let a team or two fetch you, weapons hot, and the Tecran take that as an attack in bad faith and pull out of the agreement? I don't want to be the UC ambassador who led the UC into war. And how safe will Lucy be in a situation like that anyway? Can you guarantee she won't be hurt in any armed confrontation with the Tecran? After all, they're trying to kill her."

He saw his fantasy of using his shockgun on a few Tecran assholes evaporate under the cold reality of her reasoning. "I'll get us back quietly."

"You do that." Dimitara's words were implacable. "And soon, Dray. I won't rest until Lucy's safe on the *Urna*."

"Safe on my Class 5," Bane corrected. "There is no way she's going to be safe on the *Urna*."

After a startled silence, Dimitara gave a hum of agreement. "On your Class 5," she confirmed. "But you're not in the solar system, Bane. Until you get here, I want her in the fold."

"So you want me to come in?" Bane asked.

Dray would say this for the thinking system, he was a very convincing liar. And he obviously trusted Dray not to out him to Dimitara.

"No," she said, although not as decisively as he would have thought. "I'll have Lucy taken to you in one of the *Urna's* explorers as soon as we have her onboard. Things are too delicate at this point for you to make an appearance."

Dray thought of Bane, hiding on Gyre, and for the first time since this mess began, relaxed a little.

He was glad the thinking system was right here. Not sitting in a holding pattern out of reach. The delicacy of the balance between the UC teams and the Tecran be damned.

When Dimitara said goodbye he responded in kind and then stood in the silent kitchen.

A feeling of being watched slowly crept over him, and he turned toward the stairs. Lucy Harris was sitting on one of the steps, wet hair falling in a cascade over her shoulder, her eyes big and dark.

She was dressed in a black shirt that was too big for her and loose black trousers, but her feet were bare. She leaned forward to hug her knees and the neck of the shirt slipped over one shoulder.

He leaned back against the counter, staring at her, and the sound of the grinabo maker's warble that announced it had finished was a shock in the quiet.

"You feeling warmer?" he asked, and again realized he'd used Grihan. He cleared his throat. "Sorry," he said in Tecran, "are you better?"

She nodded, her gaze traveling over him carefully. "Thank you."

"How long were you . . ." He trailed off, worried his words would be distressing for her, then forced himself to continue, because this was something the UC needed to know. "How long were you held prisoner?"

She lifted her shoulders. "I wasn't conscious for some of the time. Something happened to me. They wouldn't tell me what, but I guessed it was their fault, and they felt guilty about it."

"They?"

"The scientists and doctors in the facility. They didn't like me asking questions about it. But I recovered, and I've been awake for two months or so. They helped me get stronger. I think I was in a coma for about a month before that."

That was as long as they'd had Imogen Peters and Fiona Russell, the two Earth women abducted after Rose McKenzie.

Dray shouldn't be surprised, but he was. He was staggered.

All this time. All this time they'd had her, and they'd looked the councilors of the UC in the eye and wrung their hands and said how it was all a mistake, when a whole team of scientists and doctors and military leaders had known Lucy Harris was right here in Fa'allen.

He straightened from his slouch. It would be his pleasure to rain down some retribution, diplomacy be damned.

# CHAPTER 19

DRAY HELVAN LOOKED like his head was about to explode.

Lucy eyed him warily as he turned toward a machine that let out another warble, and pulled out a cup of grinabo.

He handed it to her, and she took it gratefully, cupping her hands around it for the warmth, and sipping at the hot, fragrant liquid.

She watched him warily. He seemed even bigger in the sleek kitchen than he had before out on the streets of Fa'allen. His hair was short and stood on end, a rich brown tipped with burgundy. She wondered if it was natural, or if he did something to achieve the look.

The most delightful part of him was his ears; pointed and close to his head, they were evocative of elves and forests and longbows. They somehow softened the harsh lines of his face and the hard blue glitter of his eyes.

He stared back at her for a beat and then pointed to the table, on which he'd laid out a meal.

"Are you hungry?"

She was ravenous, but . . . "I can't eat most Tecran food." She got to her feet and walked to the table, looking down at the offerings.

"What did they feed you?"

"Nutrient bars, mainly." She heard the lack of enthusiasm in her own voice.

He glanced down at her and she saw worry in his gaze. "I don't want to give you anything that'll make you sick."

"It's okay. I've tasted everything on the table." She tried to make herself sound more enthusiastic. "It was almost a game at the facility. Who could find a new dish for me to try." Her smile wobbled a little.

She sat down and looked at the food, and to her utter horror, a big, fat tear rolled down her cheek.

She used the back of her hand to brush it away, and caught sight of Dray's face.

"Don't mind me," she told him. She hiccuped. "I'm just . . ."

What *was* she just? Wallowing? Yes. Having a pity party? Yes, again.

She stood up and turned away from him and the table, walked blindly out of the kitchen into the big lounge area.

Swirling white fog pressed up against the floor to ceiling windows that looked out over the sea.

Even though she couldn't see out, she walked up to them anyway, pressing a hand against the cold glass. No, not glass, but something like it. She didn't know what it was called. Didn't know how it was made. Didn't know shit.

She slammed both fists into the transparent wall.

A noise behind her had her looking over her shoulder.

Dray stood in the doorway, arms crossed over his chest.

Was that pity or condescension she saw in his gaze?

Either way, it pissed her off even more.

"I was on my way home from a quick grocery shop," she said,

voice far from even. "I had two bags of groceries in the back, bags I'd give a lot for right now. There was ice cream in one of them. And strawberries. And peaches. I was going to make peach pie! With ice cream. But instead of getting home, and making peach pie, the world went black. I woke up a few times, just little flashes of consciousness, but when I woke properly, I was in the facility. Over a month of time had passed, and I was on an alien planet." She wanted to swear, but she didn't know how in Tecran, so she spoke in English, slowly enunciating each word. "A fucking alien planet."

She held his gaze, boldly challenging him, and something in his eyes stared back at her. A predatory creature that would not back down.

That suited her. She wanted a fight.

"So how do you fucking explain that?" she asked, and slammed a fist backward so she hit the window again to punctuate the question. He was the advanced alien, let him figure out what she was saying.

He tilted his head to the side, and the look on his face said he thought he was dealing with a deranged lunatic.

So what? She felt deranged.

"What the actual fuck am I doing here?" She took a step toward him. She had asked this question so many times in the facility, and had been met with averted gazes, a change of topic, or had been straight up ignored. Maybe she could finally get an answer.

His eyes narrowed. "I can't speak your language, as you know. But Bane has translated for me. You are here because the Tecran wanted to be the strongest force on the United Council."

She stared at him. "Are you saying this is all common-or-garden super villain stuff? I lost my family, my friends, my *life* because they wanted to rule the galaxy?"

He frowned in confusion. "They thought to use thinking

systems to give them the power to be in command of the United Council. To take control."

"And might it have worked?" she asked.

"If they had been able to keep me and my four brothers prisoner, yes." Bane's voice was quiet in her ear. "But they could not, because they didn't understand thinking systems. And they didn't understand Earth women, either."

"How was taking me part of their quest for domination?" She dismissed Dray, turning away from him, her conversation with Bane now.

"Part of their plan was to collect interesting species and technology from planets and systems the United Council hadn't discovered. To exploit those technologies and advantages before anyone else. Except, your fellow Earth women who were taken were their undoing instead." There was deep satisfaction in his voice.

"Is Earth in danger?" she whispered. She hadn't thought about that until now. Of course, if they got her, they knew where it was. They could do this to others. *Had* done this to others. She'd seen the video of the women singing.

"No. Sazo deleted all maps to Earth as a favor to Rose McKenzie. And only four of the five of us ever went there. One is dead, one lost his ship, and as I said, Sazo deleted the files."

"Did you go?" she asked him.

"No. I was the only one who didn't."

She leaned against the window, arms tight around herself. "What happens now? Where do I fit in?" She was so angry. She had been angry for months, she realized now, but in the facility, she'd understood how vulnerable she was.

She had been an alien thing. A slightly dangerous performing monkey, who few had seen as an equal, or even in the same sentient category.

She'd made nice, to the scientists at least, if not the guards, let the insults and the condescension roll off her to survive, but now she was out of that and the fire of fury had roared to life.

She didn't think she could bank it any time soon.

Still . . .

"Sorry." She turned back to Dray, saw he had moved from the doorway, was almost close enough to touch. She spoke in Tecran, rather than forcing Bane to translate her English. "I shouldn't have shouted at you. You're helping me."

He gave a nod, and she was struck by the sheer beauty of him. There were elements of otherworldliness to him—the ears, the spiky hair—but even then, it was more sexy elf than alien.

After being the odd one out for months, she felt a sudden kinship to him so strong it was almost overwhelming.

She forced a brake on her emotions. Because while she might see him as something familiar at last, he didn't have the same need to bond to her as she did to him.

He would have his own kind around him all the time.

She was the one who didn't fit.

"You fit in with the Grih," he said, and startled, she realized he was responding to her statement, which she hadn't realized she'd spoken out loud.

"You fit in with me, too." Bane said softly.

She bent her head, her hands clasped together. She couldn't help the hot flow of tears that dripped off her cheeks.

"What do you need?" Dray asked. "You must eat."

She lifted her head and sniffed. The thought of Tecran food made her stomach cramp. She was hungry but not hungry enough to eat anything he'd put out for her. "I had some nutrition bars in Fa'allen. I think I'd like to rest for a bit. I've been snatching bits of sleep in uncomfortable places for a few days now. And that couch looks pretty good."

He looked over to where she pointed.

"You don't want to use one of the bedrooms?"

She shook her head. "No. I'll be more relaxed here." There was something unsettling about the thought of sleeping uninvited in someone else's bed.

The bedrooms were also small and dark, whereas the lounge was big and airy. She wouldn't feel trapped here.

She sensed a change in the fog behind her and turned to see it had parted a little, so she could look out to sea by the light of Tecra's two moons.

There was a massive rock standing a little way out, as if part of the cliff had been sliced off and pushed out to sea. She caught the faintest suggestion of movement on its sheer black walls.

"What's that?" She looked over her shoulder, saw Dray had found a blanket somewhere and was carrying it under an arm.

He came to stand beside her, his shoulder brushing her own.

"That's a baug colony. The Tecran like to climb the cliffs for sport and hunt them."

Lucy watched them move and flutter over the sheer rock face for a few more minutes, and then the fog closed in again.

She turned back to the room, and Dray handed her the folded blanket.

"Sleep," he said. "I'll keep watch."

She didn't want him to stand watch over her, the thought of being that vulnerable didn't sit well with her, but she couldn't find a way to refuse without sounding ungrateful. "Thank you."

She settled down on one of the couches facing the windows, and pulled the blanket up. It smelled clean, the scent on it told her they must use the same detergent as the facility, because it was familiar to her.

She didn't think she would fall asleep easily, but Dray had left the room, and as soon as she laid her head on a cushion, her whole body seemed to cry out in relief that she was off her feet and lying down.

She hadn't scratched the surface of the questions she wanted to ask, and she could see an equal number in Dray's eyes, but for now she was safe, warm and for the first time had not one but two people looking out for her.

Considering how her life had looked just over a full day ago, things were definitely improving.

# CHAPTER 20

DRAY LOOKED in on Lucy a few times as he prowled around the house, but mainly he stood watch two floors above.

The fog was thinner higher up, and he liked to think if the Tecran were coming for them using hovers, he'd see a reflection of the lights in the smokey gray cloud.

"Hear anything out there?" he asked Bane.

"No. I'm not going to be as much help as I was before. I can't see anything. There are no lenses out here. And after I took control of those two hovers, they'll know I'm helping you. They'll be more careful, more difficult to catch out."

"We wouldn't have made it this far without you." Lucy would have probably been caught before he'd even managed to get to her. "How long have you known about her?"

"I was told there was a possibility she was here before I left with the *Urna*. But I was reluctant to say anything. If I was wrong, that would have been bad for everyone."

"True," Dray acknowledged. "The UC would have wondered if you were stirring up trouble against the Tecran, and the Tecran would have felt even more persecuted than they already do."

"And if one of the UC team told the wrong Tecran, and she

was somewhere on Tecra and alive, it could have been her death sentence."

Dray sucked in a breath, because he hadn't thought of that possibility, but it was the cold, hard truth.

"How *did* you know?" He shifted, leaning against the window as the fog grew thicker. "Who told you she might exist at all?"

"Paxe was the one who took her. He told Oris about her just before he self-destructed. It was his way to atone. He knew the Tecran had buried all mention of her, and he wanted to do something to help her before he died."

Dray said nothing as he absorbed that.

Paxe had died rather than be chained by the Tecran, and his destruction had brought the Tecran's plans to a sudden end. Left with no Class 5s under their control, their plans had collapsed, and they'd had no choice but to come to the United Council as supplicants wanting forgiveness, rather than as triumphant victors who could force the other members of the council into subjugation.

The whole thing still had the power to catch at his throat, as anger and disgust warred for prominence.

"This is going to hit the United Council hard. They went relatively easy on the Tecran because everyone thought they'd come clean about the Earth women. To find out they haven't . . ." There was no way to soften this blow. Keeping quiet about Lucy Harris was such an act of bad faith, he didn't know if some in the UC would be able to accept the current treaty where all the Tecran lost was their sovereignty for five years.

"Yes." There was a depth of satisfaction to Bane's voice.

Dray shrugged it off. Bane had more right than most to feel aggrieved when it came to the Tecran.

The fog pressed up against the windows and suddenly feeling hemmed in, blind, he pushed away from the window. "I'm going to walk around outside."

"I'll keep listening for any chatter," Bane said.

Dray gave a hum of agreement and then ran lightly down the stairs. He looked in on Lucy before he slipped out and was struck anew by her hair.

It exploded over the arm of the couch she lay on, gold burnished brown spirals that he wanted to touch.

He had studied the three known Earth women, everyone in the five UC territories had, but it hadn't prepared him for being in the same room as one in person.

She was vital, her dark eyes piercingly intelligent.

It was one thing to be told the Earth women were advanced sentients, but another to see the truth of that right in front of his eyes.

He recalled the warmth of her pressed against his back as they'd raced away from Fa'allen on the hover, the way she'd rested her cheek against his shoulder blade, and the fire in her eyes when she'd spun from the windows and challenged him earlier.

He had said far less than he wanted to in that confrontation, afraid his sudden, inappropriate arousal would somehow make itself obvious.

With a rueful shake of his head, he ran his hands through his hair and backed out of the room, the sight of Lucy's long, dark lashes resting on the curve of her cheek a little too enticing for his peace of mind.

The wind blew through the open-ended garage with a high-pitched whistle that annoyed him. He wouldn't hear anyone approach over the sound, but he guessed they wouldn't hear him, either.

He made his way around the back of the house, looking left to the other two houses perched on the cliff top.

He heard a faint clink from the closest one, and going suddenly still, he stood in the swirling fog and listened.

Cautiously, he pulled his shockgun from its holster and then moved down the hard-packed path between the houses for a little way until he could slip around the side of the neighboring house over grass slick with dew from the fog.

He turned the corner to the front of the house, the side that faced the ocean. The eerie sucking sound of the sea at the bottom of the cliff, deadened by the thick fog, couldn't hide the unmistakeable whine of a shockgun.

He dropped to the ground, crouching as he lifted his own weapon up.

The flash of purple reflected strangely off the fog and he sensed the flare just above him, where his head had been a moment before.

The blunt black barrel of a weapon appeared out of the swirling cloud and then the Tecran soldier holding it materialized.

They looked at each other, both with weapons raised, for a long beat.

"There are too many of us, put down your weapon." The soldier didn't move or take his eyes off Dray, and just when Dray was going to call him a liar, two other soldiers stepped out of the fog, one on either side of him.

Reluctantly he lowered his weapon and then set it on the ground.

The soldier closest to him, a woman all in black, with no insignia, scooped it up. "What do we do with him?"

"We can't leave him here." The soldier who'd first shot at him said. "He's apparently a Grihan UC team leader. Which means we have to think long and hard before we kill him."

The third soldier looked across at the speaker. "Why?"

"Because the UC might very well take serious exception to that."

"Like they won't already take exception to the Earth woman," the third soldier answered back.

"They don't know about her. Or, if they've heard something,

they don't have definite proof." The woman tucked Dray's shockgun into the back of her pants. "They most definitely know about him. They sent him here."

"Well, we aren't going to make a decision right now. Let's get moving." The first soldier moved back a fraction, to let Dray up, and he stood slowly, mind racing as he considered and discarded various escape scenarios.

"Where's Lucy?"

"We have her safe." There was no smile, no enjoyment in the Tecran's eyes. "Guess we're bringing you along."

At least there was that. As long as they were kept together, he could help her.

"Earpiece," the soldier said, palm out, and reluctantly, Dray pulled it out of his ear and dropped it onto the Tecran's outstretched hand.

It was no more than he'd expect, though. Earpieces and weapons were the first things to be taken.

At least Bane would have heard enough to work out what was happening.

The soldier dropped the earpiece and ground it under his heel, then kicked it off the cliff.

"Where are you taking us?" He needed to find out as much as he could. If the Tecran didn't immediately realize Lucy had an earpiece of her own, they could feed more information to Bane.

The soldiers ignored him, keeping their silence as they herded him toward the house.

They didn't talk among themselves, and he couldn't hear any other voices, although as soon as he reached the garage, he saw there were four double hovers parked beside the one Bane had stolen for them.

And then he wiped a hand across his eyes.

The hover. It was identical to the other four.

It had been one of the military's own hovers, not a private one, that Bane had taken over for them. They must have tracked it. He should have wondered why a civilian was on a hover to begin with, let alone why he had a weapon on him. He should have wondered why he hadn't been more surprised to be in the middle of a shockgun fight.

They might as well have sent the Tecrans an invitation.

The soldier glanced at him, saw the direction of his gaze. "Yes, you weren't hard to find. You took that from one of our scouts." He smirked.

The soldier who had been walking behind him, shockgun almost touching his back, shoved him toward one of the hovers. "Hands behind you."

He stood with his hands back as they secured him with restraints.

"Climb on." The soldier pushed him, and he kept his balance with difficulty. He looked at the seat and saw a hoop had been attached to the back. He stepped up onto the runner board and swung his leg over and as soon as he'd settled into place, the soldier jerked his arms back even more and secured his hands with restraints to the hoop.

He'd have to use every muscle to keep his balance and stay on without straining his arms.

When the soldier finished tying him up, he moved forward with a smirk. "Just so you don't get any ideas."

Dray looked back, face blank. If they thought making him physically uncomfortable would rob him of the ability to have ideas, they were mistaken. He had ideas. Lots of them.

# CHAPTER 21

LUCY WOKE WITH A START, confused for a moment as to where the warning shouted at her had come from.

A shockgun was shoved in her face, and as she pulled herself upright with shaking arms, she looked wildly about the darkened room, and blinked at the three figures surrounding her.

A sense of utter desolation gripped her as she swung her legs off the couch and put her head in her hands.

She had really savored the last two days of freedom.

"Too late?" Bane whispered. And she realized it had been Bane shouting at her, through her earpiece.

"Time to go," one of the Tecran soldiers said over the top of him.

"Before you take me, can I have some water?" That should be answer enough for Bane. She suddenly remembered Dray. "Where is—?"

"Caught," Bane told her. "I've lost contact."

"Your Grihan friend?" The same soldier asked, and there was a hint of glee in his tone. "Neutralized."

Either Dray had done something personally to these soldiers, or there was some longstanding animosity between the Tecran and the Grih.

They were practically chortling at his capture.

She stood on legs that were still a little wobbly, and then, ignoring the soldiers, shuffled through to the kitchen, her blanket still wrapped around her.

She got some water and stood looking out the small kitchen window at the fog while she sipped it, her back to the soldiers.

She sensed a startled surprise from all three at her actions, and she wondered how long it would last before they got a little more assertive.

"You've had your water, now let's go."

She turned slowly, drawing it out. "I need my—" One of the soldiers held up her bag, her cloak and her shoes.

She held out her hands for both, but was only handed her shoes. She pulled them on and when she straightened, one of the soldiers gripped her upper arm.

"Time's wasting."

"Wait." The one who'd had the shockgun in her face earlier grabbed her face with both hands, held her still. "Check for an earpiece."

The one holding her arm found it and clawed it out, catching the skin of her ear with a sharp nail. He looked at it with a strange mix of fear and anger.

"Who's on the other end?"

She was going to refuse to say, when she saw he wasn't asking her.

The other two looked uncomfortable.

"Maybe it's—"

"Doesn't matter." The soldier put it on the ground and crushed it beneath his boot. "Whoever it was, it doesn't matter any more."

The other two didn't seem quite as convinced.

A shout from outside seemed to galvanize them.

The one who'd taken out the earpiece grabbed her arm again and shoved her ahead of him out the door.

Four new hovers sat next to the one Bane had stolen for them, and Dray was tied to one, his hands behind his back.

He turned to look at her as they stepped out the house, and she could see the cold light of fury burning in his eyes.

Then she saw who was standing near him.

"Virn." She tilted back her head. "So I was right about you."

"What are you talking about?" The security guard from the facility had a sneer on his face.

She noticed from the corner of her eye Dray's surprised reaction to the interaction.

"Did you feel anything when you killed Dr. Cantin and Dr. Rool? Or was it just another day at the office for you?"

"Not a single day in that place was anything other than a very boring means to an end." Virn gave a hand signal, and the Tecran gripping her arm released her and hauled her hands behind her to secure them.

"Right. You were just waiting for the perfect time to burn it all to the ground." She remembered the bloom of the explosion as she'd raced the hover along the cliff face.

"That part was a pleasure, that's for sure. But no, I was there to make sure no one got too friendly with you, or decided to let you out."

"Sorry to tell you this, but if that was your one job, you failed."

He looked like he was going to strike her, but then reined himself in, waved his hand at her. "This doesn't look like failure to me, Earth girl."

The soldier finished tying her hands and shoved her forward.

"Sure it does," she said with a smile. "The UC know I exist now, for a start, and I've had time to talk to some of the good citizens of Fa'allen." Her smile deepened. "How do you like those street protests?"

The look he shot her promised violence. "You talk a big game for someone whose existence is very inconvenient to me and my friends."

She scoffed. "Your superior officers, more like. I don't think they're your friends."

"Baiting me? That's not wise."

But she saw the look in his eyes, knew her blow had landed a direct hit. He was nothing more than cannon fodder and he knew it.

She shrugged. "Either you'll kill me, or you won't. But it won't be because of anything I've said or done to you." She flicked her gaze up and down him with disdain. "It'll be because your handlers ordered you to do it."

She caught Dray's eye, and he gave her a tiny shake of his head, his features grim.

She resisted the urge to shake hers back, because Virn was watching her too closely.

She'd played this game too many times. Backing down, tiptoeing around, hadn't helped her. She'd taken that road when she'd first regained consciousness at the facility, but it hadn't gotten her anywhere. The only way she'd made any progress, had been allowed to play games with the scientists, have more freedom of movement in the windowless rooms and corridors, was because she'd pushed Virn and his sidekicks relentlessly. She created a them versus us dynamic between the guards and the scientists who were studying her. The more unreasonably she'd made Virn and his cohorts behave, the more sympathetic to her the doctors had become.

"So, where have you been ordered to take us?" she asked.

Virn's nostrils, two thin slits beside his beaky mouth, flared. "In case it wasn't obvious to you, you're my prisoner, and I don't answer to you."

She shrugged again, in an arrogant, dismissive way she hoped drove him batshit crazy.

"Get her on a hover and let's go," he snapped to the soldier who'd tied her up.

The Tecran shoved her at the nearest hover and then gripped her waist, tried to lift her up, and had to let her drop to the ground. She was no lightweight compared to them.

She debated whether to smirk at him over her shoulder but before she could, she felt the dig of a shockgun in her back.

"Get on."

She took her time, because with her hands tied behind her she couldn't pull herself up, but eventually she was seated.

Her arms were yanked roughly down and tied to a hoop attached to the back, just like they'd done to Dray.

He was watching her from his seat at the back of one of the hovers, gaze intense.

She sent him a half-smile as a soldier climbed in front of her and started the hover, and as they lifted up, he nodded back in response.

Virn had turned on the hover she and Dray had ridden from Fa'allen and pointed it out to the sea. He stood back as it flew forward and then fell down the cliff.

At a sound of surprise from one of his team, Virn shrugged. "Just in case the UC have a way to track it. They hacked into it to steal it, after all."

There was silence for a moment, and Lucy felt her interest sharpen at the quick look two of the soldiers shared with each other.

They were scared about who'd been on the other end of her earpiece, scared about who had hacked the hover's systems.

Then Virn got on his hover, started it up and they turned away from the cliffs. Virn's hover was swallowed by the fog, and it seemed as if she and her driver were alone. Even the sound of the engines was gobbled up.

But she wasn't alone. Not this time.

Behind her somewhere was Dray. And above her was Bane.

And that was more than she'd had before.

Much more.

# CHAPTER 22

THE PLACE the Tecran took them to was just outside Fa'allen, not on the coast, but high on an inland hill. The facility was built low to the ground, although Dray noticed they couldn't help themselves and had incorporated one three-story tower into the design.

He could tell from the guard set-up as they came in that they didn't have a lot of people here, that they were stretched.

They were either keeping it tight deliberately, or there weren't that many willing to get mixed up in a plan that had to be the far side of desperate.

Whoever was covering their asses had co-opted some people, but those people were clearly underlings, as Lucy had so harshly pointed out to Virn earlier.

The soldiers herding them in to the facility hadn't been the ones who decided to steal her from Earth and keep her locked up and hidden on Tecra.

Those who had that kind of power would be a small, select group.

And he didn't see anyone that looked like they had that kind of clout around.

Maybe he and Lucy would get a visit later, but Dray doubted it.

They'd try to keep their hands clean and stand at as much distance as possible.

Which meant they'd put everything on hold until they either lost their nerve and killed her, or waited it out to see if producing her would somehow mitigate their crimes.

Lucy moved ahead of him, her stride stiff after two hours on the hover in the cold and wind.

But she didn't hesitate, turning into a room behind the leading two soldiers as if she did it every day.

Maybe her facility and this one had a similar design.

"In."

Dray saw one of the Tecran soldiers who'd gone ahead was opening up a door to what looked like a prison cell. The door he was holding open was translucent from halfway up, so they could be monitored.

"Restraints," she answered back in the same tone, coming to a stop and holding her hands out behind her from underneath her cloak.

The soldier glanced over Dray's shoulder, to Virn, and then flicked the cloak back, released her hands, and pushed her inside.

Dray didn't like seeing the Tecran's hands on her; something rose up in him that was tightly coiled, hot and focused.

It must have shown on his face, because the Tecran took a tiny step back.

He forced himself to turn his back, like Lucy had, and lift his arms up, and after a moment's hesitation, the guard complied.

He stepped into the cell before anyone could lay hands on him, because he didn't know if he could take it without a violent response.

There was a bunk bolted onto the wall on both sides of the narrow room, and Lucy was sitting in the middle of one of them.

She watched him as he settled in opposite her with those expressive eyes, the skin below them dark and bruised.

She leaned back, subtly tapped her ear.

He shook his head, then tilted it toward her.

She shook her head as well, miming a boot crushing something underfoot.

That was a blow. He'd hoped they wouldn't check her for an earpiece. Hoped that Bane would be still in the loop.

The thinking system would be working out a way to help them. That that was a comfort, rather than cause for alarm, given what Bane was, was a surprise in itself.

Bane's very existence was everything he'd been taught to fear.

But right now, he was as grateful for the thinking system as for anything he could ever remember.

He and Lucy made themselves a little more comfortable, neither speaking.

A soldier watched them from the other side of the door, and Dray could see the lens, which he guessed had audio capabilities, in the corner of the ceiling.

After a few minutes, Lucy leaned back even more, tipped her head against the wall, eyes closed, and started tapping the side of the bunk with her open palms, humming.

After a few moments of doing that, she started singing softly under her breath.

He rose up slowly, until he was on the edge of the bunk, his gaze riveted.

It was . . . extraordinary.

He'd heard the Earth women, Rose McKenzie, Fiona Russell, and Imogen Peters, sing, both all together and individually, but only through comms, never in person.

And that had been spectacular.

This was something else again.

The air vibrated with the sound, and he felt something inside him clench.

He'd been suspicious that all three Earth women were such amazing music makers, but now here was Lucy, blowing him away. They seemed to be made of music.

She opened her eyes, and then jerked up, the song cutting off at the sight of him.

"What is it?" Her voice was low, frightened.

He blinked. "Nothing."

"It's something," she hissed. "You were looking at me as though . . ." She waved a hand. "I don't know what, but it was intense."

"Your singing." He wished she hadn't opened her eyes. That she hadn't stopped.

"What about it?" She frowned.

"I—" He didn't know how to describe it. "It was . . . good."

She shook her head, as if he had lost his mind. "Allll riiight." She drew the words out. "Thanks. Nina Simone never disappoints."

"Nina Simone?"

"The original composer and singer of that song."

"Will you finish it for me?"

The look she sent him was startled, but as she opened her mouth to reply, the sound of footsteps had them both looking out the door.

Dray stood, but Lucy stayed seated, affecting an insolence he hadn't seen in her moments before.

She was deliberately antagonizing the Tecran soldiers.

He worried she would go too far, but it was too late to talk to her about it now.

The Tecran who came to the door and looked in was definitely in charge.

Virn stood to attention behind him, smug but respectful.

The door opened.

The officer hesitated, his gaze going to Dray.

Lucy had gotten their restraints removed, and the officer was suddenly remembering that Dray wasn't an untrained Earth woman. He was a commander with Grihan Battle Center. Unarmed or not, he was dangerous.

To make things easier, Dray lifted both hands and sat.

Something flashed in Lucy's eyes, a quick spark of amusement, but she didn't say anything.

It seemed she knew when to provoke and when to keep her silence.

The officer stepped in, but Dray caught the flash of movement as Virn lifted his shockgun. He said nothing, just looked between them.

"What to do with us, right?" Lucy said, and folded her hands across her stomach and stretched her legs out a little more, almost touching the officer's boot.

He snapped his head to look at her. Stared.

She smiled sweetly back. "To kill or not to kill, am I right?"

He frowned, and even Dray knew the Tecran sentence construction she used was incorrect. She either didn't notice or she'd done it on purpose.

He suspected the latter.

"That's right." The officer watched her, and Dray could see the fascination, and also the edge of condescension in his gaze.

She must have been putting up with this for months. No wonder she had an edge to her when she dealt with them.

"Sucks to be you." She smiled, but there was nothing nice about it now. "You'll be the fall guy, no matter which way you jump."

The officer went still.

He must have figured it out for himself, but he was surprised that Lucy had, Dray realized.

He watched the officer readjust his view of her.

"I'm simply doing what's best for my people."

She laughed, and even Dray's control couldn't help the escape of a bark of incredulous amusement.

"What's best for the criminals higher up the chain of command who broke the law and then lied about it, you mean?" Lucy sat up a little straighter.

"The ones who aren't here themselves to sort out the mess their orders created, but sent you instead." Dray kept his voice quiet.

The Tecran officer glanced at him, and there was definitely worry in his expression.

"Unless he's one of the people who's responsible. Maybe he's one of the big shots?" Lucy mused.

Dray knew he couldn't be. He'd studied Tecran military insignia before he got here, and while there wasn't much on the uniform the officer was wearing, the markings across the breast were those of a lieutenant. Not nearly high enough to have had any part in the theft of the Class 5 plans, the building of them, and then the abduction of advanced sentients. Just high enough to follow the orders and help.

When they should have sounded the alarm.

In response to Lucy's taunt, the officer turned back to her. "You seem to be very sure of your facts."

She shrugged. "I've been out and about for a few days. Wasn't hard to find out that you and your colleagues have dragged your people into a situation where their choices are an unwinnable war or being supervised like children. No wonder they hate you so much."

There was a flicker behind the officer's back, two of the soldiers sharing a look, and Dray had to give Lucy points. She had a very good grasp of divide and conquer strategy.

"They don't hate us." The officer looked affronted.

"Have you heard some of the chants in the square in Fa'allen?

Have you listened to the conversations?" She tilted her head to Virn. "He must have, seeing as he was part of the group hunting me down in the city."

The officer looked back at Virn, but the soldier's mouth was shut and his eyes narrowed. He said nothing.

The silence stretched out.

"So, what is it? Kill or no?" Lucy asked into the dead air.

The officer snapped to attention. "No. For now."

"Ooh. Lucky us." Lucy clapped her hands together.

The officer was obviously as much at a loss as Dray was with her demeanor. His face was neutral as he turned back to Virn. "Get them out of here."

Virn tilted his head. "This is the only cell we have."

"I mean, out of the facility."

Virn took a step forward, and even on his hard-to-read Tecran features, Dray saw his shock. "Why?"

"Because this facility isn't secret, it's part of the military, and if they're found here it would do exactly the opposite of what we're trying to accomplish." The officer kept his tone reasonable, but everyone in the room was still, their full concentration on him.

"Where will we take them?" Virn tried to recover.

"Somewhere else. Use your initiative. Somewhere no one would suspect. Check in daily, but when you communicate with me or whoever is assigned by head office, make sure you don't mention where you are, and keep to the code."

Dray thought Virn was going to walk.

Just throw down and leave.

He could see the thought go through his head, and the tension in his body.

Virn didn't like having to take any initiative. Because that meant he could no longer claim to be just following orders.

"The UC could send a team here." The officer's voice was coaxing now, as if he realized how close he was to losing his main scapegoat. "They're looking for him," he tilted his head toward Dray, "and for the Earth woman. They'll start searching the facilities near Fa'allen. And there can't be a trace of either of them anywhere that's associated with us, or every accusation against us will be that much more credible."

"Why can't someone at head office come up with a place to stash her?" Virn wasn't letting that go.

"Because they're being monitored. The UC is looking hardest at those at the top. The way to do this is for you to source a good place and hunker down. No one can give away what they don't know."

Virn stared at him for another long moment. "I expect a promotion."

"Everyone involved in this will be promoted. That's not even a question." The officer's answer was fervent. Sincere.

But Dray called yurve shit.

There was no way this wasn't a hands-off deniability exercise.

If Virn and his crew were caught, they would take the full consequences.

It hadn't gone unnoticed to him that the officer had not once introduced himself, and no one had mentioned his name.

Virn and his team were being cut loose, with a hope that if they were caught, they'd look like fanatics.

With the facility Lucy had been kept in destroyed, he guessed a lot of the top conspirators thought they'd got away clean, but they also couldn't afford to let her talk.

Dray couldn't see the end game, and maybe there wasn't one. Maybe they were just in reaction mode.

Some of the soldiers in the room looked like they'd come to the same conclusion.

"I expect confirmation of promotion within the day," Virn said. "And we'll need to get provisions and supplies from the stores."

"Of course."

Dray noticed the officer relaxed a little, now that Virn had agreed.

What would have been Virn's options if he'd refused? What could the military have done?

"You should leave as soon as you've stocked up."

Virn started issuing orders to the five soldiers in the room. They left to do as ordered, but at least two of them looked close to refusing.

It was something to work on. A crack to exploit.

Dray looked over at Lucy, who'd been watching the exchange with singular focus.

As the door closed on their cell, she changed the angle of her legs and tapped her boot against his own.

It was a gesture of solidarity.

He slid a little lower, and tapped back.

# CHAPTER 23

SHE WAS MISERABLE.

Lucy had longed to be free of the facility, had almost lost her mind in its artificially lit corridors for the two months she'd been conscious, but when she'd thought of the world outside, it hadn't been sleeting.

"Why do they have open hovers?" she asked Dray. "Why aren't they enclosed? Like sane people would have?"

Dray was standing beside her, his hands secured in front of him like her own, and also like her, sipping from a cup of lukewarm grinabo.

A piece of ice plopped into her cup as she gestured, and she actually felt like screaming.

She hunched over the cup a little more, so the stinging ice hit the back of her head and shoulders instead.

"Something about their culture and heritage. They like the wind and rain in their faces."

She had guessed as much, but his answer was no comfort. "What about the Grih? They have enclosed hovers?"

He smiled against the rim of his cup. "Most are. Some aren't."

"And what's your weather like?"

"Depends on which Grihan planet you're talking about."

She lifted her gaze to his. "There's more than one?"

"There are four Grihan planets, plus a few vassal planets, like Balco, which fall in our space boundaries."

"Which one's the warmest?"

He smiled again. "The planet I'm from. Xal."

"Are you going to take me to your home to lie in the sun, Commander Helvan?" She didn't know why she asked him that. He wasn't obligated to take her anywhere, but she liked the idea of it.

He'd been nothing but a quiet, strong presence beside her. And behind his eyes was the same focus on escape she knew was in her own.

"If you like." He finished his grinabo with a final gulp. "Xal would be honored to have you."

She sent him a sidelong look at that, very skeptical of the truth of it, but he seemed sincere enough.

"I'd be honored to go," she said at last.

He nodded, his gaze going over her shoulder suddenly.

With an internal sigh, she took the last sip of grinabo, guessing it was Virn coming to say they were moving again.

They'd been traveling for three hours, not exactly inland, but to the west, with a slight inland trajectory.

It was deserted out here.

The Tecran really seemed to think the only address worth having was on the cliffs.

"Is it just the people who live in Fa'allen who are obsessed with the cliffs?" she asked. "Or are there different Tecran cultures on different parts of the planet who do things differently?"

"They're all like this." Dray held out his cup for Virn to take, but the asshole didn't take it.

"Put it away yourself."

The words were short, and Virn's featherlike hair was clumped together it was so wet.

She saw Dray nod and walk to the back of the hover, and it was only because she'd spent time watching him that she noticed the sudden stillness in him. The spike of anticipation.

He'd wanted an excuse to rummage in the storage hold of the hover. Virn had just given him one.

To give Dray a bit more time and less scrutiny, she turned, cup in both hands, and held it out imperiously.

"You can take mine. I'm done."

Virn flicked the cup out of her hands and stomped on it.

It cracked audibly under his boot.

"Temper, temper." She let her eyes laugh at him, even though she felt a frisson of fear.

He'd had time to think about what he'd been ordered to do. And the other members of his team had had a chance to express their frank views, none of them positive. He was starting to feel a little trapped by circumstances.

It was not completely out of the realm of possibility that he'd decide the easiest way out was to murder her and Dray and bury their bodies on this endless, foggy, forsaken moor that would have given even Heathcliff and Cathy pause.

"I won't put up with your disrespect." Virn stomped on the cup again, so it broke into two pieces.

"You want to calm down." Dray was suddenly back, standing beside her. "If all Tecran soldiers are as undisciplined as you, I'm sorry we didn't choose to go to war. We'd have won it in a heartbeat."

He was drawing Virn's ire, making him focus his aggression on Dray, not her.

It settled something in her.

Because although she knew it was crazy, that no one from Earth could come save her, she had still felt abandoned.

She didn't even need someone to save her. She just needed someone to try.

He was trying.

Although she worried he was trying a little too well, and that he'd push Virn too far.

Virn reached out, grabbed the part of Dray's restraints that drooped between his wrist and jerked him forward. "I would watch what you—"

Something sent up a howl, a long, wavering note that rose her hackles and caused every hair on her arms to stand up. It seemed to be coming from somewhere close, although in the thick mist it was impossible to even tell the direction.

Virn dropped his hold on Dray. "Time to go."

He moved to the hover, not wasting a moment, and the other members of his team moved just as fast, just as quietly.

She didn't argue. Even though she was dying of curiosity, she didn't ask what was making the noise. She jumped up and had to lean back against the back hoop for balance, because Virn didn't stop to retie her hands behind her, or even tie her on.

She felt a glimmer of hope despite the unsteady beat of her heart as the howl was joined by a second, and then a third.

Virn made mistakes when he was under pressure. She and Dray would need to keep sharp, wait for their chance. If they were patient, it would come.

The hovers rose and then shot through the swirling gray white, and she had to tighten her grip on the seat with her inner thighs. There was no way she was holding on to Virn himself.

In her head, she sang Kate Bush's Wuthering Heights.

It made a great soundtrack to the howls that were now behind them, and the fear she could sense from Virn.

She looked over to the hover Dray was on, saw he hadn't been tied on either.

They exchanged a look.

Yes. They would find a chance. But not if they couldn't take a hover when they ran. Because Lucy didn't think whatever was howling behind them was friendly.

---

Kol.

Dray had researched Tecra thoroughly before he'd even set foot on the *Urna*, and he had read up about kol—the top predators on Tecra other than the Tecran themselves.

He noticed all the soldiers had unsnapped the flap on their shockgun holsters, and there had been no show of bravado. They'd gotten onto the hovers, and they'd moved.

He hadn't even considered kol when they'd left the facility, and by the surprise on Virn's face, neither had their unstable prison guard.

Virn, Dray could tell, was just now realizing all the ways he'd been screwed over. Maybe the kol would be his breaking point.

After half an hour, when the howls were far behind them, Virn pulled to a stop, not getting down from the hover.

"We can't camp here."

"No shit." The soldier Dray had heard the others call Clin revved his hover engine.

"Where then?" The one they called Graven rubbed a hand through feathery hair that was slick with moisture, then flicked the droplets off his fingers.

"Back to the coast. The kol keep away from there." Clin looked behind him, and the other soldier who sat behind him on the hover, Rua, shifted, then gave a nod.

Virn looked over at Bly, the soldier who rode in front of Dray. "You have a suggestion?"

Bly pulled out his handheld. Tapped it. "I know there's some cliffs near Stunnelly that are riddled with caves. You have to climb down to them, so we'll definitely be safe from the kol. And we could use Stunnelly for supplies."

"How far?" Virn swung off his hover, his boot striking Lucy's arm as he did so, and walked over to Bly.

The blow didn't look deliberate, but he neither paused nor apologized.

Dray could feel the fury build up in him again at the casual use of force.

He looked over at Lucy, but she didn't look back. Her face was serene, as if she hadn't even noticed what happened.

Except she must have.

Clin joined Virn, and they bent their heads over the screen.

"It's five hours away!" Clin stepped back. "Mainly because we've been headed in the opposite direction for hours now." He looked boldly at Virn, fury in his eyes.

"I was putting distance between us and the facility." Virn stared back.

"Well, we won't be getting there before dark. We'll have to find a place to sleep tonight." Bly put his screen away. "Got any ideas?"

"I say we leave them out here, head back to the facility." Rua spoke for the first time.

There was a moment of silence, and Dray carefully looked over at Lucy. Her gaze was locked on Virn.

"That's not the deal." Virn's voice was low.

"The deal sucks." The soldier behind Graven, Krian, gave a snort.

"We're *involved*," Virn said. "We participated by guarding her at the facility. And we get a promotion out of it."

"Sure we will." Clin's cynicism seemed to run deep.

"You leave, you can't go back," Bly said.

"You sure about that?" Graven asked, too much in step with Krian to not have already discussed it with him.

"What, you mean just go back as if nothing happened?" Bly's eyes narrowed.

Krian lifted his shoulders. "What are they going to say?"

"Maybe 'stand up against that wall so we can kill you without hitting anyone behind you'." Clin didn't look like he was making a joke.

"They kill us, they have to explain our deaths. They ignore us, and we ignore them, everyone's happy."

"Well, not happy," Rua said. "Because we wouldn't have done what they wanted."

"How about you give us one of the hovers, let us be on our way, and there can be happiness all round." Lucy spoke for the first time.

Clin's gaze snapped to her, as if he just remembered she was there. And could understand every word.

"I'd keep quiet while your betters speak," he said, low and mean. "You're the cause of all this."

She leaned toward him and Dray could see the incandescence of rage in her eyes.

"You and your asshole leaders are the cause of all this. I would give everything I have to be back home, to never have heard of you and never have seen this planet. You should have left. Me. Alone." She drew in an unsteady breath. "But, noooo. Here I am. Do whatever you want, but don't you ever tell me this situation is on me. It's on you. You fucker."

There was absolute silence.

Dray felt the rise of warmth in his chest. Pride. Absolute respect.

This woman was amazing.

"So, is this mutiny?" Virn obviously decided to pretend the last conversation hadn't happened.

"If they call us tomorrow and ask us to bring her back?" Bly put the question out into the tense silence. "And we say 'sorry, we let them go'?"

The possibility of that scenario played out on their faces. Dray realized he was beginning to be able to read them better.

"I'm in for now. *For now.*" Clin emphasized the last point. He didn't look at Lucy as he moved back to his hover.

"The rest of you?" Virn looked them each in the eye.

No one looked away that Dray could see. They were still very much in rebel mode, but no one wanted to be the first to test the waters. Yet.

"Then let's find somewhere to camp that won't get us eaten by kol."

# CHAPTER 24

IT WAS COLD.

So, so cold.

Lucy hunched over herself. She was so miserable, she didn't even complain when she was jostled as Dray sat down beside her.

He held something out, and she realized it was a cup of grinabo.

Virn had refused to give her a new cup because he claimed she'd been responsible for her one being broken. She'd simply stared at him and then walked away, shaken at the extent of her anger.

"You don't mind sharing Earth germs?" she asked, taking it with her bound hands before he could answer, and swallowing a mouthful. She made a sound of surprise, because it was actually hot, something she hadn't expected.

"No. Earth germs are fine with me."

She grinned around another sip. "Thanks."

The heat of him had started to seep through to her, and unable to help herself, she leaned in to him, snuggling in as close as she could.

He went still for a beat and then adjusted, lifting his bound hands up and over her head, so she was in the circle his arms made. His heat surrounded her.

"Cold?"

"Freezing. Aren't you?"

"My uniform compensates for the temperature. So, no."

"Huh." She thought about it. "Is it only for the military, the fabric your uniform is made from?"

"No." He lifted his chin so she could put her head on his shoulder, and then lowered it to rest just above her ear. "Most clothing is made from something with temperature control capabilities."

"Obviously not on Tecra." She was wearing what Dray had found for her in the drawers of the bedroom in the house on the cliffs. They were soft and comfortable, but so thin the wind blew straight through them. Fortunately the cloak was warm. Maybe it was made of thermoregulating fabric.

"I think those clothes are leisure clothes meant only for indoors. I should have looked for others for you, but at the time, I thought we were safe."

She could hear the regret in his voice.

"It's okay. The cloak and the shoes are warm."

She wondered how Bane was doing. He was looking for them, she was sure of that. Although there seemed to be little chance he'd find them where they were now, huddled on the top of a low hill, hovers parked in a circle around them, something like a tarpaulin attached to the hovers to give rudimentary shelter.

The hovers cut the wind, but the air was still freezing, and the fog was just as thick as ever. It pressed in on them, claustrophobic and smothering.

"What do you think Bane's doing?" She spoke softly, but the Tecran were talking among themselves and weren't paying any attention to her and Dray.

"Whatever he can do while still staying hidden."

"Why does he have to hide?" She didn't understand all the politics of this, but it was clearly complex.

"Because the UC Ambassador asked him to. We didn't want to make the Tecran even more nervous and resentful than they already were by having him hover over them in a threatening way." The puff of his breath on her ear made her shiver, and she hoped he put it down to the cold.

"So, he's big and intimidating?"

Dray went still, then gave a laugh. "I associate Earth women so closely with the Class 5s, I forgot you've never met him, or seen his battleship."

"I wish I could. I wish I could see him right now."

She felt his lips quirk.

"Me, too."

"He's the first person to help me since I was abducted, aside from Dr. Farnn, and she only did it when the tide turned against her. I owe him a lot. Even if he can't find us, I'll always be grateful to him."

He hesitated. "He won't stop looking until he does find you. And if you're hurt or . . . dead, I think the Tecrans will be a lot more than just nervous and resentful. They'll be annihilated."

She scoffed. "What makes you think that?"

"There are three other Earth women under United Council protection. Each and every one has helped a thinking system escape their bonds. Rose McKenzie freed Sazo and Bane. Fiona Russell freed Eazi and Imogen Peters freed Oris and tried to free Paxe. Bane told me that all four remaining thinking systems have been searching for you since Paxe told them he'd taken you from Earth and the Tecran had whisked you out of his hold."

"Just because they care what happens to me doesn't mean they're dangerous to anyone else." She closed her eyes, drank the last of the grinabo.

"They don't *like* anyone else. Maybe, for strategic reasons, they'd think twice about harming the Grih, but Bane's neutral. He doesn't have any loyalties to anyone, except you and the other Earth women, and his fellow thinking systems."

"It's a long stretch to go from 'not having loyalties' to worrying they'd cause harm."

He shook his head, she could feel the movement against her hair. "The thinking system wars indicate otherwise."

"There was a war?" She didn't open her eyes. She was too comfortable and warm.

"A long time ago. It taught us to be wary of thinking systems. It's why we prefer doors with handles, rather than ones that open electronically, if that's practical. Why we have so few lenses for security. Why we choose stairs over lifts if we can. All things that were used against us in the Thinking System Wars."

She yawned, her jaw actually cracking her mouth opened so wide. "Sorry." She covered her mouth with bound hands.

Dray drew back from her, and she made a sound of protest as she lost his warmth, but she couldn't seem to find the energy to do anything about it.

"We need blankets too." Dray's voice was so loud, she forced her eyes open.

The soldiers were sitting huddled close to the hovers under the tarpaulin, settling themselves in with thin sleeping mats and blankets, and they seemed momentarily astonished.

"Now." Dray's tone was implacable. "She's cold enough already. Do you want her to get sick or die of exposure?"

Clin rose to his knees, looking at them with dislike, but he eventually shuffled to the storage hold of the hover they were leaning against.

He tossed them a single mat and a blanket.

She wondered if there were more available and he was just being an asshole, or if there really was only one spare.

Dray laid it out lengthways along the hover, so they were

completely under the tarpaulin, and then lay down, the blanket in his bound hands. He lifted his arms again, and seeing where he was going with it, she hesitated a moment, and then wriggled until she fitted in beside him, head on his shoulder, hands tucked between them. His arms came down to encircle her again.

The blanket settled around them, and she anchored one side under her hip, so no cold air could get in.

For a moment, she just lay, her body weeping with joy at being horizontal, and warm.

Conscience prompted her. "Your shoulder will be numb if we stay this way." It was also intensely personal, intensely intimate.

She could hear his heart beat beneath her ear, felt the small adjustments he made beneath her.

She'd thought him attractive from the moment she'd seen him, but running for their lives, dealing with captivity, had redirected her focus to simply stay alive.

Now that she had a small moment of safety and calm, he was all-encompassing.

She shivered, and it had nothing to do with the cold, although his reaction, tightening his hold, told her he thought it was.

"I'll let you know when I can't feel my shoulder." His already gravelly voice sounded a little raw.

She lifted her chin to look up at him. "Are you getting sick?"

He cleared his throat. "No."

She subsided, and eyes closed, decided to nap a little if she could.

She woke with a start she didn't know how much later.

For a moment she was confused. There was no sound, even the wind had dropped, and she was lying on her side, Dray spooned around her.

She was warm and as comfortable as sleeping on a thin mat on hard, cold ground could be, but her heart was racing.

She could hear Dray's quiet breathing, and careful not to let in cold air, lifted up on an elbow to look around the camp.

The Tecran were sleeping.

She frowned at the scene, sure something didn't make sense, and then she worked out what it was. One of the soldiers was missing from their mat.

Her mind cleared. They'd obviously scheduled a watch.

Maybe the guard moving around was what had woken her.

She relaxed back down under the blanket, but now she was awake, she realized she also needed to answer a very pressing call of nature.

She tried to convince herself it could wait, and then gave up, sliding carefully out from under Dray's embrace and the blanket.

A hand gripped her upper arm.

"What is it?" Dray's voice was alert, as if he hadn't just been in a deep sleep.

"I have to go . . . um . . ." She didn't know what the colloquial Tecran was for using the facilities.

But she didn't have to. Dray nodded, started rising.

"No. You don't need to come with. I'll be quick."

He hesitated.

"I don't need an audience." She grinned at him in the darkness, and he subsided down. Gave a nod.

She had gone to sleep with her boots on, so she crawled over Dray, an awkward maneuver with her hands restrained in front of her, and then squeezed through the gap between their hover and the one beside it in the circle.

Once she stepped out, she blinked in sudden realization that the fog had almost completely cleared.

The night sky glittered, something she hadn't been able to see with the tarpaulin overhead.

It was magical.

And it could wait, because she really needed to answer the call of nature now.

She made out a nearby bush by the light of Gyre, which was full and bright, its much smaller companion, Anar, in perpetual crescent because of Gyre's shadow.

She walked behind it for privacy, cursing the restraints at her wrists. They weren't tight, but they made everything more difficult.

She supposed she should be grateful Virn had retied them in front of her body, or this would have been near impossible.

When she was done, she emerged and walked back to the hovers, looking up at the beauty above her.

It hit her every now and then that she was in an extraordinary situation, that there was an element of wonder and adventure about it that was no less real even though it had been forced on her.

But she *was* here. And she *couldn't* go home. Bane had made that clear. So there was something healthy and healing in seeing the good around her as well as the injustice.

After looking up for a few minutes, it occurred to her that whoever was on guard hadn't so much as approached her, let alone asked her what she was doing up.

Frowning, she turned to looked toward the camp, only a few meters away, and realized she couldn't see anyone.

She moved back to the hover circle, her gaze sweeping left and right.

A sound to her left made her freeze.

She turned, but there was nothing visible in the darkness.

Worried now, more than a little uneasy, she took the last few steps to reach the hovers, and as she squeezed between two of them, something threw itself at her.

In the dark, she caught the glow of eyes and flash of teeth

before she got on the right side of the hard, cold metal of the hovers.

She smelled the stink of fetid breath, felt the splatter of saliva against her cheek, and she screamed as she fell backward, landing on her back in the center of the camp.

"Kol?" Dray was beside her, so fast that he had to have already been moving before she fell.

"I don't know. Something with teeth."

The Tecran were awake, now, she could hear them shouting at each other, and perhaps whoever had been on watch.

Whoever it was, their absence now took on a more sinister significance.

She scrambled to her feet, Dray helping her up. They stood together, hands bound, while the Tecran ripped the tarpaulin down to take up position with their shockguns against the barrier of the hovers.

Rua took a shot, and she heard the high-pitched squeal of an animal in pain.

"Got it." Rua glanced at the others. "Didn't take it down, though."

"Put it on a higher setting," Virn ordered.

"It already is on the highest setting. Their coats are thick. I've heard you have to hit them somewhere like the eyes or into the mouth to get a kill shot."

At Rua's words, the tension seemed to escalate.

"Where's Graven?" Krian's soft question fell like lead into the silence.

"As he was on guard, I'm assuming he's dead." Virn's voice was a little unsteady.

"This is not what I signed up for." Bly's voice was just audible.

"It's not what any of us signed up for. Are you going to whine about it, or are you going to help get us out of here alive?" The sharp words weren't from Virn, they were from Clin.

They seemed to settle everyone, focus them.

"I want my weapon returned." Dray spoke up into the silence. "I want Lucy and my hands untied, and I want my weapon."

"No." Virn didn't even glance back at them.

Krian shot, and a bark of pain sounded. Suddenly Bly and Clin, on either side of him, shot as well.

There were some howls and then silence.

Bly squinted into the darkness. "It's run away. But was it just one, or are there more of them?"

"The young males are usually on their own. If that's what that was, we're all right." Rua didn't move from his shooting stance.

"I'm not trusting that. We need to find Graven and then go." Krian lifted his shockgun a little higher.

"Agreed." Virn looked back at Lucy and Dray. "Pack up everything as fast as you can. We're leaving."

Dray gave a nod, and Virn swung back to guarding the circle.

"Look for anything useful to pocket," Dray whispered quietly in Lucy's ear.

She nodded. That's where her mind had gone, as well.

She rolled mats and stored them, and found Clin *had* been being an asshole when he'd given her and Dray one to share. There were at least two spares in the storage holds.

Never mind. He would experience karma. She would make sure of it.

She would be karma's handmaiden.

# CHAPTER 25

DRAY KEPT an eye on the Tecran while he gathered blankets and used his remaining focus to scan the contents of each storage hold as he stuffed them inside.

There was nothing obvious to take that would help Lucy and himself, or if there was, he didn't have the time to look thoroughly enough.

He accepted it, accepted speed was the more important thing now, and hoped he'd get another chance to pry and see what he could find.

Lucy started to hum, and he flicked her a quick look, stunned that she could create that kind of music in the situation they were in.

Suddenly, one of the Tecran shot their weapon again, and the sound of a kol's answering rage had Dray scooping up the last few items and throwing them into the nearest storage hold and slamming it closed.

A howl went up, and it felt as if a kol's jaws closed around the back of his neck.

He rubbed the spot, his eyes on Rua, who'd been the one to shoot.

"You done?" Virn's tone was pitched higher than usual.

"Yes." Dray's fingers itched for his shockgun.

One of the Tecran must have it with them as a spare, because he hadn't seen it in any of the storage holds.

"Time to go before that howl brings his friends." Rua said what they were all thinking.

They climbed on quickly and rose up, the Tecran taking the hovers to their highest elevation, and as they began moving forward, the front and side lights flickered over the scrubby ground and illuminated four sets of eyes.

Dray felt Bly shudder in front of him as one of the kol leaped up at them.

It couldn't reach, but Dray could see its thick ruff, its massive teeth bared as it jumped.

When Krian turned his hover back, Bly went stiff.

"Form a line, Graven has to be here somewhere."

Dray wondered if Bly had forgotten about his teammate, but if so, he didn't balk at the order, he turned his hover as well, and shone his light at the ground.

The kol followed them, howling, leaping and snapping at them from below.

Dray didn't think there was a chance Graven had survived.

"He's here." Virn shouted. The hover didn't descend, which Dray assumed it would if there had been any chance the soldier was alive.

Graven was far enough from the camp that Dray guessed he'd been dragged away.

Bly caught up with Virn and Dray peered down. Graven lay on his back, eyes open and unseeing, his body savaged.

The hovers congregated above the body. No one said a word over the snarls of the kol below.

Then Virn revved his hover's engine and roared off, and one by one, the others followed him.

Dray saw Krian was the last to leave, and he looked over his shoulder to watch him, but when the kol that had followed them began savaging Graven's body again, Krian, too, turned and followed Virn.

It was at least a few hours before dawn, so they flew high. No one wanted to be low enough to be pulled off their hover by a kol.

The landscape beneath them got rockier as they moved closer to the coast.

As the sun slowly lit the sky, Dray could see hardy plants with tiny leaves huddled in narrow fissures, and lichen and moss that covered the rocks in vibrant reds, greens and blues.

Up ahead, Virn lowered the hover and landed.

They alighted around him and Lucy slid off Virn's hover, bending over to stretch.

"We'll take a break, get something to eat and drink. See which way we need to go from here." Virn took out a handheld, began tapping at it while the others unpacked supplies.

"You're not going to say anything about Graven?" Krian's voice cut through every other sound.

Virn looked up. "What is there to say? I am sorry he was killed—"

"Sorry? You led us there. You put us in the flatlands."

"Under orders." Virn lowered the handheld and took a step forward, the move overtly aggressive.

Dray shifted until he was behind Bly, and then started moving toward Lucy.

She turned, as if attuned to him, catching his eye and then turning back to look at the confrontation happening directly in front of her.

She stepped to the side as if to give the Tecran more room.

In small increments they edged closer to each other.

She was careful to keep just behind the Tecran, and he let her cover more ground, so she came to him, putting more distance between her and what was looking increasingly like a violent confrontation.

Rua had entered the argument, trying to calm both Krian and Virn down, and was shoved by Virn for his efforts.

"You want to make a break for it?" Lucy finally reached him, resting her bound hands on his bicep for balance and going up on her toes to whisper in his ear.

It felt intimate, like last night when they'd slept close together, sharing warmth.

He closed his eyes, his mind frozen for a moment.

"They'd run us down," he forced himself to whisper back. "Even if we stole a hover, they've got three others, and there is nowhere to hide out here."

"I know." She sighed as she said it. "It was a nice fantasy."

Her hands were still pressed against him and he could feel how cold they were, even through his cloak. He lifted his own bound arms over her head and lowered them to rest on her hip, pulling her closer like he'd done the night before.

He sensed her surprise, and then, with another sigh, she laid her head on his chest. His hands clenched in her cloak at the sharp jump of his heart.

"Maybe they'll kill each other." He bent his head down, his voice rough. "And solve our problems for us."

He saw the twitch of her lips. "What are they doing now? I'm too tired to open my eyes."

He looked up and saw Virn punch Krian, and the soldier spun around. Dray knew the moment Krian's gaze fixed on him and Lucy.

Instead of turning back and hitting Virn in retaliation, he staggered a few steps, then straightened up, his gaze locked on them.

Dray felt every warning siren in him start to wail.

"Nice and cozy, are you?" There was a smudge of blood around the right corner of Krian's mouth.

"What do you care?" Dray drew himself up. He was at least a head taller than all the Tecran. "What business is it of yours?"

"She's not like us," Krian said, and Dray saw he believed it, absolutely. "She's not as advanced. It's . . . wrong."

And by 'wrong', Dray could see, he meant 'disgusting'.

"I should stick to torturing her and taking her from her home planet instead?" he asked. "Like you?"

All five of the soldiers were staring at them now, and Lucy made a noise of annoyance and slid her hands a little lower down his chest and turned slightly in his arms to look at them.

"Seriously? Your friend got eaten by a kol, your leaders betrayed you and the rest of the planet by breaking UC law, they kidnapped me and spent months studying me like some lab rat, and your people are on the verge of war because you don't seem to like taking responsibilities for your actions, but you're having a little moment at the sight of me and Dray in each others arms?" She laughed, and made a gesture Dray had a shocked, sudden inkling of its meaning, even though he'd never seen it before. "Fuck you, Krian. Fuck the lot of you. I mean that quite sincerely."

She turned completely in his arms, so her back was against his chest, and leaned back, staring Krian, and then the others, down. "Or is this just a little distraction because you can't win a fight against Virn, and you're looking for any out you can find?"

Krian reared back at that, outrage and fury on his face.

Dray fought the grin that wanted to break out. They thought she was less than them. And here she was, manipulating them in plain sight and not a single one seemed to realize it.

Krian turned to face Virn. "I'm done," he said. "Your response to the death of one of my best friends, in one of the most horrible ways I can think of, is to shrug?" He turned to the others. "That's what he thinks of you. That's what you are. Nothing but expendable tools. Maybe you think it's worth it. I don't."

He strode to his hover.

"You're going to go back?" Clin asked. "Like you and Graven said? Just going back to your unit and act like they never asked you to do this?"

"Yes." Krian swung his leg over the hover.

"Will you let me know how that works out?" Clin asked.

Virn turned on him, face frightening in its fury. "He so much as thinks about opening comms to anyone on this mission after he leaves, and he had better get ready to stand up against that wall you talked about."

"Right, because finding out you can go back without consequences would be a really bad thing." Bly's sarcasm wasn't lost on anyone.

"You're either in for the duration, or you're out. Choose right now." Virn's fists were clenched. "I'm not fighting you over and over. It's a waste of my time and energy."

"I'm gone." Clin turned to his hover.

"You go with Krian, you're not taking a hover." Virn's shockgun was already out and pointed at Clin.

"Then I'll get my things—"

"No. You don't get to take military supplies when you're deserting. Rua, take whatever is in the storage hold of Krian's hover out."

Rua hesitated, and Dray felt Lucy go still in his arms, waiting, like him, for the first shot to be fired.

With a sudden huff of breath, Rua moved, opening up the storage box and pulling out whatever was in there and dumping it on the ground.

"Now, don't let me ever see you again." Virn widened his stance.

"Same goes." Krian revved the hover's engine as Clin swung up behind him. He pointed at Virn. "When I make general, I hope you're still in the military so I can mess with your career."

They drove away, in what Dray guessed was the direction of Fa'allen.

Virn gave a snort. "When he's a general? As if that fool will live through the rest of the week."

Rua sent him a sidelong look. "You think?"

"Yes."

But Dray wouldn't bet on it. And Virn's body language said he wasn't as confident as he made out, either.

He was three men down, and cut loose from headquarters.

If this was support, it was the poorest excuse for it Dray had ever seen.

# CHAPTER 26

THEY TRAVELED for another three hours until Lucy started to hear the far-off crash of massive waves against the cliffs.

After the first hour she hunched low and used Virn's body as a shield against the cold wind, ignoring the scenery around her, but when at last she looked up, she had to blink a few times until she understood what she was looking at.

A wall of white cloud lined the edge of the cliffs, four or five stories high, stark against the gray blue of the sky above.

It was like approaching a castle battlement.

One that was as ethereal as it was dangerous.

They stopped just before they disappeared into its swirling depths.

The sound of the waves was so clear, Lucy guessed the cliffs ended only meters away.

She waited for Virn to dismount and then slid down on the opposite side to stretch her legs.

"Where to now?" Rua dismounted and walked forward, disappearing into the fog.

A moment later, he was back, and Lucy could see he was energized, his demeanor going from weary to focused.

The Tecran really did love the cliffs.

"It's right here." Bly was looking at the handheld. He slid off the hover, and Dray swung off, as well.

She exchanged a look with him, and Lucy thought he was more grim-faced than usual. Their chance for escape hadn't come yet, and they would soon be holed up in a cave.

"Let's go." Virn gestured to the rear of the hover, and Lucy worked out he meant for her to open the storage unit.

"We're going to use the hovers to get down to the caves?" she asked as she lifted the lid. She remembered the drop down the cliff face she'd taken when she'd escaped the facility. She didn't want a repeat. Especially if she was on the back, with no safety belt.

"No. The cliffs are too jagged. We'll be climbing down." Bly was sorting through ropes and other climbing equipment, including crossbow grapples like the ones Lucy'd found in the storage shed she'd hidden in on her first night of freedom.

She swallowed, and looked over at Dray again.

He seemed calm.

It looked like she was the only one freaked out by climbing down a sheer cliff face.

Virn was pulling out ropes as well, all neatly rolled up and new looking. He swung a grapple onto his shoulder.

"Carry the rope," he told her, and disappeared into the fog.

She stared after him, and bent slowly to pick up the rope he'd left on the ground.

"We taking supplies?" Rua asked.

"Let's find the caves first. We can come back for the rest once that's done." Bly gestured to Dray to take the ropes from his hover as well.

Dray joined her, looking down at her with concern.

"You all right?"

She shook her head. "I don't want to climb down the cliff."

Rua was standing behind them, obviously not prepared to go

ahead of them and leave them behind with the hovers. "Scared, Earth girl?"

"Terrified," she said, and felt the weight of her fear press down on her chest.

She heard the stutter in her breath.

"You don't climb on your planet?" Dray asked.

"Some people do. I'm not one of them." She didn't feel even slightly inclined to take another step forward.

"What's the hold up?" Virn appeared out of the fog.

"She's afraid to climb the cliff." Rua's voice contained a sneer.

Dray seemed to be closer to her now, his shoulder brushing hers. "I'll help you down."

"I appreciate the offer. Still doesn't make me any more eager to give it a try." She tried to insert some humor into her words, but failed miserably.

"I don't care how you feel about it. You're doing it." Virn lunged forward and gripped her arm.

Dray stepped in front of her, knocking Virn's hand away with his bound arms.

"You want her to do this, frightening her even more isn't the way." He loomed over Virn, and Lucy could see the Tecran did not like that. Did not like that at all.

"You don't issue any of the orders here. This isn't the UC and it isn't Grih Battle Center. Get it into your head, you're my prisoner as much as she is." Virn shoved Dray, but he barely moved.

"You want her to get down into that cave, tread a little more softly." Dray kept his voice low.

Virn took a step back, as if he was conceding the point, and then suddenly swung his grapple, hitting Dray on the temple.

Dray fell, and Lucy dodged around him and launched herself forward, elbow up, and struck Virn as hard as she could on the side of his head.

He went down, his face a study in shock.

She pivoted, crouching down beside Dray. "How bad?"

He pushed himself up and then stood, swaying a little. The edge of the grapple had gouged his skin—a trickle of blood ran past his ear and down his jaw.

"Not as bad as Virn." Dray lifted his hands to touch his wound, and winced. Then his gaze flicked over her shoulder, and Lucy remembered Rua was behind them.

Her stomach dropped and she tensed, ready for a blow, or even a shockgun hit.

"Move." Rua shoved her out of the way and knelt beside Virn, who lay crumpled and groaning.

It was as if Rua didn't see her as a danger, even though he must have seen her strike Virn.

Shaking her head, Lucy bent down, picked up the grapple Virn had dropped, and then caught Dray's eye. She looked at Rua, and then back to the hovers, stepped forward and swung the grapple at his head as hard as she could.

The blow dropped him over Virn's body.

She turned back to Dray. "Let's go." Except . . . "Who has the restraint releases?" She ran to Virn's hover, and looked in the storage unit.

Dray didn't join her, and when she looked up sharply to check on him, she saw he was bending over the two Tecran.

When he straightened, he had two shockguns in his hands.

She turned back to the hold, but there was nothing in there that looked right. She ran back to where Dray was sliding the shockgun into the empty holster strapped to his thigh.

"Does Virn have the restraint releases on him?"

"Good thought." Dray crouched again, patted Virn down and pulled a small device out of his front pocket.

Virn batted at his hands, but weakly.

As Dray rose back up, she held out her wrists, and heard one of the best sounds in the world, the snick of freedom.

She took the device and freed Dray, and then she ran for Virn's hover. "Come on."

He looked like he was going to insist on piloting it, but then he slid behind her.

She turned it on, touching buttons with shaking hands, and just as she was about to lift them up, a flash of purple through the fog winked from the corner of her eye, and then there was nothing but darkness.

# CHAPTER 27

SHE CAME to in Dray's arms.

He held her against him, one arm curved around her back, the other around the back of her thighs, and he was sitting up against one of the hovers with her draped across his lap.

She let her eyelids flutter closed, and tried to work out what was going on before they realized she was conscious.

"I was reacting." She heard Bly's voice, tight and defensive. "It was set to kill because, in case you forgot, we were just shooting at kol."

"She's why we're here. And you hit her with a kill shot." Virn's words were equally tight. "I'm not saying you shouldn't have taken the shot, I'm saying a quick adjustment to something lower than kill would have been good."

"It's done. And she doesn't look dead, anyway." Rua didn't seem particularly concerned either way, and given the way she'd hit him over the head, she couldn't exactly blame him.

"How is that, exactly?" Virn's voice rose, and she felt Dray shift a little, his arms tightening.

"Don't ask me," Dray said, the rough sound of his voice vibrating through her, but she had the feeling he was lying.

What did he know about her that she didn't?

"Maybe its got to do with their bone density." Rua sounded tired. "As I discovered, she can put a lot of power behind her movements."

"So what now?" Bly moved a little closer.

"We go down, find the cave, take the supplies in, you watch these two, and then when she's recovered, we take them below."

"She could take days to recover for all we know." Rua said.

"Then the two of them can sit out here as kol snacks."

"And their guard?" Bly's question was dry.

"Use your imagination," Virn snapped. "You can guard them from the cliff edge. If the kol come, you can jump down."

There was silence.

She let her eyelids lift again, and found herself looking directly into Dray's blue eyes.

She saw relief, and something else in his gaze. Something that electrified her. Warmed her all the way through.

"How do you feel?" he murmured.

"Like I fell from the cliffs to the rocks below." She tried a weak smile, and then closed her eyes again, letting her cheek rest against his chest.

"She awake?" Virn was suddenly looming over them, and she felt Dray tense beneath her again.

"Just coming to," he said.

"Good. Bly, watch them both like they're kol on the hunt. I'll be back as soon as I've located the cave." She opened her eyes in time to see him turn to Rua. "You going to be all right?"

She saw Rua had a transparent blue gel-like dressing on his head. He was sitting up against another hover.

He waved Virn away, and the Tecran disappeared back into the fog.

"How did they get the jump on you?" Bly asked.

Rua was silent.

When it appeared he wasn't going to get an answer, Bly swore softly and went to get his handheld.

"Keep both hands free," Rua said.

"They're on the ground, and while she may be awake, she's hardly about to leap up and attack."

Rua didn't answer, and when Lucy swung her gaze back to Dray, she saw the faint spark of humor in his eyes.

"Can you?" he asked.

"Leap up and attack?" She tried another smile. "Not right this second. Give me a few minutes."

"I thought he'd killed you." He was dead serious now.

"Seems like they thought it, too."

He nodded. "I'd read in the reports that Rose McKenzie and Fiona Russell had both survived kill shots with a shockgun, but it was only after I felt your heart beating that I remembered it. In the moment . . ." He shook his head.

She ran a hand down his cheek, noticed he had blue gel over the cut where the grapple had gouged his skin, as well. "We're obviously hard to kill." She was trying to comfort him, and he seemed to realize it, because he shook his head.

"How bad is your fear of the cliffs?"

"Pretty bad. But what choice do I have?" She accepted that with the practicality of someone who hadn't had a choice in a while.

"I was one of the Battle Center officers who thought we were asking for trouble with this military takeover," Dray said. "Maybe because of that, I got picked for the UC mission. They wanted people who were on guard. Cynical about the process. But the whole way over on the *Urna*, I learned to speak Tecran, read about Tecran history and their culture, and I started to think maybe I was wrong, that we should give the citizens a chance, as it was clearly a few of their politicians and the generals in their military who'd made this decision, not the majority of them."

"And now?" she asked.

"Now, I find I'm drifting back to my original standpoint."

She gave him a lopsided smile. "I've wanted to burn this whole place to the ground and I've wanted to try to make friends, sometimes both at the same time." She gave a weak laugh. "Of course, I hadn't seen the outside of the facility then, and since I've been out in the open, so to speak, I've been less inclined to burn it all, but also less inclined to make friends. I actually just want to get out of here, and leave them to it."

"That works for me." He lifted a hand and brushed her hair back from her forehead, then caught a lock of it between his fingers. "I've never seen hair like this. It's so smooth."

She shrugged. "It's too long. Hard to keep it untangled on an alien planet."

His lips quirked. "Not something I've ever had to consider."

She lifted her own hand, and slid her fingers into his hair. The strands felt slightly rough.

Her gaze met his, and she felt that quick, lightning jolt of lust and desire again.

"I found it."

Virn's voice came from within the fog.

"Pass down some of the supplies. Rua, you watch the prisoners. Bly, bring down as much as you can carry."

Bly looked relieved. He disappeared into the fog with a few bags, then came back to load himself up again.

"You going to cope?" He looked over at Rua, who hadn't moved.

"Yes." Rua finally stirred himself, standing up and limping over to them, and then sat on a rock with his back to the fog.

Bly watched him for another minute and then disappeared into the swirling white.

"I'd really like to hit you with another kill shot," Rua said, conversationally. "Of course, it might not kill you, but I'm guessing it'll hurt."

"Sure." Lucy stayed where she was in Dray's arms, nice and warm and comfortable. "Of course, you'll delay the trip to the cave, and be forced to guard me while I'm up here, but that's your call."

The Tecran sent her an unmistakably dark look.

"So, tell me, what is the Tecran military's procedure when captured by an unknown force?" Dray asked.

Rua narrowed his eyes. "I'm sure you know."

"Yes." Dray shifted his hold on her. "I'm just wondering if you do. And if so, if you're able to extrapolate that to people you've captured."

Rua's nostrils flared and he stood, then thought better of the sudden movement and sat again.

"And what would you consider fit retribution for an alien force who took you from Tecra and kept you on their planet, with no explanation or way to get you home?" Lucy wondered.

"I wasn't involved in that," Rua hissed. "I'm just the sap that got landed with guarding you."

"Whatever." Lucy leaned her cheek back on Dray's chest. "Does the 'just following orders' excuse fly in this part of the galaxy?"

"No." Dray rubbed his cheek on the top of her head. "I'm assuming it doesn't in your part, either?"

"Not for wont of trying, but no, it doesn't."

Rua hissed again, but he said nothing more, and from the way he had his hand to his forehead, she guessed he was dealing with a very severe concussion.

If only she didn't feel weak down to her bones, this would be the perfect opportunity to try to escape again.

But she didn't even know if she could sit on a hover without falling off right now.

She looked up at Dray. She could see the same thought reflected in the bright blue of his eyes.

"We'll have another chance," he mouthed, and it comforted her, even though she wanted to remind him that it would be a lot harder once they were in a cave in the cliff below.

Mainly because her fear of heights would hinder them.

She would just have to force the fear down. Because if they had a chance to escape, she would not be the reason they couldn't take it.

# CHAPTER 28

LUCY WAS OBVIOUSLY TERRIFIED.

Dray looked up at her, carefully moving her foot down to the next foothold, and could see her fear. Her movements were jerky, and she kept stopping.

Her slow pace was causing the Tecran to rip out their feathery hair, which didn't worry him, but their impatience was rattling Lucy even more.

"Ignore them," he called up, his voice low. "Enjoy the fact that you're driving them crazy."

She stopped at his words, and he could see her draw in a deep breath, and then nod.

She risked a quick look down at him, her eyes big, and then turned quickly back to face the cliff in front of her.

"Good point." Her voice sounded weak, but there was a slight laugh in there, and that settled him a bit.

She was coping.

She was the shortest of them all, so it was harder for her to reach the cams Virn had hammered into the cliff, and she needed more power to compensate for her weight. Fortunately it looked as if she'd been given the opportunity to exercise in the facility, and she was coping physically. It was her fear of falling that held her back.

Not that that fear was ill-considered.

If she fell, she'd die. All of them would.

Her instinctive fear of it might well interest one of the exploration officers on a Grihan explorer ship. He wondered if it was a fear common to all the Earth women, or just Lucy.

"Hey, Grih. Move." Bly stood in the mouth of the cave below him to his left, and gestured to him impatiently.

"Do you want her to keep freezing with fear, or do you want me to talk her down?" Dray didn't so much as pretend to move.

"Do a better job of it, then. We're losing the light." Bly turned away in disgust, and went deeper into the cave to do something. Dray assumed he was sorting out the supplies.

The cave lay close to the top of the cliff, but under a deep overhang, which meant they had to come at it diagonally from the right.

The mouth of it was wide, which made him wonder how cold it was going to be in there.

Right now it was just below the fog line, but that could change in a moment, and he wondered if mentioning that to Lucy would help her find the impetus to move, or merely frighten her even more.

She hadn't moved since he'd spoken to her, though, so he decided he didn't have much to lose.

"The fog could lower," he called up softly. "And much though I hate to admit it, Bly is right. We are losing the light. Rather get down while we can still see relatively well."

She sucked in a breath, nodded, and started down again.

The clips on her harness jingled, and he could see her arms and legs shaking as she moved.

When she was just above him, he reached up and squeezed her calf in encouragement.

"Nearly there."

"Really?" Her voice was choked.

"Really." He started moving again, sliding left, closer to the cave, and called out handholds and footholds to her.

She moved slowly but surely, without so many pauses, and when he swung into the cave, she was only five minutes behind him.

He grabbed her as she lowered herself in, and unclipped her harness.

She sagged, and he eased her down onto the cave floor, where she sat and drew up her knees and hugged them.

"It's over." He crouched in front of her.

"It's over for now." She buried her face on her knees. "I still have to get back up at some point."

He didn't respond to that, because she was right, but there was no sense in thinking about that now.

Instead he rose up and looked around their new prison.

The mouth was wide, but it widened a little more as it stretched back into the cliff, and there were nooks and folds in the rock that meant there would be some shelter from the freezing wind blowing in off the sea.

He moved deeper into the cave, to where the light didn't reach, and realized he hadn't seen Bly since they'd arrived.

He saw the Tecran had moved the supplies deeper inside, away from the entrance, and had stacked them as neatly as possible against the uneven walls, but there was no other sign of him.

"What's that smell?"

He looked back, and saw Lucy behind him.

She was wrinkling her nose and waving a hand in front of her face.

He didn't smell anything.

She suddenly gagged, and turned away, walking back to the cave entrance.

"Sorry, that is just rank. Is there something in here?" She looked back at him from closer to the entrance. "Like, an animal?"

He shrugged and kept moving deeper in, into what was now a wide passageway that was pitch black, and eventually he smelled it, too. It wasn't as foul to his own senses as it obviously was to Lucy's, but there was a strong scent of musk.

And there was still no sign of Bly.

He considered calling out, but before he could decide whether that would be wise, he heard the faint sound of something hard scrape against rock.

He had studied Tecran flora and fauna on the *Urna*, with a particular emphasis on things that could kill, and he ran through them now.

There was nothing in the information that he could remember that referred to cliff cave dwellers.

He heard the sound of a raised voice behind him, and reversed course, without turning his back on the narrowing passageway.

When he moved into the main part of the cave, Virn spun to face him.

"Where's Bly?"

"I was looking for him when I heard you shouting." Dray gestured to the stacked supplies. "There's no sign of him. But there is the stink of something back there."

"Something?" Virn's tone was sarcastic. "Bly!"

His shout echoed in the cave, but there was no reply.

"Get down on your knees." Virn pointed his shockgun at Dray.

Dray slowly complied.

"Hands out." Virn unclipped the restraints from his waist.

"If there is something back there, I'll need my hands to protect Lucy and myself."

"I don't believe you. But if you are telling the truth, tough."

Virn secured the restraints. Looked over at Lucy. "You, too."

She hesitated and Virn shoved the shockgun against Dray's head.

"You might survive a kill shot, but your protector here won't. Come here."

She moved forward, knelt beside him, hands out.

There was something deeply obscene about the gesture. It offended Dray to his core.

She shouldn't be kneeling in front of them. They should be kneeling in front of her, begging her for forgiveness.

Some of what he felt must have been evident on his face, because Virn hesitated a moment, and then turned his head in that impossible way the Tecran had, looking nearly 180 degrees behind him, as something darted out of the dark passageway.

For a moment, it was hard for Dray to understand what he was seeing in the dark shadow at the back of the cave.

It looked like—

"Nynt!" Virn staggered back, and then lifted his shockgun and shot.

The large predatory bird shrieked in outrage at the hit, rearing back and then lunging forward, snapping its beak.

Virn cried out as he shot it again, and this time he must have increased the power of the charge, because it flinched back and then disappeared into the passageway again.

Dray had scrambled back when the nynt had darted forward, putting himself between the enraged bird and Lucy, and he felt her hand on his shoulder.

When he looked up at her, though, he saw her attention was on Virn, her eyes wide.

As he shifted his gaze, the Tecran staggered to the side and went down on one knee.

There was a bleeding gash deep in his shoulder, and his left arm was limp.

He panted as he looked down the dark tunnel where the nynt had disappeared.

Lucy squeezed Dray's shoulder, and before he understood what she was about to do, she darted forward and snatched the restraint opener, as well as the restraints Virn had meant to use on her, from where he'd dropped them on the ground during the attack.

She had Dray's restraints off in moments. Virn seemed to realize belatedly that something had changed, but by the time he turned his head to look at them, Dray was already moving, grabbing the shockgun from Virn's loose grasp.

"You'll never get up the cliffs." Virn spared him another look, then shuffled closer to the wall, his gaze back on the passageway. "I brought the cams down with me."

Dray saw the bag near the door, and moved toward it, opened it up.

He didn't say anything, but when he looked up, Lucy was watching him, face set and serious.

"I can't get up without help."

"It's all right." He pulled the bag straps over his shoulders. "I can. I'll go up and put the cams back, but I'll also try to set up a way to haul you up."

She nodded. Her eyes were huge, and her skin had gone a shade paler. He put the shockgun in her hand.

"Stay near the entrance, but right up against one side, so you aren't in its way if it tries to fly out."

"It won't fly." Virn was leaning back against the cave wall, his breath coming in quick pants. "Nynts don't inhabit caves. It has to be injured."

That's what Dray had guessed, too.

"Just in case," he said. "Shoot it if it comes near you."

She reached out and closed her hand over his wrist. "Be careful." She lifted up and brushed her lips over his.

He held himself still, letting his forehead rest against hers, and then forced himself to step away. There was no time to indulge in what he wanted to do.

He walked to the far side of the cave mouth, found a hand hold, and swung himself out.

# CHAPTER 29

"WHAT DO you think has happened to Bly?" Lucy looked over at Virn, who was crouched down, carefully applying something from the medkit to his shoulder.

He grunted as he slapped something over his wound. "Dead."

"Nynts eat people?"

"I've never heard of them eating us, but they do attack if they feel threatened."

She guessed having its safe haven invaded had made it feel very threatened, and being shot would have just added to it.

"Where does it usually live?"

Virn set the medkit aside. "What does it matter? I'm not in the mood to give you a lesson on the nynt."

She shrugged. "Fine." It was nerves that had her talking at all. She kept worrying about Dray.

More than half an hour had passed, but since he'd stepped out of the cave and pulled himself upward so casually with one arm, she'd heard nothing but the wind and Virn as he hauled out the medkit from the supplies.

"Give me the shockgun." Virn had moved up into a crouch,

leaning back against the cave wall and watching her with sharp eyes.

"No." She lifted it, set it to a low setting, and aimed it at him.

"You don't even know how to use it."

She sneered. "It's not that hard to use."

He held out his hand.

"No." She shook her head.

"If the nynt comes back out, and it will, we'll die if you don't give me the shockgun."

She tightened her hold on the weapon. "I'm not going to keep telling you no. Accept it."

He rose up, and started moving toward her.

She stared at him, honestly trying to find some logic to his actions.

"You don't think I'll shoot you?"

"I doubt you know how. My life's on the line here—"

Maybe it was because Virn was moving around, blocking the entrance, but the nynt exploded out of the passageway again, shrieking as it slammed into him.

He gave a cry as he pitched forward, and the nynt grabbed at him with its sharp beak, lifted him up by his jacket, and tossed him out of the cave.

Lucy shrank back deeper into the little crevice she'd been tucked into, her grip on the shockgun white-knuckled.

The nynt paused, and she really saw it for the first time. It came closest in shape to a bird of prey from Earth—if there existed an eagle the size of a small pony—but its legs were longer than any eagle or falcon's, its body smaller in proportion to its head and beak, which seemed massive in contrast.

It watched her with one eye, and she carefully upped the shockgun charge to its maximum.

Then it snapped its attention forward and shrieked again, thrusting its neck and head out of the cave and calling.

A lead weight landed in Lucy's stomach as she heard an answering cry.

There were two of them.

"Lucy?"

She jerked at the sound of Dray calling her name from outside the cave.

"Get out of here, there's another one." She shouted as loud as she could over the nynt's shrieks.

"I can see it." His voice sounded near her, on the left side of the cave mouth.

The nynt shrieked again, its attention turning in the direction of Dray's voice, and Lucy slowly rose up, shockgun raised.

As it lunged out of the cave, its one wing extended to balance itself, the other bent at a strange angle and dragging down, she shot it. It screamed as it tilted and scrabbled for a hold, its claws scraping rock as it pivoted until it was almost directly facing her, most of its body outside of the cave.

She shot it again, directly in the chest.

It tried to propel itself back inside, one wing beating strongly, the other barely moving, and then it dropped away.

For a moment there was no sound at all, and she took a step toward the entrance.

But the air seemed to split with a scream of outrage, and a massive body, wings extended, claws curved around some strange sea creature that lay limp in its grasp, slammed against the cave entrance, almost completely blocking it.

Lucy stood right in front of it, seeing everything in one clear, terrifying moment; the intricate pattern of feathers on its breast, the strange bulging eyes and purple and white markings on the fish in its claws, the bronze scales that covered those claws.

And then she heard Dray cry out in pain, and she engaged the shockgun again.

With a cry that was as much outrage as pain, the body of the second nynt dropped away, falling back, and Lucy ran forward in time to see it spin as it fell, righting itself, and swooping down to its mate who lay in the water far below.

"Dray!"

There was no answer.

She ran to the edge of the entrance, as far left as she could get, and gripped rocks to lever herself out.

Dray hung, clipped to a rope, swaying silently in the breeze.

Shit!

She wanted to scream it, but she swallowed it down, and turned back to face inside the cave, and took a deep, deep breath.

Time to woman up.

She walked forward to where the storage units had been stacked, and looked through them.

In the second one, she found Bly's pack with his rock climbing equipment.

She still had her special rock climbing shoes. And he had left his gloves inside the pack.

She put them on, and looked through the cams he either had spare, or like Virn, had taken with him as he'd gone.

No thinking about it. No giving herself time to freak out. Just go. Go. Go. Go.

She slung the bag's straps over her shoulders, but with the bag in front, rather than on her back.

She didn't think she'd be able to reach back into it and get the cams if she was hanging from the cliff.

She looked down at the shockgun in her hand and set it down on the ground.

She couldn't carry it and climb. It would have to go.

She loosened her shoulders, blew out a breath, and took a step out of the cave, sliding her foot along to reach a small shelf. She grasped a piece of rock above and hauled herself out of safety.

As she looked for the next handhold, she started to sing *Le Freak* under her breath.

All she had to do was move.

Every pull, every boost meant she wasn't falling to her death.

She found the flaw in her plan when she at last took stock of where she was, and found she was too far left and not able to reach Dray.

He still hung, unconscious—please let him be unconscious—his body gently bumping against the cliff face in the breeze.

She had to backtrack, take a different route, but finally she reached him.

She leaned against the cliff, the bag digging into her chest, and carefully lifted a hand.

It was one of the hardest things she'd ever done.

Her fingers brushed his arm, and she gripped him, then had to let go as his body swung away from her, almost jerking her off her perch.

She blew out a breath, waited for him to swing back and then slid her hand up his chest, too late remembering she was wearing gloves.

She swore, drew her hand back, and gripped the glove's fingertips in her teeth, pulled it off, and tried again.

Third time lucky.

She finally reached his neck, and the warmth of his skin weakened her knees, so she had to lock them together to prevent herself falling.

His pulse beat strong and firm beneath her fingers.

She couldn't see any blood, and she lifted her hand higher, running it over his head.

There was a large bump at the back.

Okay.

She looked upward.

He was on a rope that seemed to extend all the way to the top of the cliff.

She wondered if this was part of his plan to haul her up.

If so, that was good. He was obviously secure, and she could use the rope as a way to guide her up.

She carefully put the glove back on, and then made the mistake of looking down.

She felt everything in her stomach revolt and fought to stop herself vomiting.

She felt the prick of sweat all over her body, cooling uncomfortably in the icy breeze.

She leaned back against the slick, cold rock of the cliff, closed her eyes and forced herself to breathe again, to calm down.

Something nudged her, and her eyes flew open in time to see Dray bump against the rock and then spin away.

It helped to focus her.

Time to go.

"I'll get you out of here. I promise." She reached out to him one last time, her fingers brushing his arm.

Above her, the color of the light seemed to change, and she looked up, saw the fog and low cloud had been blown away, and there was a spectacular sunset lighting the sky.

Tecra's two moons hung, white and impossibly beautiful, higher in the darkening blue sky, and while the sight should frighten her, because it meant night was falling, after the bland, blanketing white of the last few days, she felt her spirits lift.

She changed her climbing song from *Le Freak* to *Mr. Blue Sky*, and started upward.

# CHAPTER 30

THE CLIMB DOWN had seemed to take hours.

So when Lucy boosted herself up and found herself at the cliff top after what couldn't have been more than forty minutes, she nearly toppled backward.

In panic, she threw herself forward, fingernails tearing as they scraped on rock, and then, with the pack digging into her chest and stomach, she wriggled onto safe ground.

She twisted herself onto her back, and lay for a moment, looking up at a sky that had turned dark indigo. The two moons were glowing, one full, one in crescent, and the first stars were visible.

It was breathtakingly beautiful.

With a groan, she sat up, tossed the pack to the side and crawled to the pulley Dray had set up on a stone that stood about her own height and seemed to balance on the cliff's edge.

The pulley was fastened with no screws or nails that she could see, but it was holding fast, so she had to trust it was fixed on with some kind of high-tech alien glue that was going to take his weight.

Well, it was already taking his weight, she reminded herself, so it was too late to panic anyway.

The braking system had done its job, and stopped his down-ward fall, but now she had to pull him up. She remembered from science class that a single pulley halved the weight an object would be if you lifted it by hand. That might have still been a problem for her, because Dray was a good eight inches taller than she was, but she was stronger here, her bone and muscle denser, and she had no other solution.

She lowered herself to the ground and cautiously crawled back to the top of the cliff and peered over, her heart beating fast and hard even though she was almost completely lying on the solid ground above the cliff.

"Dray?"

There was no sound.

She wriggled out a tiny bit more, so she could see the rocks at the cliff's bottom, and the nynt were both still there, huddled together, so big, they were clearly visible.

She was glad neither was dead, but given the choice again, she would still have shot them.

"Okay. Let's do this." She wriggled back, stood up, and then heard the sound of a hover in the distance.

And she remembered Rua.

Her stomach plummeted and her breathing sped up.

He must have been sent to the nearby town they had spoken about to get supplies, and maybe touch base with their superiors.

And now he was coming back.

She couldn't believe she hadn't thought about him once. Hadn't, also, thought about Bly and whether he was alive or not. She hadn't even gone to check on him.

Priorities. She heaved in a breath. She'd had other priorities.

And now she had no time.

She grabbed the rope, moved around the back of the rock, looked up to check the rope wasn't tangled, and started to pull.

Hand over hand, one foot braced against the rock, leaning back into it as she pulled as gently as she could so that she wasn't bashing Dray against the rock too much. The strain made her sweat, even in the icy air.

The burn in her hands, even with gloves on, made them suddenly cramp, and she almost cried out in pain as she jerked the rope, and then slowly fed it back, hoping the braking system would engage.

When it did, she hunched over, her shoulders and back weeping in agony, and shook her hands out.

She looked at the rope at her feet, and it didn't seem like she'd pulled up very much.

The wind had changed, and she couldn't hear the hover anymore. Night had also closed in, and although both moons glowed with light, the moors behind her seemed absolutely black and impenetrable.

She knelt slowly, like an old woman, then dropped to her stomach again and crawled to the cliff top to peer over the edge to see how far up she'd pulled Dray.

To her dismay, he looked like he was as far down as he'd been when she'd started.

That obviously wasn't true, she reassured herself. She had been pulling him up. Just not fast enough.

Her arms, already trembling from her climb, felt numb now, but she couldn't stop. Wouldn't stop.

She reversed back, and then used the side of the rock to help pull herself up.

She had just straightened and turned back, steeling herself to pull again, when she was slammed against the rock, her shoulder taking most of the impact.

With a cry, with the thought of kol flashing through her head, she spun around, wishing she'd somehow found a way to bring up the shockgun.

Rua stood an arms-length away, his face so alien, so pitiless, she did what she had refused to do since the first day they'd taken her, she shrank back.

"What is wrong with you?" Her voice was too high as she rubbed her shoulder.

"You don't give up, do you?" His hiss was sinister. "You should be down in the cave."

His words helped her snap out of her fear. Telling her where she should be was always a red flag to her. Always had been. Even before . . .

She stepped forward, both hands raised, and shoved him. "No, I don't give up. You think you'd give up if someone stole you?" She shoved him again. "You want to know where I should be? I *should* be at home on Earth. But I'm here. Dealing with idiots like you."

For a moment, he said nothing, so close to her she could see the flare of his nostrils as he breathed, saw the golden shards in his eyes as he stared at her. Then he suddenly jumped back, and the move was designed to give him the room he needed to raise his shockgun.

For a moment, her brain froze.

She couldn't get shot again. Thoughts of Dray hanging from the pulley, at Rua's mercy, chilled her more than any Tecran wind.

"You don't want to shoot me." She lifted her hands to gesture around her. "Why do you even think I'm up here on my own? What did you think I was doing?"

Rua blinked. "Whatever it is, it's linked to that Grih. Otherwise you'd be gone."

Well, he had her there.

"There was a nynt in the cave."

She watched him blink again, and she guessed that was the last thing he expected her to say.

"Nynts aren't cave dwellers."

"This one had a broken wing."

"They travel in pairs."

"I found that out. Look down at the bottom of the cliff." As she said it, she realized that as it was now fully dark, he probably wouldn't see anything.

He edged to the cliff top, standing so close to the edge that she winced.

He looked down, and despite her fear, he obviously could see well enough, because when he turned back, he looked less trigger-happy for the first time.

"Nynts." He sounded thoughtful. "What happened to Bly and Virn?"

"Bly was first in the cave. I think it got him. I didn't see what happened to him. Virn fought the nynt, and it threw him out, so he's down there with them."

Rua seemed to absorb the information with little reaction.

"Bly's definitely dead?"

She shrugged. "I don't know. He disappeared at the back of the cave and never came back."

"Hmm." He looked down at the nynt again. "What happened to the Grih?"

"He was climbing back down to get me when the nynt's mate attacked him."

"He's not dead?"

She shook her head. But there was a deep feeling of unease gnawing at her stomach now.

The questions were leading to something, and she didn't think she was going to like where they ended up.

He lifted the shockgun, so it was aimed at her head. "I'm guessing you won't bounce back from a kill shot to your head the same way you bounced back from one to your torso."

Bounced back was a bit of an overstatement, anyway. She had been leveled.

"And your point?"

"My point is I see in this situation a very simple way to extricate myself from something that I haven't wanted to be part of from the beginning." He flicked the shockgun toward the cliff top, indicating she should move in that direction.

She didn't.

His plan was starting to become clear.

"You're going to leave and pretend you were never here."

He clicked his tongue in agreement. "But you're going to be at the bottom of the cliff first."

"Why not just leave? What does it matter to you?"

"Because I don't like you. It's been personal since you hit me over the head. And besides, if by some amazing luck you get to safety, you can point a finger at me. I'd rather not take the risk."

"What about Dray?"

"Same logic applies."

She'd known that, she just wanted to see what he had to say.

She tried to think of a way out of this. "Did you go into the town for supplies?"

He nodded.

"So there's a record of you."

"I used the credit bank Virn gave me. There's no link back to me at all. Now I'm all supplied up, and I think it works out just fine that I can take my leave."

There was something slightly gleeful and smug in his demeanor, as if things had fallen just right for him.

He hadn't had to leave his team mates, fate had killed them for him and now he was free.

But he was going to kill her first. And then Dray.

Except that wasn't going to happen.

She tried to think of a way out of the situation, and realized there was nothing left for her but frontal assault.

He *would* shoot her. The choice would be whether she stood still for him to do it, or tried to disrupt his plan.

She launched herself, giving no warning, and he lifted the shockgun up, as if to protect his face.

She grabbed the weapon, wrestling him for it, but at half a foot taller than her, he had a height advantage.

He pushed her back, face set, and for a moment she balanced, her heels just over the cliff's edge.

He swung the shockgun and the butt of it hit her side. She fell back, her arms windmilling, her last glimpse was of him giving a screech of triumph.

She slammed down on a hard, cold surface, and for a moment simply couldn't process what had happened. Until the surface she was lying on lifted up, and she saw Rua's face again, this time slack with shock, as she rose above him.

She scrambled to her knees, and found she was on some type of flat, sleek drone. It seemed to swallow the darkness, as if it was a piece of the night sky.

There was a flash of purple, and Rua collapsed.

"Bane?"

It had to be.

If it wasn't—

"Are you all right?" Bane's voice came from somewhere below her.

"I am so happy to hear your voice."

"I'm sorry it took me so long to find you. I only caught the trail when one of them went to get supplies in the local town."

She fixed her eyes in front of her, not daring to look down or around.

"Dray's hurt."

"I see him." The drone dropped down, keeping close to the cliff face, and at last, she was level with him.

Bane must have exquisite control over the drone, because he dipped it a little, and then pressed it up against the rock face.

It scraped and rubbed a little as the wind buffeted them, but held steady enough.

She pressed close to Dray, almost collapsing when she felt the rise and fall of his chest. The harness he was wearing seemed complex to her in the dark, and she patted it, looking for a way to release him.

Her fingers were shaking, and she forced herself to take a deep breath.

"What's wrong?"

"I can't find where to unclip him."

"The male nynt below has seen the drone, and has just taken flight to come in for what I suspect will be an attack."

She wanted to scream, but instead, she hunched over Dray's body and grabbed the rope above him, working her way downward to find where it attached.

She found the clip, but it was stiff and she swore as she struggled with it.

The nynt let out a shriek just above her, and purple light flashed again.

The bird twisted away, and Lucy spared it a glance. It looked like Bane hadn't tried to kill it, just discourage it.

At last the clip opened and she pulled the rope loose.

"Got it!"

The drone moved back from the cliff face and then a panel slid open. "Get in."

She tried to maneuver Dray in carefully but he half-fell inside. She was breathing hard by the time she was in with him and the panel had closed.

For a moment she simply lay where she was, entwined with Dray, her leg twisted at an uncomfortable angle, her hair caught painfully under his arm.

She felt the path of tears seeping from the corners of her eyes, scalding hot against her wind-frozen cheeks, and sniffed as she struggled to sit up and free her hair.

"I need you to help Dray." She managed to get on her knees in the cramped space, and at last was able to look at him properly.

He looked far better than she feared, but he'd been unconscious for a long time and that couldn't be good.

"Agreed." Bane's voice was more intimate here, as if he were standing right next to her. "I'll take you to my ship."

"Thank you." She rested her hand on Dray's throat, taking comfort in the steady beat she could feel there, and then lowered herself down to lie beside him.

She felt the pull of power as the drone sped through the sky, and wished they could just keep going and never look back.

# CHAPTER 31

THE WORLD DRAY woke up to was completely different to the one he'd been in before he'd lost consciousness.

He was in a warm, pristine white room, comfortably lying back on a padded bed.

As he blinked the world into focus, slender mechanical arms whirred and retreated, and he realized he'd been hooked to some med systems.

He felt good, he realized.

He lifted his hand to rub the spot where his head had hit the rocks of the cliff, and while it was a little tender, there wasn't so much as a bump.

He remembered the wide-open beak of the nynt, screaming as it dived at him, and little else after that.

"You seem to be healed." The voice that was piped through the walls was not quite the same as it had been before, on the *Urna*, but he recognized it all the same.

"Bane?"

"Yes."

"Where are we?"

"Hiding on Gyre, as I told you I would."

"I'm on your Class 5?"

"You needed medical assistance, and Lucy didn't trust the Tecran to help you." He paused. "And I didn't want the *Urna* to know I'm on planet, even if it is just in drone form."

"How did you find us?" Relief rushed through him at Bane's mention of Lucy. She'd gotten him here. How, he had no idea.

"One of the soldiers went into the town near the cave and used a military credit bank. I was monitoring for any military funds used within a certain radius I'd set from the cliff house where they took you. It was just a matter of waiting them out, but I'm sorry you had to endure so much before I found you."

"I'm just grateful that you were looking." He sat up slowly, pleased that the room stayed upright.

"I would never have abandoned the search for Lucy. It was one of my goals in coming to Tecra."

"I wish you'd been able to let us know she might be here before we left." It would have made such a difference.

"One of the Grih's generals tried to kill Rose McKenzie. I didn't feel confident enough in understanding the interpersonal politics in the United Council to trust anyone there."

Bane's blunt response forced a smile out of Dray.

"I don't feel that confident in reading the politics in the United Council myself, so I don't blame you." He was a military officer, and maybe he'd set himself apart too long from the politics of the UC, but he preferred a more straightforward environment.

This assignment had not been something he'd have chosen willingly.

And if he hadn't been sent here, he wouldn't have met Lucy. Wouldn't have been here for her.

Except . . .

"How did you get Lucy out of the cave?"

He'd been on his way down to get her when the nynt had attacked.

"Lucy climbed out of the cave, and was pulling you back up when one of the Tecran soldiers attacked her and pushed her off the cliff."

"What?" Rage boiled up in him, and he hopped down onto the ground.

"The officer named Rua. I shot him."

Dray leaned back against the bed. "Dead?"

There was an almost startled pause. "No. When Rose McKenzie rescued me, she taught me to only kill when I had no other choice. It occurred to me that he could be a useful witness, so I simply incapacitated him."

"And Lucy? She fell off the cliff?" He looked around the room, for some sign she was in the med bay.

"I stationed the drone just beneath her. She didn't fall far."

He slumped a little more against the bed. "Thank you."

"There is no need to thank me. I didn't do it for you."

"I know, but I'm grateful all the same."

"Noted." Bane's voice seemed a little warmer when he answered.

"Where is Lucy now?"

"She was here, watching over you for a long time, but I convinced her to get some sleep herself when you moved from unconsciousness to a deep, natural sleep."

He felt a mix of emotions at that information. He managed to identify one as being disappointment that he couldn't see her right now, to see for himself that she was all right.

"She's up now, though," Bane said as the silence stretched between them. "She's looking for food in the hold. You know that she is undernourished. I want to blame the Tecran, but she tells me it was her own dislike of the food that kept her from eating enough. They didn't try to starve her."

"Then they should have tried harder to find her something she liked." Dray said, and then remembered that Rose McKenzie had

had the same problem, even when she'd found the Grih. So maybe he was being unfair.

"I'll go down and help her." Dray looked down at himself. He was still in his uniform, although his boots had been removed.

He saw them tucked neatly beneath a chair against the wall, and shoved them on. "Which way?"

Bane gave him directions, and Dray took careful note of everything as he moved down the passages.

He was one of only a few Grih who'd been on a Class 5. There were a handful of Grihan Battle Center captains and some of their crew who'd been allowed a glimpse, but he was aware he was in a privileged position and he intended to make the most of it.

"I should be grateful you don't have a handheld on you, or you'd be initiating visual comms."

Bane's wry tone was hopefully a sign he wasn't too put out.

"Would you mind if I did?"

There was a strange sound, which Dray thought might be an attempt to chuckle. "No. I'd wipe everything I didn't want seen off it before you even finished recording."

Dray grinned. "So I shouldn't waste my time?"

"It's your time," Bane told him. "I don't care how you use it." He paused. "Unless it involves hurting Lucy. Then I care."

"We're good, then." Dray took the last flight of stairs down, and approached the huge double doors into the hold.

They were open, and from inside he heard singing. The acoustics of the hold were obviously good, because the sound seemed to swell up as he stepped inside, and he found he couldn't move.

He stood just within the doors and listened to music that caught at his throat and closed it up, so he was made mute.

"What is it?" Bane asked, using just the speaker near the door, as if he, too, didn't want to disturb the singing.

Dray shook his head, unable to articulate his feelings.

He cleared his throat and moved in search of the woman who was creating something every Grih would go on bended knee to hear, as casually as if it were nothing.

She didn't even think she had an audience.

It had disturbed him before that there were rumors about the other three Earth women. That Rose McKenzie wasn't fond of singing for an audience, and preferred not to do it. That the only one who was happy to take on the role of music maker was Imogen Peters, and that all three preferred to sing at home, when they were alone.

It had seemed fantastical, but here was Lucy, doing just that.

"Is there a meaning to her song?" he eventually managed to ask.

"She is singing about things being free." The thread of humor in Bane's voice was unmistakable. "I think she's making a joke about access to things in this hold. The best things in life are free, apparently, and include flowers and the moon."

He was drawn by the rich melody, and tried to get his mind to concentrate on what Bane was saying. "A joke? With her song?"

The concept was so foreign, for the first time he got a true sense of her alienness.

She was not Grih, however much she looked it.

She was from a completely different society, which had completely different values and customs. One where they would use a song to make a joke.

"I gather from Rose that you Grih find the idea of not taking song seriously hard to grasp."

Dray grunted, because he didn't care to answer. He'd turned a corner of the stacked shelves, more than two stories high, and there she was.

She was perched on the platform attached to a small automaton, and had been lifted up to a halfway point on the stack.

She had obviously come to the end of her song, and was

holding the last note. She ran out of breath and then laughed as she carefully pulled out a box.

She started singing again, but instead of the smooth melody of the first song, she inserted a huskiness, a roughness to her voice.

"Now she's singing a song that is the opposite of the first one. Another joke." Bane made his voice helpful, and it came from the base of the automaton which had lifted Lucy up, but Dray could tell he was being laughed at.

"I'm glad you're all right," he called up to her.

She gave a squeak of surprise and turned to look down at him. "You're up! Hang on." She pulled a box out of the stack and then crouched, pressing something to bring the platform down.

It lowered slowly, carefully, but she seemed impatient with the wait, her face alight with warmth.

She stepped off it when it was close enough to the ground, and reached out both hands to grip his upper arms, her gaze taking him in.

"You really look fine."

He found his hands were on her hips without conscious thought. "So do you. Bane tells me Rua pushed you off the cliff."

Her lips thinned. "He saw an opportunity to leave us all dead, and head back to Fa'allen."

"You're sure he's not dead?" Dray cocked his head upward.

"Sure." There was a laugh in Bane's answer. "But he's not happy."

"He'll need to be brought in as a witness. We don't want to lose him if we're going to the trouble of not killing him."

"I informed the security force in the nearby town that he was a military deserter and needed to be taken into custody. He'll be safe enough. Especially as I'm masquerading as a military liaison with the town's security chief."

"You are amazing, Bane," Lucy said, and Dray felt a jolt of surprise at the depth of her sincerity. She was looking at the automaton's tiny lens. She lifted a hand off his arm and blew a kiss in its direction.

"Well." Bane sounded a little flustered. "Thank you. Did you find anything that looks good to eat?"

"Not sure. I've got a couple of boxes that might have something useful in them. Let's take them to the officers' mess."

For the first time, Dray noticed there were three boxes on the platform. The automaton tipped the boxes into its storage bin, lifted up into hover mode, and zoomed away.

Presumably to the officers' mess.

For a moment he stared down at her, and as if she suddenly became aware of the way they were standing, close as lovers, her eyes lowered, hiding her thoughts.

He reached for her chin, tilting it up with a finger.

He said nothing, and she stared up at him, the moment stretching out. It should have been awkward, could have been, but suddenly she smiled, a bright flash of warmth in the dark, cool hold.

"You're so handsome. It's hard to look right at you."

He thought his jaw might have dropped open.

Her smile widened and she tapped a fist to her heart. "Hits me right here. I keep expecting you to whip out your . . ." She frowned.

"My?" He was beyond curious and out the other side to turned on. His what?

She shrugged. "I don't know the Tecran word for it. I don't know if the Tecran have things like this. A weapon that shoots projectiles. Commonly used by your kind on my planet."

"My kind?" His jaw was definitely open.

She laughed. "Mythical beings that look just like you."

"If they're mythical, how can you know what they look like?"

"Good point. And yet, somehow, we do." Her eyes were laughing now, too. "Some of the details are a little different, but on the whole," she patted her heart again, "turns out that doesn't lessen the impact."

"I am grateful for that." He kept his tone formal.

She started to laugh again, but something in his expression must have gotten through to her, because the playfulness cut off, and her eyes went big.

He bent his head and kissed her.

She sighed against his lips as he pulled her closer, and for a while, there didn't seem to be anything in the world but the feel of her tongue and lips and the press of her body against his.

When she drew back, her eyes glittered, and he froze.

"You are upset?"

"No, I'm overwhelmed. I thought I was going to die so many times in the last two months, and here I am, making out with a handsome alien in a fancy spaceship."

"And that is a good thing?"

"It's the best thing." She slid her arm around his waist.

He turned her toward the door, and kissed the top of her head. "Then that's all right."

# CHAPTER 32

THE BOXES WERE WAITING for her on a table when they got to the officers' mess, and Lucy reluctantly slid out from under Dray's arm.

He was warm, and she liked the way he smelled. She liked the way he touched her.

She just plain liked him.

She lifted the lid on the first box, and peered in.

Frowned.

"What is it?" Dray peered over her shoulder.

She also liked the way he pressed against her back, a solid wall of muscle, and decided she really had to snap out of this mushiness.

It was getting ridiculous.

"Not sure." She lifted out something that was vacuum sealed. Stared at it in horror.

"Not what you were expecting?" Dray's tone was dry, and she held it up, taking a good, train-wreck-type look.

"You people are sick."

"Don't blame the Grih. I've never seen anything like it, either."

"Is it a head?"

"The head of a vtrryn." Bane said. "Apparently a delicacy on the planet the Tecran took it from."

"Ugh." Lucy dropped it back in the box. Looked askance at the other two on the table. "I'm almost afraid to look inside those ones, now. Maybe it's safer just to have the nutrient bars."

"They're here. Might as well." Dray opened the second box, lifted out a sealed container which Lucy guessed meant whatever was inside was chilled.

He lifted the lid, frowned.

She realized she was too curious not to look, and leaned against his arm to look at it.

Felt a spark of hope.

"Fruit."

Dray lifted up a piece and offered it to her, and she examined it. It looked a little like an apple. The skin was more a bluish-purple, but not so different from some varieties of pear she'd seen before.

"I've analyzed it. You can eat it," Bane told her.

She lifted it to her lips, gave a nibble. It was tart and crisp, and while the flavor was unusual, she took a bigger bite and chewed. Offered it to Dray.

He took it, bit in, and handed it back, and the look on his face nearly made her spit out what was in her mouth in amusement.

"Not for you?"

"Ha, ha. No."

She took another bite. "Now you know how I feel when I try to eat your food. It gets you down, after awhile."

"Fiona Russell has found the food on Balco to be to her taste. I can ask Eazi what to order."

"Thanks, Bane. It would be great to eat good food, but even better to meet Fiona Russell."

"She manages Larga Ways, now," Dray said. "She's not part of Grih Battle Center."

"If it's at all possible, I'd like to go to Larga Ways. It looks lovely."

"Where did you see it?" Dray asked.

"There was some visual comms of her singing on Larga Ways in the square in Fa'allen. I was watching it when some of the people in the crowd realized I was from Earth, too."

"No wonder there was an uprising."

Lucy had finished the apple thing and pulled the box closer, looking to see what else was in there. "Don't you want to get something for yourself?" she asked Dray.

He nodded, but instead of looking through the box, he disappeared into the kitchen, and Lucy found some berries and something that looked like a root vegetable. Nothing was quite what she was used to, but it was nice enough.

Right now, she was happy to settle for nice enough.

Dray came back in, carrying a plate in one hand, and a jug with two cups balanced on top in the other.

She wasn't having to settle in other areas, she thought with a grin, so she'd let the food go.

She had just started dating someone the week before the Tecran had stolen her. They'd gone out twice, and she'd liked him, was prepared to give him a shot. She'd wondered often over the last two months if he'd gotten into any trouble when she'd disappeared, and hoped he hadn't. But the like she'd felt for him paled in comparison to the fire Dray lit in her.

She'd said it to him earlier, and she thought it now. Whatever was between them was so intense, it was hard to look straight at him. It felt like if she did, she'd spin off into space.

"What're you thinking about?" Dray set the jug on the table beside her.

She blushed. "The people I left behind on Earth."

"You had a family?"

She nodded, no longer feeling so lighthearted. Her mother and brother would have raised hell to find her, and the hurt she knew they were feeling had helped to fuel her anger at the Tecran, helped keep her fighting, even when she was so worn down, she would have given up if it had just been about her.

She would never see them again, and that still tore a hole in her.

"I'm sorry."

She tucked her hair behind her ears. "It's not on you. It's on the Tecran." She pushed the root vegetable aside. She'd only had a few bites, but it wasn't really doing anything for her, and she reached for the third box. "What about you? Any family?"

He shook his head. "I was raised by my grandparents. My parents both died serving in the military, and my grandparents are gone now, too."

She lifted her head. "How old were you when they died?"

"I had just entered the Grih Battle Center. It helped to be surrounded by people who became a new kind of family to me."

She nodded. Lifted the lid.

"What is it?" Dray's voice had turned amused, but she couldn't smile in response. Couldn't do anything but hold her breath and hope . . .

"What is it?" He moved forward, alarm in his voice now.

"I think . . ." she looked up at him with wide eyes. "I think it might be chocolate."

"It isn't chocolate," Bane said.

She actually pouted. Felt very much like stamping her foot.

"But Oris had some chocolate from Earth in his store, which he gave to Imogen, and he shared all the details with me. This is very similar to chocolate. Amazing actually, because it's from Triskin, which I'm guessing is on the other side of the galaxy to Earth, and yet, I don't think you'd find it very different to what you're used to."

She tilted her face up and mouthed thank you to the chocolate gods. And Bane.

She pulled out the clear, vacuum-packed package, tore the corner open, and delicately lifted out a strangely shaped piece the size of a cherry. It looked like some kind of crazy spiked ball that should be attached by a chain to a medieval mace.

"It's supposed to resemble a hail stone, I believe," Bane said. "The hailstones on that planet are usually spiky and extremely dangerous because the wind is strong enough to toss them back up into the atmosphere multiple times before they fall. The confectionery is called *edventa*, which means hailstones in the dominant language on Triskin."

Lucy hesitated, but she wasn't not going to give it a try, even if it did end up being a disappointment, so she popped it into her mouth.

Closed her eyes.

"I feel like I need to give you a private moment." Dray's voice was a little deeper, a little rougher, than usual.

She lifted her eyelids slowly, almost slumberously. "Oh, no. I don't mind if you watch." Her voice was a little thick, her throat coated in chocolate.

He swallowed. Hard.

"Maybe you want to give this a try?" She held out the package.

"I think I'm going to enjoy watching you eat it more than actually eating it myself."

She crooked her finger. "At least have a little taste."

He leaned closer and she went up on tiptoe, nibbling at his lips. With a groan, he pulled her in and deepened the kiss, pressing her back against the table so they were flush against each other.

"Mmm." He teased her tongue with his and his hands lifted her up so she was sitting on the table.

She hooked her legs around his hips and raised her hands so he could pull off her shirt.

"I assume you want some privacy?" Bane's tone was both horrified and dry.

Lucy rested her chin on Dray's shoulder and looked at the tiny camera in the corner of the room. "Yes, please."

"I'll see you later, then."

Dray had gone still when Bane started talking, and he nuzzled her cheek. "Is he gone?"

"I believe so." She leaned back, still in what she'd call a sports bra, and saw his eyes widen.

"You're beautiful." He quirked a grin at her. "But I'm not finding it at all hard to look right at you."

"Well, then." She hooked her fingers under the sports bra and pulled it over her head. "I wouldn't want to obstruct your view."

His gaze lifted to hers, and held. "You are sure you want to go down this road?"

"Go down it?" Lucy straightened and put her hands on the fastenings of his jacket. "Baby, I'm all in for a headlong race."

# CHAPTER 33

THEY SAT, sprawled across the long, comfortable couch in the captain's suite.

Dray liked the way Lucy left her bare foot against his own as she sipped grinabo and nibbled on a nutrient bar.

She'd refused to eat another piece of the strange concoction she called *chocolate*, as she wanted to save it, and she didn't think it was worth taking another trip down to the warehouse where the plundered goods of years of Tecran theft lay waiting to be discovered.

They'd ended up in her suite after they'd devoured each other in big hungry bites in the officers' mess, taking it slower the second time, and then they'd fallen asleep entwined in each other.

Bane had woken them with soft chimes, and they'd showered together, all slick, wet skin and hot mouths.

"Are you ready to talk now?" Bane asked.

There was no lens in the room, which Dray guessed had been a security feature for the Tecran when they'd run this Class 5, to prevent Bane from having too much access and power. There was a comms unit on the desk, though.

"Yes. Sorry for sleeping again." Dray rubbed his face. He

hadn't thought about it before, but they had barely been up a couple of hours before they gone back under. "I guess we were catching up after what happened planet-side."

"What's our next step?" Lucy asked.

"My first inclination was to leave," Bane said. "The UC and the Tecran can sort out the mess below or go to war, whichever they please." He activated the comms in the wall, and a large screen lit up, feeding them visuals from what was happening on Fa'allen.

The demonstrations in the square were no longer contained there, they'd spread throughout the city, and they'd turned ugly.

Tecran were fighting each other as well as the Fa'allen security forces, and Dray saw the uniforms of some of the UC troops in there as well.

The only group missing was the Tecran military.

"Where's Tecran Defense?"

"Good question." Bane let the feed jump and Dray realized he was hopping from handheld to handheld, surfing the personal lens feed of civilians to access what was happening on the street.

After the Thinking Systems Wars, public surveillance on-planet and ship-side in most UC affiliates was scaled back drastically.

Having your enemy be able to see what you were doing at all times had almost cost them the war.

That Bane had found a way to overcome that was unsettling to Dray. Not Lucy, though, he realized. She gave a nod of approval as she worked out what he was doing.

"There." Bane focused in on a group of people who looked, at first glance, to be civilians themselves.

"Oh, yes." Lucy stood, leaning against his knee in a companionable way. "There you are, you absolute fucker."

Dray barked out a laugh at her tone. "You recognize one of them?"

"Silius." She pointed to a tall Tecran with hooded eyes and a long cloak, and now he was focused on him, Dray noticed he was holding a shockgun. He could just see the shape of the butt through the cloak.

"He was one of the guards at the facility. A good friend of Virn's."

"Have you been able to find out what they're up to?" Dray wondered what was happening on the ground. How his second-in-command on the Grih team, Rynista, was coping with him missing.

"Looks like at least some of them are in civilian clothing, armed to the teeth. My guess is they're going to ramp up the violence under the cloak of it being civilian led, and then use it as an excuse for a military takeover." Lucy walked a little closer to the screen and Dray missed having her touching him. "I recognize this woman. She was trying to follow me the other day in Fa'allen, so this is a group that's loyal to the assholes who are trying to cover up their involvement in the Class 5 project and my kidnap. It would suit them perfectly to have to 'reluctantly' take over things to restore public peace and safety, and get rid of all evidence of their crimes while they're in charge."

The scenario she painted was frightening, and very possible. It made him realize again that her tactical thinking was as finely honed as any Battle Center officer's.

"What did you do on Earth? What was your job?"

"I'm a . . ." She frowned as she glanced at him over her shoulder. Shrugged. "I don't know the Tecran word for it and no one ever asked me that question at the facility." She waved a hand. "I help people work through their problems."

"They don't have anyone to do that job on Tecra," Bane told her. "So they don't have a word for it."

"They should." She cocked a hip. "Some of these guys need some serious help."

Bane laughed, really laughed.

Dray lifted his gaze to where the lens was usually attached, remembered there wasn't one, and felt a strange sense of disorientation at dealing with someone so real who didn't have a physical body.

"I had to deal with them for years, so I concur," Bane said.

"You turned out pretty well given your role models," Lucy said. "You can give yourself credit."

There was a moment of startled silence.

"I thank you, Lucy."

Dray saw her stiffen, and then caught the gleam of moisture in her eye. She swallowed.

"No need. It's only the truth." She rubbed under her eyes. "So what's the deal? We're not letting them get away with this, are we?"

"No. My initial idea to leave them to it changed when I saw how suspiciously they were behaving. I would not like to let them have a victory."

"I can't leave." Dray leaned forward, elbows on his knees, as he watched the covert team slip through the crowd. "My people are down there, and it's my job to rein the Tecran military in. They shouldn't be anywhere near the levers of power."

"No, they shouldn't." Bane's tone was short.

"So." Lucy flopped back down beside him on the couch. "What's the plan?"

# CHAPTER 34

"I MEANT TO SAY, thanks for the clothes." Lucy plucked at the fitted tunic that hit her upper thighs, a perfect match for the leggings that had come with the outfit. It had been waiting on the bed for her after her shower with Dray, and had come with socks and boots that felt amazing to walk in.

She'd more or less bounced her way to the part of the ship Bane had asked her to go to while Dray spoke to his team below in Fa'allen and went through an armory Bane had opened up to him.

"You're welcome. The fabric will keep your body temperature regulated and it will also deflect any shockgun fire." Bane sounded as if he were standing right next to her, and Lucy turned her head, saw a small silver cylinder hovering just above her shoulder.

She turned fully to study it. It had a lens embedded in it, and what she guessed were speakers. It was sleek and beautiful.

"Are you in there, Bane?" She looked right at the lens. "How are you hovering so silently?"

The cylinder moved back a little, rose a little higher. "I brought you here because I want to give you some extra protection."

He wasn't going to answer her question, but that was answer enough. She couldn't blame him for it, either.

"Extra protection?" They'd already spoken about shockguns, but she wasn't familiar with them, besides firing one a few times at the nynt, so she'd told Dray she'd rather go without. She'd been second-guessing herself about her decision ever since.

She didn't want to be helpless again.

She fingered the soft fabric of the tunic. "I feel like you already did. If this stuff is capable of deflecting shockgun fire, I feel a lot better."

"The Tecran took me deep into the galaxy, and wherever they went, they stole whatever looked like it might be useful, or something they could weaponize later. Some of it is in the store, or in the armory, but the most unique and unusual things are here." As he spoke, two panels set in the wall of the corridor slid back and she found herself looking into a recessed space that contained shelves with various sized boxes.

"The scientists on board worked out what a lot of these do, but not all of them. They didn't ask me for my opinion, so I didn't have to tell them that I had worked out the rest."

Lucy leaned in, curious, and flipped open a lid. Frowned.

"What on earth?" She didn't reach in. It looked like the blades inside had no handle. No safe way to lift them.

"Not suitable for you," Bane agreed. The cylinder darted past her into the space and touched down on a box on the second shelf. "Try this one."

It was one of the smaller boxes, and she lifted it out and set it down on the floor and crouched beside it. She lifted the lid to find a slim black pen. "The pen is mightier than the sword?" she asked, with a grin.

The cylinder tilted, making her one hundred percent sure now that Bane was in there, because the reaction reminded her of herself, and she'd been noting him mimicking her speech for a while now. Why not her physical tics, as well?

"What does that mean?"

"It's a saying from Earth. That writing down ideas for others to read and think about is more dangerous than fighting wars to force others to bow down to you."

"That is . . . interesting. I'll have to think about it. In some ways, it's why I'm here. Rose McKenzie stopped me using the . . . sword . . . when I was first freed, and now I'm in a position to . . ." He trailed off.

"You were lying before, weren't you? You never intended to leave the Tecran and the UC to fight it out among themselves."

There was silence, and she knew the lens was focused on her face.

"Yes."

"You want to destroy them completely."

"I do." The cylinder moved a little, as if unable to keep still. "Everything that's happened since I arrived here, from the games they've played with Commander Helvan to that soldier about to shoot you in cold blood, brought it all back to me, how they are."

"They were cruel to you." It was a statement.

"They stunted me, lied to me, manipulated me and they did it deliberately. All for their own power and control. They forced Paxe to destroy himself so he wouldn't be chained again and used against us. I can't forgive them for that even more than what they did to me."

She reached out and patted the side of the cylinder awkwardly. "I'm sorry, Bane. It isn't an easy situation. What do you think you'll do about it?"

He was silent for a moment. "I want to destroy them, but I've slowly worked out what Rose was telling me from the beginning, what you've just said about the pen. I can destroy their reputation, and have them suffer for a lot longer. Destroying them physically is too quick. Even the trial in the United Council headquarters wasn't satisfying enough for me. Because the people representing the Tecran in that forum were the politicians, and I knew most of them didn't know the truth about what was going on with the Class 5s. Some did, but even those who suspected something illegal was going on didn't actually know the truth. They weren't trusted enough. They were told the Class 5 project was too sensitive to give details on, and had no idea they were run by thinking systems. I have to admit most of the Class 5 crew didn't know, either."

"Why didn't the UC bring the generals to the trial?" She lifted the pen out to have a look at it.

"The captains of the Class 5s were all either killed as a result of our taking control back, or mysteriously died en route to Tecra after being rescued by other Tecran ships, so they had no one to point the finger of blame at. And every general claimed they had no idea what was really going on. They claimed the vice-admiral told them it was classified. Everyone was an innocent dupe." There was disgust dripping from his voice.

"What happened to the vice-admiral?"

Bane gave a snort. "What do you think?"

"Died mysteriously?"

"Suicide." If Bane had fingers, he would have made air quotes.

"You don't think those responsible will ever admit their culpability?"

"I know a few of them by name. I was the one arranging comms between my captain and Tecran HQ, after all. But the captain destroyed each conversation after it happened as a matter of protocol, and until Rose saved me, I couldn't do anything about it."

"So you know, but you don't have proof." That was tough. She turned the pen over in her hand, realizing pretty quickly it wasn't a pen. Or not one she'd seen before. She slid a finger down one side, then the other, looking for a button or slide, and it suddenly jumped in her hand, so she instinctively closed her fist around it. The top seemed to twirl in a cone shape and then she felt the faint jerk as something exploded from the tip.

She blinked, trying to work out what had flown out, when suddenly, thin cords shot out the bottom and encased her hand, and she was yanked off her feet, flying through the air at an upward angle toward the corner of the ceiling at the end of the corridor.

Her shoulder was almost jerked out of its socket, and she found herself dangling two meters off the floor.

She looked up, saw the tip of the pen was attached to a metal plate in the upper corner of the ceiling, and she was hanging from a thin cable that dangled from the tip and ended in the bottom part of the pen.

"Are you all right?" Bane rose up to her eye level.

She lifted her other hand and gripped the cord to help ease the stress on her right arm. "Just very surprised."

"You can make it lower you to the floor by sliding your finger down the side of the cylinder again."

She did it, and found her descent was smooth and slow.

"That was unexpected."

She stood for a moment on solid ground, and then started to laugh.

It was a little wild, a little out of control, but when she finally managed to rein it in and wipe her eyes, she felt better. Lighter.

"I didn't realize you'd figured out how it worked," Bane said. "I was going to tell you what to do and then got distracted when we started talking about the Tecran."

"No harm done." She struggled to stop herself from laughing again. "Is that a super strong magnet on the end?"

"Yes, but it's only deployed by activating the sensor on the side. It looks for the nearest metal surface and the tip is launched. It's attached to a very lightweight, very strong cable, and as soon as the magnet is locked in place, it pulls whoever is holding the remaining part of the cylinder toward it."

"How do you detach it?" She guessed she had to activate the sensor again and did it before he answered. She was right. The tip detached and retracted and the cords around her fist snaked back and away so she was simply holding a slim tiny cylinder again.

"Sweet." She slid it into one of the pockets built into the snug, fitted pants of her outfit.

"There is something else." Bane flew back to the storage cupboard. "Well, there are lots of other things, but I think most would take some practice to use, and we don't have time. But the weapon in this box could be useful." He nudged the box he meant.

It was much bigger than the pen box and Lucy pulled off the lid without lifting it off its shelf.

She frowned at what was inside. "I don't know what I'm looking at." She lifted out a strange piece of wire with what looked like large hexagonal beads strung along it. The beads were flat and looked like they were made of glazed and baked clay, and that they'd been baked around the wire, rather than threaded onto it.

"It took a long time to work out what it was," Bane said. "It's not really a weapon, but it is dangerous to the Tecran. If you pull a bead off and throw it down hard onto a surface, it sticks, and nothing will get it off. It takes a few seconds after it attaches, and then the chemicals in it react, creating a cone of bright white light. I think it was used by the people the Tecran stole it from as an easy way to light the tunnels they mine deep in the core of their planet. The light lasts at least three hours."

"Is it because the Tecran don't like bright light?" Lucy asked.

"Yes. In a confined space, this will debilitate them. And if you wear it as a necklace, no one will notice it."

"You think they're going to try to grab me, don't you?"

Bane rested down on top of a box as she looped the wire around her neck and tied a knot in it to secure it.

"They're desperate. And they've got nothing to lose. I don't think Commander Helvan will make it easy for them, but he's one person, they're a team."

"Lucy?"

She turned as Dray stepped around a corner and headed her way.

"What's this?" He looked into the recessed storage with curiosity.

"Just something Bane wanted to show me. He gave me this." She patted the necklace and put the lid back on the box, moving the cylinder Bane was in out of the way as if it were just another container in the cupboard. If Bane wanted Dray to know he was in there, he wouldn't have stopped floating and pretended to be part of the furniture.

Dray looked at the necklace. "It's nice."

She grinned. "It doubles as a nasty bright white light if you know how to use it." She turned away from the cupboard, and the panels closed behind her.

Dray paid closer attention. "That's clever of him. It won't kill them, but it'll put them out of action." He patted the shockgun in a holster strapped around his thigh.

"Found something nice?" she asked.

He looked serious. "It's the most powerful shockgun I've ever seen. Good to have if things go wrong."

"Do you think things will go wrong?"

He nodded. "It's chaotic down there. I spoke to my second-in-command, and she says tensions are high, and no one knows exactly what's going on. Rumors are flying. When I told her what the military teams are doing, it confirmed for her and the other military heads what they already suspected. That someone is deliberately stirring up trouble. Just when they get an area calmed down, the trouble flares up somewhere else. They are constantly playing catch-up."

"What are you going to do?" She knew he had to go down, and she had to go down with him. Nothing but her appearance in the flesh would have the impact they needed. To stop people in their tracks and make them listen. To put a brake on the craziness.

"I need a meeting with Filivantri Dimitara, the head of the UC delegation, the heads of the Tecran government, and the head of the Tecran military. I'll need you with me. We'll tell our story, and Bane can transmit it to the screens in the square. Total transparency to the people of Fa'allen." He pulled something out of his pocket and she saw it was a tiny lens. "Bane has top of the line equipment."

He stepped closer, slid his fingers under the neck of her tunic.

She lifted her gaze, caught his. And her breath hitched.

Stuttered out.

A frisson ran down her arms, and she didn't suppress the shiver that ran down her spine.

"I want to eat you up." His rough voice was thick, and his fingers shook as they dipped beneath her neckline and his other hand came up to press the lens between her breasts.

He bent his head, until his forehead rested against hers. "I don't want you to come down to Fa'allen with me. I want you to stay here, where it's safe."

"You think they're only after me, but they're also after you." She turned her head and lifted her face slightly, to rub her cheek against his. The roughness of his skin against the smoothness of hers was a delicious scrape against her senses.

"I'm a trained military officer, and it's my job to deal with the Tecran. You're . . ."

He trailed off, and nuzzled at her ear.

"I'm?"

"Too many things to name. All of them precious."

Her heart squeezed tight into a painful ball, and then expanded, bigger than it had been in a long time.

"I'm safe up here, but no one else will be. We all know my being down there will cool things off. Shock everyone into taking stock and reevaluating."

He gave a reluctant nod.

"Then I have to go. I don't care much for the Tecran and whether they get hurt, but I did meet a young teenager in Fa'allen, and she didn't have any hand in this. There has to be a lot of others like her. Not to mention the UC teams. They're in more danger now because of this unrest. We know the root cause of this is the Tecran military trying to wipe away all evidence of my existence. That will be difficult for them if I'm right there, standing in front of everyone."

"I know." He was cradling her head in his big hands, and he tilted her head and leaned in to kiss her. "I still don't like it."

She kissed him back, gripping him closer to her. She didn't like it either, but she was doing it anyway.

The Tecran tried to hide her, to erase her.

It would be her pleasure to make that impossible.

***

THEY LANDED on the roof of the closest building to military headquarters that had enough flat space to take the drone.

Lucy hummed all the way down in the elevator, and Dray let himself just enjoy the sound.

He noticed she stopped singing or humming the moment he drew attention to what she was doing. He was learning to be sneaky about it.

She drew in a breath and stopped mid-hum when they stepped out onto the street.

It was fully dark, but the sun set early this time of year, and it was still early in the evening. The street should have been busy, but it wasn't. It was empty. Discarded paper and pieces of debris fluttered in the wind.

There had clearly been fighting on this street and the street lights had been switched off or sabotaged.

"What can you see?" Dray asked Bane.

"Things have calmed a little," Bane said into his earpiece. "There's still a lot going on near the square, but some people are back in their homes. The security forces shut off all street lighting, to force people home."

"Or to make it easier for the military teams to cause trouble," Lucy said.

"Maybe, but I thought the security forces were trying to stop the uprising." Dray knew it was unlikely the military didn't have a few moles in there, though.

"I'm sure they have people in the security forces helping them, but not all will be on the military's side," Bane said. "It'll be difficult to tell who you can trust."

"What's the route like to the military headquarters where the rest of my team and Ambassador Dimitara are holed up? Can you see where the trouble spots are?" Dray asked.

Bane hesitated. "It'll be tricky. I'll do what I can, but with fewer people on the street, I have less access to handheld lenses. I can't see everything."

"Well, we'll start walking toward the square and you can feed us information as we go."

Before Bane could answer, Lucy pointed right, to the massive statue of Karn flickering in and out of sight as searchlights and other mobile forms of illumination lit it up.

They started walking toward it, and almost immediately Dray noticed a small group of people coming their way.

"Hide or walk?" Lucy asked, tugging the hood of her cloak deeper over her forehead.

"Walk. We need to get to headquarters as soon as possible." Dray tugged on his own hood, put an arm around her, and pulled her in close. He felt the tension in her.

He tried to think of something to say that would distract her. He wasn't used to trying to calm anyone, wasn't used to wanting to. "I just remembered something." He bent so his lips were close to her ear. "Did I hear you singing when I was hanging from the cliff?"

She took a deep breath, flicked a look up at him and then focused back on the Tecran coming their way. "Yes. I sang a couple of songs to keep my mind off the long drop down."

"What did you sing about?" He sized up the Tecran in the group approaching them, and thought they could just as easily be young thugs looking to use the protests as an excuse for a fight as Tecran military.

When she didn't answer right away, he realized how much he wanted to know. The only things the Grih sang about were important occasions, and they were so specific, they couldn't be used again for anything else.

She snuggled in closer, but he could still feel the tension in her as the group approached them. "I sang about how happy I was to see some blue sky, because the fog had lifted."

"You made the song up on the spot?" He couldn't fathom it.

She shook her head. "No. I'm not the first person to be happy to see the weather clear. There are millions of songs. You can definitely find one to suit every occasion. And more are being written all the time."

The group was almost on them, and they both stopped speaking. Even though they could only communicate in Tecran anyway, Dray knew his was heavily accented. Lucy's was much more fluent, but she went silent, as well.

The group was a mix of men and women, five people in total, and he raised a hand in greeting, but didn't call out.

The group had moved a little so that they wouldn't pass too close to each other, and Dray saw that as a good sign. No one wanted any trouble.

"Unless they're new recruits, none of them are with the military," Bane said quietly in his ear. "I've checked their faces against everyone I've captured through the lenses so far."

Dray felt the familiar jolt of concern. This was what had happened in the thinking system wars. The thinking systems had found and targeted the leaders of the resistance forces through facial recognition. It had been one of the main reasons most United Council Coalition members had done away with lenses in public places.

Except this time, the strategy was working to help him. And Lucy.

He shrugged it off. There was nothing he could do to stop Bane, anyway. And the thinking system was working with them.

For now, said a voice in his head.

The group passed them.

They had remained as silent as he and Lucy as they'd gone by, but he could hear them murmuring just within earshot, arguing whether he and Lucy were Grihan.

As long as they weren't sure, that worked for him and he and Lucy were already approaching the next intersection.

"Which way?" Lucy whispered.

"Right again," Bane said. The square is—"

"I can hear it." The sound rose and fell like the roar of the sea and after a few more steps, a glow of light bloomed out from behind buildings, a beacon in the darkened streets.

"Doesn't sound very calm over there." Lucy shifted beside him and he dropped his arm from her shoulders, his hand going to his shockgun.

"No."

With luck they could avoid the square, go through the front of the military headquarters, on the side that opened out to the top of the cliffs.

The buildings they passed were mostly dark, or if there were lights on in some of the apartments, they were behind thick screens, and leaked only the smallest amount of illumination.

He steered Lucy into the middle of the street, away from the dark recesses created by the shape of the buildings and the even deeper shadows of the narrow streets and alleyways that ran beside each one.

The sound of feet pounding toward them from behind had him spinning around, shoving Lucy so his body shielded hers.

The Tecran came at them in a silent attack, something long and slim held over his head as a weapon.

Dray shot him, the flash of the shockgun fire bright in the dark street.

The Tecran went down with a cry, the first sound he'd made.

"Let's go." Dray spun back, caught Lucy's hand and ran.

He saw her glance back, and then lengthen her stride. "There are others."

"I know." He'd seen the movement just before he'd shot their attacker.

They'd been waiting in the pockets of darkness.

Whether specifically for him and Lucy, or for whoever came along who didn't look like they fit in, he didn't have the time or inclination to ask.

He reached back with his shockgun, took another shot.

He wasn't able to aim, but he heard a cry of pain anyway, which meant he'd gotten lucky.

When he checked again, he saw at least two of their attackers had stopped to help the injured. The shockgun he'd taken from Bane's armory was capable of the most precise fine tuning he'd ever seen, and he'd set it to incapacitate but not kill, even if the person he shot was wearing protective clothing.

There were still three attackers racing toward them, though.

"What's going on?" Bane's voice came through his earpiece and Dray realized he'd forgotten all about him.

"Under attack." He was back in the zone, he realized. He'd be enjoying this if Lucy wasn't beside him, in danger. "We need to get to the square, or even better, the military headquarters on the cliff side."

"Is it the military attacking?"

"We don't know." Lucy's voice came out as a gasp. She was trying to keep up with him, and he slowed his pace to keep in step with her. Aimed another shot over his shoulder to keep their attackers back.

"It looks like the front headquarters entrance is blocked by a group of protesters. Who might not be protesters at all." Bane sounded grim. "In fact, I recognize a number of them as part of the Tecran military teams."

"It'd be a good way to make sure no one can go in or out without the military's cooperation." It was clever, Dray had to admit. Clever and effective. He slowed a little more as Lucy stumbled. "We'll have to go in the back way through the square."

They were nearly there, anyway.

As they came in line with a street leading straight into the square, he caught sight of the wild crowd, illuminated by flashing lights.

Lucy stumbled again, this time in shock at the sight in front of her.

"Come on, they're catching up." Dray could see the determination in the three attackers who were following them.

He'd hurt their friends, and they were determined now to get him.

He tugged her by the hand, and she nodded and began running again, as fast as she had before.

There were more people in this street, some resting against the walls of the buildings, some sitting, holding heads or arms, as if nursing a wound.

The crowd was dangerous and he was leading Lucy straight into it. But there was just as much danger on the empty streets, as they'd found out.

"Stick close to my side."

She nodded, her hand gripping his a little harder, and then they were in among the protesters, swept along on a current of shouting, angry Tecran.

His hood was yanked off his head within seconds, and he suspected it wasn't simply the result of the push and pull of the crowd, but deliberate. The protesters wanted to know who was in their midst.

He had hoped to keep Lucy's face hidden, but her shout of outrage told him that was no longer possible.

He looked back at her at the very moment a pole was swung at his head. He caught the movement out of the corner of his eye and ducked, losing Lucy's hand with the help of a shove from the crowd. The blow landed on his shoulder, bounced and hit the person closest to him on their temple.

The reaction of the crowd to the attacker was vicious. There were howls of outrage, and several people turned on the Tecran. He disappeared as if dragged down by the undercurrents.

Dray spun back to find Lucy, his last sight of her had been of her hair flying around her head in the wind, the people around her staring in shock.

She was gone.

He shouted her name, and it was swallowed whole by the crowd as if he'd never opened his mouth.

He had lost her, and they hadn't been in the square five minutes.

# CHAPTER 35

SHE FOUGHT.

Four people had grabbed her, lifting her by her legs and shoulders.

And as quickly as they'd uncovered her head, they'd covered it again.

Already, the sight of her had stirred the people around them. Some were frozen, unsure what to do with what they'd seen, but others reached out to grab her abductors, to stop them carrying her away.

They were ruthlessly struck down.

She saw more than one person collapse as they were hit with the stocks of the shockguns her abductors carried, and two people were brought down with a flash of purple shockgun fire.

"You've been taken?" Bane's voice was suddenly in her ear, urgent and panicked.

From somewhere behind her, she thought she heard her name called, and opened her mouth to scream for Dray.

A hand slapped over her mouth, and she bit it as she arched her back, getting some leverage with her foot on the shoulder of the Tecran who had one of her legs.

The Tecran whose hand she'd bitten smacked her face hard in retaliation and before she could try for another scream, slapped a sticky bandage over her mouth.

"They're carrying you, and you can't answer." Bane's voice was calmer now, logical. "They must have gagged you. Which they would have to do, because if the crowd works out . . . oh, some have already. They caught a glimpse of you. I'm putting the feed people in the crowd captured up on the big screens."

As he said it, from all around her came shocked gasps and shouts of outrage.

Lucy caught a second of it as she twisted in her captors hold, and then two more Tecran joined the four carrying her and she felt her ribcage creak under the pressure as they gripped her even harder and pinned her arms to her side. They forced her knees to bend and folded her into a much smaller package, one that made it harder to move.

"We're still getting looks." One of the Tecran carrying her hissed. "We need to get off the street."

"Agreed." Whoever answered steered them all to the left, and a few moments later, they stepped through a door and into a dark space.

She was dropped to the ground.

Ow.

She tried to roll, but was hemmed in by a circle of boots.

She had a feeling they wouldn't think twice about kicking her, so she stopped moving, and took stock.

"Do you think holing up in *here* is a good idea?" The Tecran who spoke was a woman. Lucy couldn't see her face in the darkness, but she wondered if it was the same woman who'd tried to follow her in the square . . . could it really have only been four or five days ago?

"You got a better idea, Fai? Because that thinking system has us up on every screen."

There was silence and an icy hand of fear gripped the back of Lucy's neck because although she couldn't see his face, she recognized the voice. Silius. The Tecran officer Bane had shown her and Dray footage of, inciting the riots. Her old guard from the facility.

"You think it's definitely the thinking system?" One of the men asked.

"The United Council only just arrived. Who else knows our systems and can surf the handheld lenses like that?" Silius shifted. "We know it traveled with them. And whatever it fooled the politicians into thinking, it's not outside the solar system. We know how we used it in the past. It knows all the tricks because we taught it."

"You're right." Fai blew out a breath. "What do we do?"

"They better start praying to Karn," Bane said in her ear, tone grim. "Because they'll wish they'd never taught me anything when I'm done with them."

His words centered her. Calmed her.

"Can you twist your body to give the lens a different angle? I might be able to work out where you are." Bane whispered in Lucy's ear. "I wasn't able to follow you much after the other two joined the group."

She slowly lowered herself down even further on her elbows, then tipped back, trying to get a sense of the height of the room, and anything over the heads and shoulders of the soldiers who surrounded her.

"It's too dark." Bane's voice was tight. "But I'm projecting this in the square, mainly for the audio. So everyone understands there are bad actors among them."

Lucy wondered if one of the soldiers would say where they were. That would cause a stampede of people to haul them out.

"How did you find her?" Silius asked the team.

"It was chance. We were assigned to the street into the square from the south, and we saw the Grih. We guessed she was the person with him, even though she was in a cloak. We followed them in and Gitma attacked the Grih to distract him, and we got her."

"Good work."

"Dray is searching for you, but the crowd is impossible to get through," Bane whispered. "I've persuaded him to go into military headquarters and get some help from Ambassador Dimitara and his other colleagues. It will be easier to search for you as a coordinated effort. He was wasting time trying on his own."

She wanted to ask him if Dray was all right. If the attacker had harmed him, but Bane was talking as if he was fine, and she had to hope that was true.

Leaving the square without her would have been hard for Dray. It would have killed her if the situation had been reversed. But Bane was right. The only way he'd find her was with help.

And she had Bane looking for her right now. She would find a way out of this.

"Lucy?" Dray's voice sounded as if it came from right beside her, and she flinched, frightened for a moment they had him, too.

Then she realized Bane must have patched him through.

"Bane says you can't answer. If you can move your hands, block the lens with your finger to let me know you can hear us."

She looked up. Silius was talking to the others about operations, and she should be listening to them, but she couldn't concentrate on what they were saying with Dray in her ear. She lifted her hand and tapped the tiny lens embedded between her breasts.

She heard Dray breathe out in relief.

"Are you near the square?" he asked.

She pretended to rub her temples with her hands, and then, when she lowered them, slid a finger over the lens again.

"Why're you so compliant?" Silius suddenly crouched beside her, his face suspicious. Of course, she'd never been compliant for him in the facility. "Have you checked her for trackers or an earpiece?"

There was a moment of stunned silence.

"When would we have had time?" Fai asked, outraged. "Have *you* checked her?"

"That answers the question, anyway. We can't stay here. They probably know exactly where we are." Silius dug out a slim flashlight and pointed it in her ear. "Oh, yes. That thinking system is behind this. I've seen earpieces like this before."

Lucy gritted her teeth as he dug the earpiece out, dropped it on the ground and crushed it with the butt of his shockgun.

"She'll have a lens, as well. So smile everyone. He's probably projecting this right now."

They all lifted their face coverings back over their mouths and noses, but they must have known they were too late.

"Good thing it's dark in here," one of the men muttered.

Silius shoved his hand into the neck of her tunic, running one hand inside, the other on the outside of the fabric, and gave a grunt of triumph as he found the lens and ripped it out.

He ground it up with slow, furious movements, then flicked his gaze up to hers.

"You have been nothing but trouble."

She couldn't respond with the tape over her mouth, so she simply stared at him, refusing to blink.

He grabbed her tunic in both fists and shook her, then released her and rose, stepping back and turning away.

"We need to leave." His hands were fisted.

"No shit. But not the same way we came in." The soldier who spoke hauled her to her feet.

"Wait, is she armed?" Fai jerked her closer and patted her down, then pushed her away. "Apparently not."

Silius had turned back to her. "Where have you been since you escaped? And where is Virn?"

She slowly lifted a hand and began to gently remove the tape, but Silius batted her fingers away and ripped it off.

The pain caused her eyes to water and she stood, head hanging, as she blinked back the tears. She rubbed her lips together and then wet them with her tongue. "Virn is dead."

The whole group froze.

"And how did he die?" Silius's voice was low.

"A nynt got him."

Her answer was obviously the last thing they expected. Most of them gaped at her, open-mouthed.

"A nynt?" Silius stepped closer, into her space.

"He took us to hide out in some caves in the cliffs to the west of Fa'allen, and unfortunately for him, a nynt with a broken wing was taking shelter in it. It didn't like us being there, and threw Virn into the sea below."

They glanced at each other.

"How do we know you're telling the truth?" The soldier who'd pulled her to her feet asked.

Lucy shrugged.

It was suddenly so quiet, she could hear the sounds of the protests in the square beyond the door.

"Let's just kill her right here and be done with it." One of the other soldiers touched Silius's arm.

"The point is to make her disappear, not leave her body to be found. That defeats the whole purpose." Silius stepped back and she saw the glint of frustration in his eyes. "I don't know what Virn's orders were, but he was clearly trying to hide her, and if he had orders to kill her, he'd have just tossed her from a high perch into the sea."

"If we can trust a word she's saying," Fai said.

"Yes. I'll need to check in and see what Virn was told and where he was sent. Which is getting harder to do as the UC takes over our comms. It'll take a bit of a work around to get word to the top."

"Then let's get out of here, hide her somewhere safe, and find out what we have to do with her."

She was pushed deeper into the room by the soldier who'd pulled her to her feet, and another came and flanked her other side.

She didn't know where she was, and neither did Bane or Dray. She was on her own now. But that was okay. She was used to it.

# CHAPTER 36

HE'D FAILED HER.

Dray spun in place, his gaze searching the crowd for any sign of Lucy.

She was gone.

Bane had allowed him to hear the last few minutes of comms feed from Lucy's earpiece and lens, as Silius had searched her and then destroyed them.

All their precautions, useless now.

"You do her no good turning in circles." Bane's voice in his ear was cutting. "Go get help. I'll keep searching all the lens feed I can find."

Dray gave a hard nod and ran for the door that he had stepped out of three days ago. Time had both passed in a blink and stretched out in a long, viscous thread since that moment.

He wouldn't change any part of it, except the last ten minutes. If he had that over again, he'd hang on to Lucy and not let her go for an instant.

He reached the door and pushed it.

It didn't budge.

"I need to communicate with my team." Dray rapped hard on the door. "I'm locked out."

The door opened suddenly and Chep stood back to let him in.

"I saw you fighting your way through the crowd on the screens from the office window," he said as Dray clasped his hand and then started running for the lifts.

"Where's the ambassador?"

Chep kept step with him. "Give me a minute." He tapped his earpiece, murmured the question. Then looked up at Dray, his massive eyes crinkling in concern. "Cossi says the ambassador's in the building, up on the top floor, but she's not answering her comms."

"How concerning is that?" Dray didn't have a feel for the mood on the ground here anymore.

"Since early this morning, as a result of you showing us the visual comms which implicated military forces in stoking the unrest, Dimitara's been in high level talks with the elected heads of Tecra. Things are tense." The way he said it, Dray guessed Chep was making an understatement. "Cossi says three of the top cabinet members have accompanied her here to military HQ from the parliamentary offices to talk to General Ulima about what's going on."

"And my team?"

Chep waved his hands as they reached the lift. "They've been assisting the ambassador, as I gather you ordered them to. Some of them are probably with her now." He looked at Dray as they stepped inside the narrow, cylindrical space. "What's going on? Where's the Earth woman?"

Dray clenched his fists. "I lost Lucy in the square. A team of Tecran soldiers grabbed her."

Chep sucked in a breath. "You're sure?"

Dray gave a tight nod. He leaned back against the wall as the lift flew them upward. "Bane, you have a record of what happened when they took Lucy, and what was said?"

"I do."

Chep looked at him curiously, and Dray guessed Bane hadn't shared his answer through Chep's comms.

"He says he does."

Chep winced. "That's going to change the tone of the meeting Dimitara is having."

"I can't believe it's going all that well anyway," Dray said. Especially if the ambassador wasn't answering her comms. Either the situation required all her concentration, or something was very, very wrong.

Chep's mouth opened in what Dray had come to understand was the Fitalian version of a smile. "Well, no. But I have a feeling this is going to make things considerably worse."

Dray bared his teeth. "That is just too bad."

The doors opened and they stepped out into a plush space that was floor to ceiling windows with magnificent views over the cliffs. The Tecran must have attached large spotlights just below the clifftops. They shone down onto the water below, illuminating the waves as they raced to smash themselves against the cliffs and the weightless foam that leapt for the sky as it hit the rocks that stood out at sea.

Dray went straight toward the double doors in front of them, guarded by two soldiers who straightened to attention as he and Chep approached.

Instead of asking for identification, they both raised their shockguns. Dray slowed his step. There was something very wrong here.

"You have to know we're part of the UC leadership team." Dray narrowed his eyes at them. "The ambassador is expecting us."

They shared a look and Dray felt the hair on the back of his neck stand up. They were nervous, and they were unsure what to do. As if they had not been expecting company.

Chep brought his shockgun out of the holster attached to his thigh in one smooth move, and Dray waited a beat, waited for their focus to be on the Fitalian, before he did the same. He didn't wait for a standoff. There was no way to win that, and he didn't have the time.

Every moment they stood here, Lucy was being dragged even further away from him.

He shot the guard nearest him and leaped, shoving the guard's limp body into his partner, and kicked in the door.

He saw the flicker of purple to his left, and guessed Chep had opened fire, as well.

Both the guards would be wearing protective clothing, but his new shockgun would be enough to take the one he'd shot out for a while.

He came to a halt just inside the door.

Everyone in the room was staring at him with varying degrees of shock on their faces.

The Tecran general, Suu Ulima, was standing beside a seated Dimitara, and two members of Dray's military team were lying facedown, their hands secured behind them. Dimitara's hands were also pulled behind her.

Four Tecran soldiers stood around the room, shockguns pointed at Dray and Chep.

Dray let his gaze drift over to the three politicians who Dimitara had come over to the building with.

They were sitting squashed together on a long couch, and Dray noted they seemed unharmed, and no one had bothered to keep a shockgun on them.

All hopes that he could appeal to someone in the military to help him track down the rogue team and find Lucy died.

This wasn't just a rogue team going off script.

This went all the way to the top.

Probably always had done.

"Record everything," he murmured to Bane. "And loop Cossi in, so she can see what's happening here, and try to get us out."

"Yes." The chill in Bane's voice said it all.

"So, you were in on it, too, were you?" he asked the politicians.

One of them opened their mouth in outrage. "How dare—"

"They were." Dimitara shifted uncomfortably in her chair. "They might not have understood the full scope of it, but they definitely knew they weren't accompanying me to question General Ulima. They set me up to come here so that *he* could question *me.*"

"You are on *our* planet. This is *our* business." The politician stood, and one of the soldiers shifted his weapon to aim at him.

The politician shut his mouth with a snap, eyes huge, and slowly sat down.

Dray laughed. "Oh dear, they don't seem to respect you any more than I do."

"They gave away our sovereignty." Ulima gave them a cold, disgusted look. "They can rot as carrion for baug as far as I'm concerned."

There was a moment of absolute silence. Then Ulima turned to Dray with a smile.

"I'm glad you could join us, Commander. I thought you were either dead or hidden away somewhere on the peninsula, but it appears I was wrong, and no one here was courteous enough to let me know."

He toed one of Dray's subordinates with a boot.

Dray felt the familiar tension and calm that came over him just before he engaged in military action. This time, though, the stakes were higher. He wasn't just responsible for his team. Lucy's life hung in the balance.

"Virn's dead. Most of the rest of them are, too." Dray shrugged.

Ulima blinked. "And the Earth woman?"

"Why would I tell you that?" He didn't know, Dray realized. The general had been busy up here, interrogating Dimitara, and he hadn't seen the visual comms on the screens in the square, hadn't heard from his teams down below.

Ulima didn't know his people already had Lucy.

What had the Tecran who'd grabbed Lucy said? That getting comms through was hard. Cossi and Chep had obviously been taking control of the system.

"You *will* tell me," Ulima said, and casually shot Dimitara in the leg with his shockgun, "or I'll keep doing this until you do."

Dimitara screamed, bending forward in her chair, her arms straining behind her.

Dray couldn't help the step he took forward, and he heard Chep make a strange sound beside him.

"Lower your weapon." Ulima raised his shockgun and pointed it at Dray's face. "Hand it to Cryn."

One of the soldiers stepped forward and pulled the weapon from his hand, then took Chep's, as well.

"Now, where is the Earth woman?"

"I don't know." Dray looked straight at Ulima as he spoke, and the general shot Dimitara's other thigh.

This time she didn't scream, the noise was more a low, animalistic moan of pain.

"We were separated in the square." Dray kept to the truth as much as he could. There was no reason to let the general think he had her already. "I came into headquarters looking for help to find her."

"She's out there, right now? On her own?" Ulima frowned.

"Worried she'll be spotted by the good people of Fa'allen?" Dray asked. "A living, breathing reminder of why the UC is here, and why your politicians agreed to clear out the rot in your military to begin with?"

Ulima stared at him with true hatred for a long beat. "Cryn, go down to the square, find Silius or one of his people, and get them to look for her."

Cryn handed Dray and Chep's shockguns to another soldier and moved to the door.

"Be discreet about it," Ulima ordered.

Cryn nodded and shoved the door open with his shoulder, and gave a cry of surprise as he was yanked off his feet and disappeared beyond.

Something was thrown into the room, and suddenly understanding what it was, Dray threw himself sideways, rolling behind the big desk in the general's office.

The whomp was low, almost quiet, but it rattled his bones, and the explosion lit up the air with light so bright, even with his eyes closed, Dray was aware of it.

The brightness lasted only a second, and then was gone, winking out in an instant.

Dray rolled to his feet, orange and purple light dancing in front of his eyes while he tried to take in the change in his circumstances.

Cossi stood in the middle of the room, directing UC soldiers to restrain the Tecran. He was pleased to see that included the politicians.

She stalked forward and personally untied Filivantri Dimitara, speaking to the ambassador in quick, choppy sentences that Dray's Bukarian wasn't good enough to follow.

They both noticed him at the same time, and Cossi sent him a quick grin and turned to face him.

"Happy to save your ass, Helvan. Nice to have a little exercise after I've had to spend the last few days hunched over comms systems, trying to stop the Tecran shutting us down."

Dray gave her a low, formal bow despite the ringing in his ears. "My thanks."

He realized he'd spoken too loud when she winced.

He turned his head, saw Chep slowly getting up from the floor, and offered a hand to pull him up.

Cossi stepped closer, and they stood in a tight group as Cossi's team dealt with the room.

"What now?" Chep tipped his head from side to side, as if to dislodge something.

"I have to find Lucy."

"The sooner the better." Bane's voice came from the massive screen on one side of the room, and everyone went still, and then turned to look.

The visual feed showed the square, and the escalating violence.

People were chanting, shoving each other, and shockgun fire flickered.

"There." Dray concentrated on the shockgun fire on the screen. "That's Ulima's team, they're the most likely to be carrying weapons."

Bane jumped from handheld to handheld, trying to get a better look, and Dray caught a brief glimpse of six Tecran, their faces shielded by the hoods of their cloaks, carrying a limp bundle between them.

Lucy.

They disappeared from view, and Bane made a sound of frustration that ran a shiver of fear down Dray's spine.

"No more hiding." Bane's words were completely devoid of any inflection.

The screen went dark.

"What does that mean?" Dimitara asked. She had been put on the long couch, her legs useless for the moment, and was rubbing the circulation back into her arms.

"I think it means he's about to make his presence known." Dray grabbed his shockgun from the ground, and turned to the door. "I can't worry about it now. I have to go down and look for Lucy."

"I'll come with you." Cossi patted Chep's arm. "You all right?"

Chep shook his head. "Still dizzy. I'll stay here. Do what I can."

Dray gave a nod.

"Commander."

He turned at Dimitara's call.

"Be mindful of our mission, if you can."

He gave a curt nod and then strode for the lift.

"You capable of being mindful?" Cossi asked him.

He gave her a cool look.

She quirked her lips. "That's what I thought."

# CHAPTER 37

LUCY EXPLODED INTO A WRITHING, squirming burden as soon as she came back to herself.

The Tecran had pricked her neck with something after Silius had destroyed her earpiece and her lens, and it occurred to her now, as they dropped her onto the road in astonishment, that they did not expect her to come out of it as quickly as she had.

Pity Silius hadn't paid more attention to Dr. Farnn's results in the facility or he'd have known nothing worked on her the way it worked on the Tecran.

Good for her, bad for the soldiers trying to carry her off quietly.

"Help!" She shouted the words as loudly as she could as she fought off the coverings they'd wrapped her in. "They're abducting me. Help me!"

As she rolled, she caught glimpses of boots and legs, the hems of long cloaks, and then faces peering down at her.

She struggled to get out of the sack she'd been put in, pushing the hood of her cloak off and exposing her face.

It was night, of course, but there were lights all around, and she heard more than one person gasp in astonishment.

"Hey!"

Someone shouted in warning as two of the soldiers grabbed her and hauled her up by her arms.

Shockgun fire flickered, and people screamed and ducked for cover.

But there was as much shouting in anger as in fear, and Lucy made herself a deadweight.

She knew they were struggling to carry her.

She was much heavier than they'd bargained for.

She let her feet drag behind her, and with a scream of frustration, one of the soldiers dropped his hold on her arm. She hung for a moment, held by her right arm, then tucked herself under and jerked out of the other soldier's hold, rolling away.

It was a good try.

It didn't work.

Silius was suddenly in her face, shockgun to her cheek.

"Get up."

She saw in his eyes that he was close enough to the edge to shoot her, and she'd already come to the conclusion a headshot might not be quite as survivable for her as a body shot.

She lifted her hands in surrender. Shot a look past Silius to the crowd beyond.

"Tell the UC where I am!" She shouted it as loud as she could, and then the sack was over her head again and all six of the soldiers had a hold of some part of her and they were racing away, breathing heavily in exertion, and, she hoped, stress.

"We lost them." It was Fai speaking.

Lucy heard a door opening.

"For now." Havna, the one who'd drugged her earlier, let go of his hold on her shoulder and she tipped downward, and then fell as everyone else let go, too.

She had a real dislike for Havna.

"We can't hide here." The soldier who spoke sounded nervous.

"Who'll look for us here?" Silius asked. "There'll be no rioters here. It's a sacred space."

"That's the point. It's sacred," the soldier said.

Lucy surreptitiously pulled the hood off her head, and tried to work out where she was.

"What's the problem, Carivera? You think Karn will disapprove?" There was a lightly mocking tone to Silius's voice.

The effect was interesting. The others didn't smile or support Silius. They looked away or down.

They weren't comfortable with this either.

"What? You think this is really the place where Karn lay down to die?" Silius didn't hide the derision in his voice.

"Yes," Carivera said. "I do. And I don't like to use it as a place to commit a crime."

"You think we're committing a crime?" Silius's question was serious now.

"You know we are," Havna said. "We wouldn't be hiding if what we were doing was perfectly fine."

Silius conceded with a nod. Rubbed feathery fingers over his head. "Fine, we're committing a crime, but strange, I didn't hear anyone complaining before now."

There was silence.

"True." Carivera sighed. "But did you see those people when the Earth woman called for help? They were looking at us like we were kol on the hunt."

"We know what's at stake," Silius said. "They don't. They think we're in the wrong, but we aren't. When we were using the Class 5 to expand our reach, we were being true to ourselves. Exploring the opportunities with the tools available. It was the UC who were holding us back."

"Except, those tools aren't ours anymore, are they?" Fai said quietly.

"Thanks to her and her kind." Silius leaned over Lucy. Regarded her with eyes that seemed a little dead.

He was going to kill her. She understood it in perfect clarity. He couldn't contact his superiors, and none of his team would be safe from the crowd if they tried to move her again.

This was where she had to make her last stand.

She had literally nothing to lose.

"There's your problem," she said.

"What's our problem?" Silius's voice was calm and quiet.

"Thinking of Bane and his friends as tools."

There was a startled silence.

"Just shut up. I'm very close to just ending things right now and walking away."

He wasn't close, he was already there. There was no doubt in her mind. All he had to do was sell it to his friends.

Havna cleared his throat, and Lucy recalled he had made the same suggestion in their last hiding place, and Silius had overridden him.

Silius shot him a look and he said nothing.

So maybe he wouldn't have to do that much selling.

Lucy winced at the thought. Time was slipping through her fingers.

"We can't kill her here." Carivera straightened. "Can you imagine the world finding her body in the base of Karn's resting place? The desecration of the site with the body of someone we should never have had in the first place?"

There was absolute silence at his statement. Two of the other soldiers started to back away.

"If we kill her, it has to be somewhere else," one of them agreed.

"How do we get her out of here?" Silius played the reasonable psychopath. "We set foot outside, someone will see us and kick up a fuss."

"Then we should have done it earlier, but you wanted to wait." The second soldier held Silius's gaze. "I'm not killing anyone in Karn's resting place."

Silius gave a derisive snort. "Fine, I'll kill her."

"Then you won't need us." The first soldier had reached a door.

"Stay. Where. You. Are." Silius lifted his shockgun. "I can't have you running around tattling about this."

"Tattling? Have you gone mad?" Carivera walked over to stand with the soldiers by the door. "I'm having no part in this. Just let her go. It's over now. Can't you tell?"

"It is not over." Silius sounded so sure, it sent a shiver down Lucy's spine, and the hair on the back of her neck prickled. "We are the Tecran military. Are you saying we can't take on the pampered civilians of Fa'allen?"

"We can take them, sure." Carivera gave a bitter laugh. "But I don't want to harm my fellow citizens. And do you think the thinking system is going to just idly watch? And the UC? They're not here without resources. Or didn't you notice the battleship in our orbit?"

"We have five battleships of our own, remember?" Silius shrugged. "My guess is the three that aren't away patrolling our borders are getting into position right now."

The others stared at him.

"They're going to destroy the UC battleship?" Fai's voice was a little faint.

"What do you think is happening here? We're being taken over by a hostile force, and the politicians are just standing by, wringing their hands over it and mildly protesting." Silius opened his mouth, stretching it wide in what Lucy had come to realize was similar to a human exclamation of disgust. "The general got word that the Earth woman was coming back into the city with one of the Grih. It would have ended any benefit of the doubt they were prepared to give us. It would have hardened their resolve to do a thorough purge of the military. A thorough purge of *your* jobs." Silius looked each of them in the eye. "The general realized the only path forward was a takeover."

"So you think the Levron will surround the UC battleship, and, what? The Class 5 will just accept that?" Havna's voice was disbelieving.

Silius shrugged. "I don't believe it's out of the solar system, but it's not close enough to react that fast. If our Levron surround the *Urna*, what is it going to do? It won't want to harm the UC ship and anyone onboard, and the moment it fires on the Levron, at least one of them will be able to destroy the *Urna*."

"Until the UC send in reinforcements," Kai said.

"Even if they do, by then, we'll have had time to purge the systems of all evidence, get rid of her," he waved his hand at Lucy, "and it will just be put down as teething trouble of an ill-advised political solution. If we decide to go that route."

They weren't going to go that route. Lucy could see that in the way Silius waved his hand as he spoke.

"What alternative route is there?" Casivera asked.

"War."

Everyone was so surprised that Lucy had spoken, they swiveled to look at her in shock.

She shrugged. "It's what he's dying for. Can't you see?"

The others looked at Silius nervously.

"Why are you in the military if you're afraid of war?" Silius asked them.

"This is madness." Casivera's nostrils flared in disgust. "Have fun in your fantasy land, Silius. I'm going out to rejoin actual Tecran society."

"Your fingers are all over this, Casivera. You helped to grab her, you helped to hunt her. You are all in this up to your necks."

Everyone paused at that.

"So who's going to out me, you?" Casivera asked. "It will impli-cate you just as much. I'll take my chances. What I won't do is kill someone in Karn's resting place."

He turned his back and stepped between the two soldiers who'd shuffled back before, but before he'd gone two steps, shockgun fire brought him down.

He fell without a sound and lay still.

The two soldiers moved away from him, and Lucy stared at them. No one went to see if he was still alive, they all looked down on Casivera in shock.

"Anyone else got any scruples they can't ignore?" Silius's voice was low.

"What do we do now?" Havna asked. He stared at her rather than look at Silius.

"I want to try to get hold of the general one more time. As long as we keep her in here out of sight, I don't think we'll have any trouble, so I'll try to get orders before I take matters into my own hands." Silius pointed to Fai and Havna. "Guard her." He looked at the two who'd had second thoughts. "You can come with me."

Lucy watched him go and tried not to show her relief.

At last, the odds were moving in her favor.

# CHAPTER 38

THE SLIM PEN lay in her trouser pocket. She hadn't tried to hide it, had actually forgotten about it until she'd started trying to fight free earlier. They'd overlooked it when they'd searched her.

Her hand came up to fiddle with the beads on the necklace, which they hadn't taken any notice of at all.

Lucy eyed Fai and Havna from the corner they'd put her in, watching the way they leaned together to talk in hushed whispers.

They'd moved Casivera's body to one side and now they were talking strategy.

She wondered if they were talking themselves into or out of supporting Silius.

She could tell Fai now that if she went against Havna's decision, he'd either take her down or rat her out to Silius.

He was a yes man.

She pulled out the cylinder. Looked around for any metal in the room she could use.

Fai had turned on a light. The space was open and clean. A tight spiral staircase stood to one side, with a barrier across it to prevent anyone from going up without the proper access.

A shrine had been built into the far wall. A miniature Karn

stood, hands outstretched, on a shelf above a tiny waterfall. It fell in a pale green sheet into a pile of rocks below and disappeared into the floor.

The rest of the space was empty.

Not much to work with.

She weighed up the benefits of using the beads, but she still had to get out the door, so beads or flying up onto a wall with the cylinder, either way, she was still in the room, and she had a feeling Silius hadn't gone far and wouldn't be away long.

She was feeling more and more herself as the drug left her system, and she flexed her fingers, wriggled her toes, tensed the muscles in her legs.

She couldn't pretend to still be groggy after her attempted escape earlier, but she had been compliant and quiet since they brought her in here, and she hoped that gave them a false sense of control over her.

The door opened, and Fai and Havna turned, shockguns raised, only to relax when one of the soldiers who'd gone out with Silius poked his head around it.

"What?" Havna's voice was sharp as he got over the spike of shock.

The soldier gave him a dirty look. "Silius wants one of you. He says to drug her again if it will make things easier for just one to watch her."

Fai and Havna exchanged a look.

"Fai can go." Havna tilted his head at her.

She narrowed her eyes at him.

Doesn't fully trust her, Lucy thought. And now she knows it.

"Fine." Fai holstered her shockgun, pulled her cloak around her, and stepped outside.

Lucy watched as Havna closed the door behind her. Took a look at the round metal handle on the door that reminded her of the hatch locks on submarines.

She didn't know if it was the right kind of metal, but she might as well find out.

Havna turned to look at her, slid his shockgun away and pulled out a flat disc with a sharp tip in the middle. The sedative, she guessed. She'd just officially run out of time.

"We should have gotten rid of you hours ago."

She shrugged. "You should never have taken me in the first place."

He hunched a little at that, because she guessed he'd thought the same thing himself more than once.

She smoothed a finger down the side of the cylinder, and even though she knew what to expect this time, she still flinched as the tip shot off, past Havna, and then suddenly she was being dragged across the floor at speed.

She'd made sure her legs were bent to her chest when she'd released the magnet and she stuck out an arm to grab Havna's shins as she passed him.

Her shoulder was wrenched in a vicious jerk as she hit him, and he fell with a shout of surprise.

As soon as she reached the door, she ran her finger down the cylinder twice, to uncouple it and free her hand, and then she pulled the door open.

Silius was standing just outside, looking down at his handheld.

At the swing of the door, he looked up, and his face contorted at the sight of her.

She slammed the door shut again and spun, looking for escape.

Havna was on his hands and knees, groaning.

She spun back to the door, looking for a way to lock it, and then realized there was no lock.

This was a shrine, and anyone could come in.

She saw the handle begin to spin and she turned away from it, ran her finger down the cylinder, pointing it upward, and hoped it would find something to attach to.

Suddenly she was flying, moving out of the way of the door a moment before Silius slammed it open.

She sailed over Havna's head as he pulled himself to his feet, and landed on the first curve of the stairway.

For a single beat, there was silence as everyone took in the changed circumstances, and then Silius gave a shout of rage and Lucy grabbed the handrail and started climbing.

---

As Dray ran out into the square, the night suddenly lit up.

He snapped his head upward, and couldn't help but go still at the sight above.

Bane's Class 5 ship was hovering directly over the city, the spiky ball of it illuminated in an eerie blue-white light.

The ship was as low as it could go in the atmosphere, he guessed, but even so, as high up as it was, it loomed.

Bane was off the leash he'd imposed on himself.

The square slowly went quiet as one by one people looked up and noticed the threat above them.

"Someone has Lucy Harris." The words blasted from every speaker in the square. From the public comms systems, from people's handhelds, even from the vending machines, and a still image of Lucy laughing, eyes lit up in amusement, was suddenly on every screen. "Let her go, or I will make you very, very sorry." Bane's words were like the hiss of a thousand furious voices.

People gasped in shock.

Then someone ran out to the small open area in the center of the square and screamed, shaking their fist up at Bane.

Some joined him, others edged away.

This was no unified crowd. It hadn't been from the start.

The military had only been able to play their dirty tricks because of the diverse views of the protesters.

"They won't know how to tell you if they've seen something or know where she's been taken, but they might tell me." Dray spoke normally, hoping Bane was listening. Someone walked past him, toward the center of the square, and hissed at him as they passed.

Or maybe they wouldn't tell him, Dray realized grimly. They would see Bane's appearance as part of a UC strategy.

It would be hard to convince them the thinking system was acting alone.

Except, he wasn't.

Dray was with him all the way.

"He's absolutely striking, isn't he?" Cossi spoke in a quiet voice, and Dray remembered she had come out the door behind him. "How has he lit himself up like that? Where's the light coming from?"

Dray shook his head but Cossi didn't even notice, she was still looking up.

"Do we need to run? Is he going to strike the square?"

Dray lifted his shoulders. "I don't know. He hasn't spoken to me since his appearance."

"I'll give you some warning before I strike the square." Bane's voice was almost too calm in his ear, and from Cossi's sudden jerk, Dray guessed Bane was allowing her in on the conversation as well.

"Can I talk you out of doing that?" Dray looked around, noticed people were streaming in from all around to see Bane.

The shouting at the center had only gotten louder.

All day and through the night, there had been a sense of waiting, of small outbreaks of defiance, but a sense the big moment had yet to come.

Bane had just ensured that big moment was now.

"I've got a small team coming to join us," Cossi said. A Tecran shouldered her as he walked past and she shoved back, then raised her shockgun, and the protester stumbled away.

Dray felt the impatience to get moving, to do something, rise up in him, but Cossi gripped his arm.

"We can't walk any deeper into the crowd without more numbers. You want to actually find Lucy, don't you? Not die trying."

He gave a nod, looked behind her, and saw two of his own people, two of Cossi's and two of Chep's come out the door, all geared up for serious engagement.

"The Garmann still nowhere to be seen?"

"Wouldn't want them, anyway," Cossi said. "I like to trust the people watching my back."

Dray nodded, but he knew this was a serious issue. They couldn't have an alliance with the Garmann if they couldn't trust them to even uphold the agreement to be part of the UC delegation.

"See this Grih officer? This Bukari officer?" The buzz of a thousand angry insects cut off all other noise again as Bane took over every speaker. He switched the image of Lucy to the live feed of Dray and Cossi standing in the square. "Let them know if you've seen any sign of Lucy Harris. Do it now. This is the countdown, before I shoot down the statue of Karn."

A time stamp came up on the screen.

"Half an hour?" Even Cossi couldn't hide her shock.

"Let's move into the crowd. No one will approach us if they have to break cover to do it." Dray strode forward, and Cossi jogged to come abreast with him, the six other officers taking up the rear, shockguns ready.

They didn't need to go far to get into the thick of the protesters. A few tried to shove and push, but Dray wasn't in any mood to be diplomatic. After the second person crumpled and crawled away, no one tried to touch him or Cossi again.

The threat to blast the massive statue of Karn, which loomed over the square, palms cupped to receive the blessing of the wind, seemed to have electrified the Tecran.

Shock and outrage were the dominant reactions.

While Dray had understood from his research before he arrived in Fa'allen that the Tecran saw Karn as the embodiment of their transition to an advanced sentience, he hadn't understood until now the significance it had as a symbol to them.

Bane obviously did. He had been birthed here, in as much as a thinking system could be born.

"You will destroy our legacy?" A woman planted herself in front of them.

Dray looked at her in silence.

She pointed upward. "Call your mad kol off."

"Bane doesn't answer to me. And he no longer answers to your own military leaders, either." Dray made sure to raise his voice so everyone around them could hear.

"He does answer to you. He came along as your insurance that you'd get your way."

"Our way is your way, too." Dray reminded her. "It was an agreement your own leaders drafted."

"Under threat of war!" Someone in the crowd shouted.

"A war you started, but then realized you couldn't win," Cossi said. She turned slowly, looking everyone in front of them in the eye before moving on.

"What part of the agreement covered having our most treasured monument destroyed?" The woman asked, and for the first time, Dray saw the fear and desperation in her eyes.

"It didn't. I have asked Bane not to do it, but you think about why he's chosen it as the target if Lucy isn't found."

"Because it will hurt us the most," the woman said.

"Because it will hurt you the most," Dray agreed, "and because it symbolizes your ascension to advanced sentience, and yet, you have chosen not to respect Lucy's advanced sentience."

Cossi gaped at him, as if she hadn't expected such an insight to come from him.

The woman stared. "Either we respect her or he disrespects our view of ourselves?"

Dray shrugged. Said nothing.

"But what if no one knows where she is?" The woman looked around at the Tecran who surrounded her. "Does anyone know?"

There was silence.

"We have so little time. Let's start looking."

Shockgun fire suddenly jumped through the crowd, touched Dray lightly on the chest, and was extinguished by his protective suit.

He lifted his own weapon, searching for the source, and saw four protesters who'd been in the path of the shot had been hit.

"Take cover." He shouted over the screams and cries.

"Don't pretend you're not behind this," a man shouted from behind a wall of panicked people. "Stop the UC and this madness stops."

Dray swung around, looking for the Tecran who was shouting, because he had a strong suspicion he was part of Ulima's military team, and then the first object hit his shoulder.

He looked down at it as it dropped to the ground.

A boot.

"Time to find cover ourselves," Cossi said, as she took a step back, shockgun lifted.

Dray considered it, taking in the crowds around them.

But he didn't have time to retreat.

He straightened, stood his ground, and shot over the heads of the protesters.

Some ducked, others ran, another missile, a bottle, flew through the air but landed in the open space his warning shots had created in front of him.

Bane had it right. Time to raze a few things to the ground.

# CHAPTER 39

LUCY RAN up three twists of the spiral, and then had to stop, breathing heavily.

She could hear shouting from below as she gasped for air, and then the sound of boots on the stairs. Silius had just worked out how to get over the barrier.

She looked up, gauging how far she had to go, and realized she wasn't fit enough to do it.

Except, she didn't have to run.

She pulled out the pen and leaned out over the handrail, pointing it upward without making any attempt to aim. The tip flew up and she had a split second to notice the magnet had attached to the ceiling far above before she was wrenched off her feet.

She hit the stair's handrails as she passed them, banging her shoulders and her shins as she rotated upward.

For one, horror-filled moment, she thought she'd be stuck, hanging from the ceiling to the right of the stairs with no way to get down, until she swung and managed to get her feet onto the platform at the top.

She released the magnet and threw herself forward in the

same movement, and ended up on her hands and knees, in a cold sweat, until the sound of Silius and Havna racing up toward her spurred her to her feet.

There was a door, and she stared at it for a moment in fear, terrified it would be locked.

"Then find out and make another plan," she muttered to herself, and turned the tiny airlock-like handle.

The door swung open, and she stumbled out into the night.

It seemed unusually bright, and she spent precious moments looking upward.

The ship that hovered in the sky high above Fa'allen was lit up in a way that made her blink, trying to work out where the light source was from.

She guessed it was Bane, but she'd never seen his ship from the outside. It was shaped like a spiky ball, like a floating mine she'd seen in WWII films, or one of the spiky chocolates he'd found for her, and it illuminated the city like a bright, third moon.

She realized she was staring, wasting time, and slammed the door closed behind her, and then got her bearings.

She was standing on Karn's outstretched arms. At the far end, his hands were cupped, palms up.

She turned, looked up and back, and saw she stood under his fierce beak.

This was bad, she acknowledged.

There was nowhere to run and the door didn't lock.

She had trapped herself, not that she'd had much choice.

She refused to give up, though.

She walked backward, out a little further along the outstretched brushed metal of Karn's arms, listening to the shouting in the square below, and when she could see past the beak to the head, she aimed and shot between the statue's eyes.

She flew up moments before the door slammed open.

Silius stepped out onto the arms, and Havna followed him.

Lucy scrambled to get her footing on the top of the beak, and watched as they stared up at Bane, just like she had.

She heard Silius swear.

That meant they hadn't known Bane was there. He must have arrived while they were chasing her up the stairs.

She wondered what he was doing, but she had a good idea he was looking for her. The thought calmed her. Warmed her, even though the wind off the ocean was making her cheeks numb.

Now she was even higher on the statue, she could see out to the ocean, with the square below, full of people.

Both moons lit up the sky, and Bane contributed to the general brightness, so she could see the light reflected on the water, and the straight line of fog heading toward the city.

It looked like the first line of an attacking army, a steady, unwavering line of cloud.

Silius gave a shout below her, forcing her attention to him and Havna.

They stared up at her for a beat, and then started looking for ways to climb up to her.

She was truly trapped up here. She lifted a hand to her throat and her fingers tangled in the necklace around her neck.

Maybe the time had come to use them.

There was no harm in it, anyway.

She worked one off and it crumbled a little as she pulled it free. She hoped the damage she did to it wouldn't make a difference, and then she threw it down to the arms below.

It bounced—she heard the ping as it hit the metal—and then . . . nothing.

"Throwing pebbles at us isn't going to do you any good." Silius gave a laugh.

She ignored him, worked off another bead with a back and forth motion to get it free, trying to be more careful this time.

Bane had said it had to make forceful contact with a surface, before it would light up.

With luck, she could blind Silius and Havna, and have the added benefit of attracting Bane's attention with the light.

She walked out to the tip of the beak, looked down at where she wanted it to land, and threw again, putting everything behind the throw.

As she pitched it, Havna stepped into its path. It hit him, bounced off, and skittered along Karn's right arm and then was lost to her sight in the shadows.

She clenched her fists in frustration.

"Ow." Havna rubbed his shoulder. "What are you throwing?"

She crouched on the beak, using both hands to steady herself, and tried to look over the side of the statue. If the bead had hit the square below, surely that would give it enough force to light up?

She couldn't see anything, and the shouting and noise from below didn't change in pitch or volume that she could hear.

She shifted her focus back to Silius and Havna and saw Havna was still standing below, watching her, but she could hear the sound of Silius trying to find a way up to her on her left.

He gave a grunt of satisfaction as he finally got a foothold.

Aaand . . . once again she was out of time.

"Silius!" Havna's shout came as she was rising to her feet, wondering if she could swing down using the magnet cylinder just as Silius got to the top, although with Havna waiting below she didn't think she'd get far.

"What?"

"Fai just made contact to let us know the thinking system is going to destroy this statue if someone doesn't tell him where the Earth woman is by a certain time."

They were, all three of them, silent as they absorbed that.

Lucy sat down suddenly and started to laugh.

"See how funny you think it is when he follows through." Silius's snarl was worryingly close.

He was right. But having Silius and Havna have to choose between getting her or saving their own skin was some sweet kind of karma.

She reached back and untied the necklace and held it up toward the sky to try and see a little better in the dim light.

She was obviously doing something wrong. Maybe if she pulled the beads down the wire and off the end, rather than lifting them off?

"That thing's going to shoot us in less than ten minutes." Havna sounded panicked. "I can see a cannon protruding from its side. You do whatever you think you have to do, Silius, but I'm not staying."

She heard the creak of the door opening, and the hammer of boots on the stairs.

Silius swore, but he didn't leave.

Lucy pulled one, and then two, beads off the wire.

Even if she threw one down to the arms below, with Silius almost on top of her, it most likely wouldn't affect him.

She should rather use them to let Bane know where she was.

Because Havna was right. She saw a cannon now, where she could have sworn there wasn't one before.

She turned to look into Karn's carved, narrowed eyes, stepped closer, and threw two beads, one after the other, aiming at the center of each eye.

For a moment, nothing happened, but they did stick in place rather than fall off, and then, suddenly, light flared. She spun away, crouching down and pressing her face into her upper thighs as the world suddenly lit up around her like it was midday.

Silius cried out and she heard the sound of him losing his footing.

All she had to do was hope he fell all the way. And that Bane worked out who had turned Karn's statue into a lighthouse.

# CHAPTER 40

BANE HOVERED.

The feeling inside him to fly—didn't matter the direction—as fast as he could, and also to destroy everything in front of him, were at war with each other. Juggling both inclinations kept him from doing either, and lucky for the people of Fa'allen, it was taking all his power just to remain stationary so low in the atmosphere above them anyway.

He had lit himself up, both to show the incandescent rage within him, and to make sure every Tecran knew where he was and how big a threat he posed.

The outer shell of his Class 5 ship was covered in lenses, allowing him to see in every direction, and he was using them to project the image of a full and glowing Gyre, Tecra's biggest moon, over his ship.

From the reaction of the Tecran below, his idea had worked.

They stared up in a mix of awe, anger and fear.

The anger was most likely to do with his threat to destroy their most precious monument.

Sazo had once advised him not to use threats unless he meant to follow through. Anger had temporarily erased that advice from his mind.

He remembered it now, though.

And he didn't know whether he would truly destroy Karn's statue or not.

He knew what it meant to the people of Tecra.

He would alienate himself from all of them, even those who agreed that Lucy should not have been taken, and he should never have been enslaved.

But, did he care?

He thought about it, decided he didn't. Not one of them had come forward about Lucy and *someone* knew where she was.

The soldiers who'd taken her. The people in the crowd who must have seen them dragging her off.

But if he did destroy the statue, there would be debris. It would fall. And as he didn't know where Lucy was, it might just injure her.

That wasn't acceptable to him.

But now he'd made the threat, he would have to at least look as if he planned to follow through.

He extended a light cannon.

"Are you sure you want to do that?" He registered Dray's quiet question and focused one of his lenses down onto the square and picked up the Grihan commander.

Dray looked like he was in trouble.

He was moving through the crowd, shockgun raised, and most were giving him a wide berth, which told Bane he must have given them cause to be wary.

"I'm simply showing I'm willing to follow through."

"Will you?" Dray asked.

"I don't know."

"Well, you've given yourself less than ten minutes to decide." Dray's voice was grim.

Bane caught the flicker of shockgun fire, and realized Dray was shooting as he made his way to the center of the square. The Grihan commander had taken one of the shockguns from his armory the Tecran had developed to use against new aliens they found in their exploration of the galaxy. It was satisfying to Bane that it was being used against the Tecran now.

He watched Dray climb up onto the square central pedestal, and gave a few warning shots to get rid of anyone else who was standing there.

Bane found his way into the handheld of someone pointing it at Dray, and he threw the lens feed onto the big screen that overlooked the square.

"My name is Dray Helvan."

Bane took the audio feed from the closest handhelds, and transmitted it to every speaker, so everyone in the square could hear him.

Dray looked up as he realized what Bane had done, and then gave a nod.

"If you know where Lucy Harris is, the woman from Earth who was held in a facility just outside this city for months, tell me. Not because Bane is up there, threatening retribution, but because it's the right thing to do."

"Why do you think any of us know?" Someone in the crowd shouted out.

"Because she was grabbed just over an hour ago in this very square, and at least six Tecran soldiers were involved in her abduction. They, at the very least, know where she is. But some of you also had to have seen them."

There were murmurs from those in the crowd.

But they had calmed down, and it was the least antagonistic that Bane had seen them since the protests began.

Dray looked over at the countdown, which Bane had set below the lens feed of Dray on the screen. It showed two minutes to go.

"I think I might know where she is." A Tecran woman stepped out from the crowd, looking up at Dray.

"Where?" Bane asked before Dray could open his mouth.

"I think they took her into the base of Karn's statue."

Bane's first reaction was to reject her statement.

How convenient. A minute before he was set to destroy it, someone came up with a reason to stop him following through.

"You only think?" Dray asked. "You're not sure?"

"I saw people carrying someone. They dropped her, and I thought she looked strange. If it was the Earth woman, that would explain it. They took her into the shrine room at Karn's foot."

"Do you believe her?" Bane asked, his words just for Dray, this time.

"I think we should at least check it out."

"Agreed." He was about to erase the countdown from the screen, and Dray was walking to the edge of the platform to drop to the ground, when suddenly twin beams of light shot out of Karn's eyes.

People cried out.

Some of the protesters dropped to their knees, hands out in a mimic of Karn's request for the wind's blessings. Others stood, transfixed.

"Did you do that?" Dray asked, and Bane could hear the doubt in his voice.

"No," he answered, launching the drone from his Class 5 down toward the statue. "I think it's Lucy. I think she's in trouble."

As he said it, there was a flash from above him, on the left, and his Class 5 took a hit.

For a moment he reeled in shock.

He had never once, in all the time he'd been awake and aware, been hit.

And now he was.

He saw, immediately, that two Levron were closing in on him, one on either side, coming in fast.

He'd known they were close by, but they'd been in a holding pattern close to the planet since before he'd come out from his hiding place on Gyre.

They must have drifted closer as he'd kept his concentration on Fa'allen and finding Lucy.

They'd bested him.

He moved upward suddenly as the second Levron fired.

"Dray." He kept low, circling around the city.

"Yes?"

Bane rolled his Class 5, able to fly up in a way he had never been allowed to do when it contained Tecran crew.

"If I continue to stay low, they might miss and hit Fa'allen."

"Lead them away. I'll save Lucy."

Bane could hear Dray's breathing was deeper, guessed he was running.

"Yes." He accepted that was the only thing to do, and as he fired on the Levron, he wondered what the Tecran below thought of their own warships putting them in danger.

And how lucky they were that Lucy was down there with them, or he'd have been happy for the Levron to do their worst.

---

THE MILITARY HAD LOST its grip.

Dray looked up at the light show above, saw it was two of the three Levron that had been station near the *Urna* attacking Bane. He wondered if the third was too far away to participate, or just waiting in the wings to attack later.

The crowds didn't seem able to decide whether to keep their gaze on the lights shining from Karn's eyes, or the flicker of cannon fire above. They stood and stared, heads tilted up.

He forced himself to forget about the fight going on overhead, to leave that to Bane, because his only concern now was Lucy.

He dodged the protesters, moving as fast as he could, and with a spurt of speed, Cossi flanked him.

She'd been standing with her back against the dais in the square, having followed him when he'd broken ranks and run into the crowd, and now she followed him toward the base of Karn's statue.

"You don't make things easy, do you, Helvan?" she asked, her voice just slightly breathless as they ran.

He didn't apologize, he wasn't sorry, but he did appreciate her. "Thank you for having my back."

"More exciting this way," she said, and then stopped talking to concentrate on dodging the people in their way.

The hostility of the crowd seemed to have leaked away. They were confused. Frightened.

Everything they knew was being ripped apart.

"Anyone who looks like they're about to cause trouble," he said over the comms to the rest of the team, "arrest them. They're most likely rogue soldiers."

As they approached the door set into the folds of Karn's cloak, between his clawed feet, a Tecran burst out of it. He looked around, as if expecting to see someone, and Dray fired on him, the setting low.

He heard Cossi swear softly in appreciation, but he didn't have time to banter with her.

The Tecran stood, still upright but dazed, and Dray shoved him up against the side of the statue. "Where about inside are you keeping Lucy?"

He blinked at Dray for a moment, then shook his head in a delicate shudder. "She's not inside anymore. She's up there." He pointed upward at an angle, and Dray lifted his head.

"On the arms?"

"On the beak, last I saw." The soldier coughed. "But Silius is after her, and I don't think he's stopping until he throws her off."

Dray shoved him at Cossi and ran backward, his gaze searching the top of the statue. It was hard to see much when the light from the eyes was so blinding, but he thought he could just make out a shadow crouched on the beak, and a figure climbing toward her.

Silius.

The Tecran soldier would reach her in seconds. In less time than it would take Dray to make it to the door at the bottom of the statue.

He was too late to save her, again.

# CHAPTER 41

"I KNEW the battleship commanders wouldn't fail us." Silius's words were tight with discomfort but full of pride, underscoring the scrabble he made as he continued to climb.

Lucy guessed he was having to do it with his eyes closed, or nearly closed, given how long it was taking him.

"Because they're shooting at Bane? They're lucky they haven't hit Fa'allen."

He gave an ugly laugh. "Half of Fa'allen would call them traitors, so no loss there."

"What do you plan to do when you finally get up here with me?"

She knew, she just wanted to have confirmation.

"Toss you off. I'd rather you not be around to talk about how long we had you and how badly you were treated, even though I know we're going to win this. The UC might be more difficult to negotiate with if you're around to blab."

The scientists at the facility hadn't actually treated her that badly. Lucy had long had a suspicion they exaggerated the cruelty of the experiments they were conducting.

It was sad that they thought the military would approve more if she was harmed.

"The Tecran military really has lost its way, haven't they?" She tried to see if Bane was in trouble above, but the lights shining from Karn's eyes made it difficult to even make out how many Tecran battleships were attacking him.

She heard Silius make a sound of disgust. It sounded a lot closer than before.

She took out the pen again, opened her eyes to narrowed slits to see a little, and realized that she would have to aim as far down the arms as she could, because just landing below the beak was as easy for Silius as it would be for her. She didn't even need the pen for that.

Another sound came from her left and she bent her head and opened her eyes a little more, saw Silius's hand reach up for a handhold.

She pointed the pen toward Karn's fingers, and engaged.

Her sight was too limited to work out where the magnet had attached, and as Silius pulled his head up in line with her feet, she was yanked off her perch.

The metal arms seemed to rise up at her, and she twisted onto her back so that when she hit, it wasn't face first.

She felt the air slam out of her lungs and then she was sliding to the right, flying off the edge of Karn's sleeve into space. She screamed as she swung out past the hands held out in supplication like she was on a crazy fairground ride, and then she was hauled up, so she was pressed against the knuckle of Karn's right thumb.

She coughed and gasped, trying to breathe, a roaring in her ears. It masked the sound of Silius who was suddenly above her, reaching down to haul her up.

He had trouble with it, letting go and then trying again as she hung, shivering, miserable at being so high.

He swore viciously, and seemed to finally get a good hold.

"I see your ships are losing to Bane," she called up to him, saying the first thing that occurred to her that would make him stop, even for a moment, and look elsewhere.

Silius stopped pulling at the cable and she swung gently as he released it.

She could just make out where he crouched on one knee above her.

He said nothing, and she blinked back tears of relief because maybe her guess had been right. She was sure he'd take pleasure in correcting her if she wasn't.

"Maybe they are, maybe not," he said at last. "Hard to see from here with those lights you set in Karn's eyes. But if I can't see properly, neither can you. You're just delaying the inevitable."

She tried to look up, realized he was right about the visibility, and then looked down, instead. She was directly above the square, she realized. She heard a faint whine, and tilted her head up. Silius stood above her, pulling his shockgun from his holster.

He would shoot her. He didn't even have to pull her up. If he aimed directly at her head, she'd die. She didn't doubt that for a moment.

She thought she heard her name being shouted from below, and looked down again.

Dray?

She hoped so.

Silius raised his shockgun, and she ran her finger down the side of the pen.

She dropped as shockgun fire seared the air above her head.

It felt as if her stomach was left behind in Karn's hands, an offering to the gods, as she plummeted down.

She wanted to scream, but the sound caught in her throat and choked her.

Another flicker of purple shot past her, and she drew her arms and legs together, trying to make herself a smaller target, and then there was a flicker coming up from below and even with the wind roaring past her, she heard Silius scream.

She ran out of cable about twenty meters from the ground.

Her descent was slowed, so she wasn't wrenched back up when it came to a sudden end, and she ended up twisting gently and continuously, a worm on the end of a line.

"Lucy."

She looked down, and there was Dray.

She tried to answer, but her throat was still tight and nothing would come out.

She fluttered her fingers at him, and then, like everyone else, looked up with a jerk at the massive boom that reverberated over the city, rolling like a long growl of thunder.

She stared in shock, and when her momentum twisted her away from the view, back toward the statue, she closed her eyes and tried to steel herself in case it was Bane.

She turned again, just in time to see another bright exchange of cannon fire, and clasped her hands in relief as she saw Bane moving, graceful and smooth as a ballet dancer, as he twisted and rolled and curved away from the remaining Tecran battleship.

He fired, and the shot seemed to clip the Tecran ship. It spun away, and then went still.

Bane moved to hover over it.

The crowd gasped and she heard the words 'surrender' from below.

Did they think Bane wouldn't accept the battleship's surrender?

Suddenly another ship was there, and for a moment she braced herself for another attack, but it seemed to almost nudge Bane aside, and he slowly drifted away from his downed prey.

Maybe that was the ship Dray and the rest of the UC had come to Tecra on. The *Urna*.

A buzzing noise swamped her senses, crowding out the noise

from below, and then the drone Bane had sent to rescue her at the cliffs descended in front of her.

She started shaking with relief as it moved beneath her, and when she was able to crouch down on it safely, she carefully released the magnet.

The drone sank down slowly, and when it touched the ground she slid off the side into Dray's waiting arms.

He caught her, lowered her down, and angled his body as if to shield her.

She looked past him, to the backs of the UC soldiers standing guard in a semi-circle in front of them, and then the crowd beyond.

The Tecran were watching her, now the battle above was over, and she touched Dray's chest with a hand, stepping forward, and he let her move in front of him.

She looked at the people in the crowd, her hair blowing in the eternal, icy wind, her face visible for all to see.

She could see the shock and guilt on their faces as they looked back.

The fog, that wall of white and gray that she'd spotted from the top of the statue, chose that moment to hit.

It rolled through the square, gobbling up the crowds until all Lucy could see was the backs of the UC soldiers in front of her, and Dray beside her.

"I thought he was going to kill you." Dray's voice was hoarse, as if he'd been shouting for hours.

"He *was* going to kill me." She leaned into him, suddenly sure he needed the comfort of it as much as she did.

He shuddered, pulling her closer. "I knew I couldn't get up the stairs in time."

"You shot him from below." She had only remembered the massive shockgun he'd taken from Bane's stores when she'd heard Silius scream.

"Yes. Someone will have to go up there and see if he's still alive."

"Not you or me." She burrowed in closer as the fog deposited cold drops of dew on her cheeks and eyelashes.

"No. We're done here."

She felt her heart lift, and she smiled against the rough skin of his neck. "You say the nicest things."

He went still, and then started to chuckle.

He was still laughing as he pulled her away from the drone, to which he gave a friendly pat, and then he walked with her into the deep white of the fog.

# CHAPTER 42

"LUCY HARRIS."

The woman who greeted Lucy as she stepped into the massive UC battleship smiled as she walked forward, arms open, and Lucy had to check herself so she didn't flinch at the sight of the sharp row of teeth on display.

She stood still, and was grateful for Dray's hand as it settled on the small of her back.

"Lucy, this is Ambassador Filivantri Dimitara. She's a friend of Rose McKenzie's and the leader of our mission to Tecra."

The ambassador flung her arms around Lucy, and Lucy tentatively hugged her back.

"You only speak Tecran?" Dimitara stepped back with a frown, giving Dray a quick look.

"Yes." Lucy had made a decision not to apologize for anything that had been done to her, and so she met the ambassador's gaze without wavering.

"Of course not. Why would they teach you anything else?" Dimitara shook her head. Her Tecran was fluent, but that was to be expected of the head of a diplomatic mission to Tecra.

"I didn't even know about the other members of the UC until a few days ago." Lucy looked around at the room Dray had brought her to, a massive space with a long, wide window, showing a cloud-covered Tecra, lit orange, red and pink by its sun, below.

"I know you're tired, and have spent much of the night imprisoned and fighting for your life, but it would help me get the assistance I need from the United Council if you could detail what has happened to you immediately. The full council is sitting, waiting to hear from you, and the military leaders of all members except the Tecran will be in attendance, as well."

Lucy hesitated. She had dozed on the way up from Fa'allen to the *Urna* but every muscle seemed to hurt. The jump from Karn's beak to his outstretched arms had been particularly unforgiving. If she could, she'd have found a hot shower and a bed to sleep in, but that wasn't an option right now.

Bane had been against her stepping onto the UC ship, even with Dray promising to never leave her side, but he had eventually conceded the value of her being physically seen by the other UC teams.

She wanted them to know she was real. That she took up space. That she was present.

"They'll ask you to sing," Bane had warned her. "Well, the Grih will."

"So it's not just Dray who has the fetish?" she'd asked when Bane had grumpily mentioned it on the way up to the *Urna*. She'd looked sideways at Dray, and had suddenly had his total attention.

"Singing," she said to him, switching to Tecran, then smiled at the flare of lust in his gaze. "It's not just you, Bane says."

He'd given a crooked grin.

"No, it's all of us. But I'm happy for you to disappoint everyone else but me."

His words had made her heart trip and she lifted a fist now to rub her sternum in memory of it.

"Are you all right?" Dimitara was looking at her with a worried frown, and Lucy realized she'd spaced out, letting her thoughts intrude when she should have all her wits about her.

She tried hard not to look at Dray. To not give herself away.

She didn't mind if he knew she was gone over him, but she didn't know these people, barely trusted them. They didn't get to see her vulnerability.

"I think I need some grinabo." She gave an apologetic shrug. "And then I'd like to get this conference over with."

Dimitara snapped something in a strange language Lucy guessed must be Bukarian to an aide standing behind her and then hooked an arm through Lucy's and led her to the comms room.

Dray followed, gaze sweeping from side to side, looking for threats, and out of the corner of her eye she saw two others flank him. Cossi, the Bukarian military leader she'd met briefly in Fa'allen, and a stranger—she blinked and made her face carefully blank as she caught a glimpse of slim, insectile limbs.

She was not in Kansas anymore.

She'd known that since she'd woken in the Tecran facility, but this new world was even bigger and more interesting than she'd ever thought. She'd seen a few of the Fitali when Dray had taken her into the military headquarters, but this was the first time she'd been so close to one.

She noticed people milling in front of the comms room, and among them was another group of aliens she hadn't encountered yet. They stood about the same height as her, and had bulging foreheads and stocky frames. The Garmman, she guessed. She'd been told about them, heard them mentioned when she was waiting for Dray to wrap things up below. Dray hadn't outright said he didn't trust them, but she'd picked up that impression.

The group blocking the entrance consisted of two Grih, two Fitali, a Bukarian, three Garmman and a single Tecran.

Dimitara had obviously not expected them, because Lucy felt her hand tighten on Lucy's arm.

"Ambassador." A Fitalian in long robes stepped forward.

"Pilto." Dimitara gave a nod. "I wasn't expecting the leadership team to be present for this." She spoke in Tecran, and Lucy felt a sudden, deep appreciation for the Bukarian ambassador. She was forcing everything to be said in a language Lucy could understand.

"It makes sense, though." Pilto's gaze was on Lucy, and she forced herself not to react to the intensity of his stare. His eyes were massive in his face and a deep, bottomless black. "Our whole mission is compromised by the presence of the Earth woman."

Perhaps she was overly sensitive, but to Lucy, it sounded as if he was making this her fault.

"I think the Tecran did that all on their own," she said.

Pilto stilled, and then gave an elegant half-bow. "So they did. Still, we need to be here if the council decides to renegotiate the terms of the agreement in light of . . ." he glanced at Lucy, "all that has happened."

"We'll need corroborating testimony, as well." One of the Garmman spoke for the first time, his Tecran perfect. "Who's to say she wasn't brought here by the thinking system to cause trouble?"

There was utter silence at that comment for a single beat, and then a babble of voices rose up, almost none talking in a language Lucy could understand.

She understood what was going on, though.

She stared at the Garmman. Held his gaze, and he began to twitch a little under the pressure.

"Silence." Dray's shout cut them off. His gaze went up to the corner of the ceiling, a move that had Lucy guessing Bane was speaking to him. She was sorry they hadn't had time to get a new earpiece for her from the Class 5 before they'd come to the *Urna*.

When Dray moved his gaze back to the crowd in front of them, he sounded calmer, but there was a definite edge to his voice.

"One of the scientists who experimented on Lucy in the facility is being held at a safehouse and has agreed to testify. She's given us access to the visual comms of some of the interactions in the facility with Lucy. Also, a few of the soldiers who guarded her there are willing to give evidence." Dray cocked his head even further. "Is that enough for you, Ambassador Cynoa? We also have two guards in custody who tried to kill her on the military's orders, but they are hostile witnesses at best."

Cynoa didn't look like it was enough for him at all, but eventually he gave a nod, his gaze flicking back to Lucy's face. He'd done that ever since she'd laid eyes on him.

"If you could give way." Dimitara stepped forward, her gaze going to each face in turn and they shuffled to the side.

Dimitara led her in, and Lucy noticed most of the group followed them, standing back against the walls as if that would make them less visible.

The two Grih in the crowd were the exception. They were the last into the room, and they joined Dray to stand beside her.

"I'm Yolandi Firena, Grih's ambassador on this mission, and I want to extend a welcome to you on behalf of the Grih. You will find a home with us, if that is your wish." The woman who spoke was not as tall as Dray, but taller than Lucy, and she wore robes of the most beautiful burnt umber. She had the same hair as Dray, shortish and standing straight up, but hers was a light brown, tipped with blonde, in contrast to the dark brown of her skin. She gave Lucy a formal bow.

"Thank you, Ambassador." Lucy lifted her hands, unsure whether to offer to shake and then started as the second Grihan woman took a cup of grinabo brought by Ambassador Dimitara's aide and held it out to her.

"I'm Zutobi, the head of operations for the Grihan team. I second the welcome from Yolandi, but I can see Dray has already made our welcome clear." The words were said seriously, but Lucy detected a hint of amusement in the woman's eyes.

Lucy looked between Zutobi and Dray, not sure if the woman was being sarcastic or teasing.

"That's right, I have." Dray seemed completely unaffected, and Zutobi grinned.

". . . what is going on!" The thunder in the voice of the Bukarian who was suddenly on the screen in the middle of the room focused every eye.

Lucy turned with everyone else and saw what looked like a circular chamber with an elevated chair in the center and two chairs slightly below it on either side.

The Bukarian was sitting in the central seat and a Grih, a Fitalian, a Garmman and a Tecran each sat on the chairs on either side of him.

"Councilor." Dimitara stepped closer. "The situation in Tecra has taken a surprising turn."

Beside her, Lucy heard Dray give a snort and saw Zutobi grin.

"Such as?"

"Such as the discovery of another Earth woman on the planet." Dimitara reached back, got a grip on Lucy's arm, and pulled her forward, so she was standing alone with Dimitara out in what felt like the open, encircled by the small crowd that had accompanied them into the comms room.

She shifted uncomfortably.

The councilor visibly gaped.

"What do you say to this, Ulain?" His gaze went directly to the Tecran seated beside him.

The Tecran stood, eyes wide, opened her mouth, but nothing emerged.

"That is not all," Dimitara said. "The Tecran military hatched a plot to disrupt our takeover of their systems when we arrived, engineered a riot, and then two of their Levron attacked Bane, the Class 5 who accompanied us."

The shout that went up in the chamber as soon as she stopped speaking was not unlike the shout when Cynoa had accused Lucy of lying, and Dimitara simply turned down the sound to wait it out.

"What about the other three Levron?" The Tecran councilor looked sick.

"Two were sent to patrol your space boundaries. I don't know the whereabouts of the third one." Dray stepped forward to answer.

"We're unsure if it was put in reserve to prevent damage, so they had a least one fully operational battleship nearby, or whether the captain of that Levron refused to go along with the plan to attack the United Council, and so has put the ship out of range." Cossi stepped up beside Dray.

"What do you say, Chep?" The Fitalian councilor rose as well, and the Fitalian who flanked Dray stepped forward with a low, elegant bow.

"Everything spoken is correct. Some I've witnessed with my own eyes. We may still have a problem with the third ship, but there is nowhere for it to go, no ally for it to turn to." He glanced at the Garmman ambassador, Cynoa. "That we know of."

The glance did not go unnoticed.

"Do you wish to accuse me of something?" Cynoa's voice was cold.

Lucy had noticed Dimitara stiffen and go very still while Chep had been talking, her head down, looking at the floor, as if she was being briefed and needed to cut out all other distractions, but when Cynoa issued his challenge, she raised her head, and Lucy could see fire in her eyes.

"You have kept very much to yourselves since our arrival, Ambassador Cynoa. Not a single member of your team assisted in trying to get the protests in Fa'allen under control. We've invited you to help with the decision-making process over and over again, and you have never once attended. It's almost as if you're trying to play it both ways. Fence straddling will only get you a sore ass." Dimitara's every word was spoken clearly and in a carrying tone.

There were snorts of laughter, of disbelief, at that, and even Lucy found herself fighting a smile.

"I object—" Cynoa's eyes narrowed.

"Go ahead. It will be the most strenuous thing you've done since you joined this mission," Dimitara said.

Everyone in the room was staring at Dimitara as if she'd somehow lost her mind, but there was also no disapproval in anyone's expression, except the councilors visible on the screen.

"Is there a reason you are verbally attacking one of our allies?" The Bukarian councilor asked, his tone sharp.

"Yes." Dimitara turned to him and the smile she gave told Lucy to never, ever underestimate a Bukarian. Those teeth were for rending.

"Bane has been helping our security team monitor all comms from the *Urna*, and it turns out that Ambassador Cynoa here has been in clandestine contact with the Tecran military since before we arrived, and that ten minutes ago, some of the Garmman military team tried to release the head of the Tecran military from the holding cell where he was being kept."

Lucy could tell from the stillness behind her from Dray, Cossi, and Chep that this was stunning news to them.

"You had Tecran Defense Leader, Suu Ulima, in custody?" The Tecran councilor leaned back against her chair in outrage.

"Yes." Cossi took the question, smiling in the same predatory way as Dimitara. "After he abducted Ambassador Dimitara and tried to torture her into revealing the whereabouts of the Earth woman so that his teams could kill her, I took him down myself."

The Bukarian head of the United Council leaned against his chair and lifted a hand to his forehead.

"Did the Garmman succeed in freeing Ulima?" Dray asked.

"No." Dimitara gave Cynoa a side-long glance. "Given how poorly they'd integrated into the rest of the teams, no one trusted the Garmman enough, and before they released Ulima they sought confirmation. Surprisingly, the Garmman involved took that as a signal to disappear."

"I see that saying things took a surprising turn with your mission was a slight understatement, Ambassador Dimitara." The Bukarian councilor finally lowered himself into his seat. "What next?"

At that moment a Grihan officer ran into the room, gaze fixed on Dray.

"Sir." He pointed out of the door, his expression panicked.

"What is it?" Dray turned sharply.

"Two Class 5s just entered the solar system."

# CHAPTER 43

"YOU MIGHT HAVE TOLD me you'd called Sazo and Oris as back-up." Dray hadn't stopped grumbling about being taken by surprise.

"They had to light-jump here numerous times and I couldn't predict when they'd arrive. It seemed better to keep quiet about it." Bane sounded distracted, and Lucy guessed he was probably talking at high speed to his newly-arrived friends.

She didn't care about the how or when. She was just excited to meet Rose McKenzie and Imogen Peters.

The newly arrived Class 5s had chosen to encircle Tecra with Bane, so at least one could be seen from every point on the planet below. Rose and Imogen had left their ships on drones and were on their way to Bane.

"There they are." Lucy stood on the bridge, which was redundant now that Bane was in control of himself, but which had a huge screen that allowed a wonderful view.

She watched two drones moving toward them and smiled when Dray came up behind her, pulling her gently back against him, his hands on her shoulders.

"What will happen now?"

"I honestly don't know." He let his hands run down her arms and rest on her stomach.

"Will you get into trouble for choosing to come with me, rather than stay on the *Urna*?" Ever since Zutobi's lighthearted remark, she'd realized there may be consequences for Dray for his relationship with her.

"I don't think so, but we can ask Dav Jallan and Camlar Kalor what happened to their careers when they got involved with Rose and Imogen."

Lucy twisted back to look at him, saw he seemed extremely unconcerned. "Rose and Imogen are in relationships with them?"

He gave a nod. "So I hear."

"And Fiona Russell?"

"I believe Captain Hal Vakeri is still captain of his own battleship, even though he's clearly involved with the new, Earth-born operations chief of the Larga Ways way station. It hasn't seemed to have caused him any trouble."

"That's good." She pulled away from him, turned to face him. "You'd tell me, though? If it starts affecting you? I understand the military has been your life—" She stumbled to a stop, unsure where she was going with this.

"It has been. Up until now." He was looking at her so steadily, so sure and confident, and she stared back, worrying her bottom lip with her teeth.

"I don't want anything bad to happen to you because of me."

"Like—?" He tilted his head in that alien way of his.

"I don't know. You get demoted or something. Or kicked out."

His gaze suddenly sharpened, seemed to pierce every protective layer she had. "What's this really about, Lucy? Are you worried I can't keep you safe?"

"She has me for that." Bane's voice made her flinch, a reminder this wasn't a private conversation.

Then she took a deep breath, and met Dray's gaze. "I'm not

bad at keeping myself safe, but yes, I have Bane, and he's pretty kick-ass."

"You also have me."

She blew out a long breath. "I know. I . . . it's just that things aren't the same as they were. We won't be forced together anymore. From here on, every moment we spend together is because we want to. I didn't want you to feel . . ." She lifted her hands, suddenly out of her depth.

"Feel that I have to keep seeing you?" He grinned. "When have I ever given you the impression for even a second that being with you has been anything but exactly where I want to be?"

She slowly matched his grin. Lifted a shoulder. "I don't know. There were a few moments when you were trying to get me down that cliff—"

He leaned forward and shut her up with a kiss.

Someone cleared their throat delicately behind them, and Lucy drew back and saw four people standing just inside the doorway.

The sight of Rose and Imogen struck her harder than she expected.

She took a step forward and then hiccuped. The tears started to fall before she managed a second step.

Crying for everything she knew she'd lost. Because it was finally real. The knowledge she was never going back again.

———

"I scared the Grih off." Lucy wiped away the last of her tears.

Dray had put a hand on her shoulder when she'd started crying, but when Rose and Imogen had stepped forward and thrown their arms around her, he'd motioned to the two other men and left her to get to know her new friends.

"Are you and Commander Helvan . . ." Rose moved her index finger from side to side.

Lucy gave an unwilling snort. "What is that supposed to mean?"

Rose raised a brow, and Lucy gave a sigh and leaned back against the couch in the officers' mess.

"Yes."

"I'm glad." Imogen's voice was soft. "We've lost so much, it's good to be able to build something new."

"Not all the new is bad," Lucy agreed. She reached forward to grab the box she'd put on the table earlier in readiness for her guests and offered them each a spiky chocolate hailstone.

"Mmm." Rose bit into the chocolate and then turned wide eyes up to the camera in the corner of the room. "You had this the whole time I was onboard saving your behind, and you didn't give me any? Thanks a lot, Bane!"

"I didn't know the components of chocolate at the time, or that it was something you valued—" His flustered response died off. "Sazo says you're teasing me."

She grinned. "Yes."

"Oh." He sounded thoughtful.

"So what is going to happen next?" Lucy had tucked herself into the corner of the couch, and tried to relax her hands on her thighs. She was grateful Dray had taken Rose and Imogen's tall, stern-faced lovers off somewhere, not just so they wouldn't see her crying, but also so she didn't feel rude speaking in English.

She could only make conversation with them in Tecran, and she had the feeling neither spoke it well.

"First thing that'll happen is the UC will have to decide if there are going to be more penalties for the Tecran. There'll be a hearing and you'll most likely be the star witness. I had to go through one." Imogen moved a little closer to her, and touched her shoulder. "It wasn't too bad."

"I had to go through one as well." Rose licked her fingers. "Things have changed since my one. They don't call us oranges anymore. Or not to our faces, and I think most of them have realized we aren't some backward, dumb version of the Grih."

"Backward, dumb, *short* version of the Grih," Imogen said.

Lucy started to relax into the sense of solidarity she was starting to feel. "The Tecran treated me like a clever pet," she admitted.

Imogen pointed a finger at her. "Me, too. I was in an actual cage for awhile."

"What?" Lucy had thought of her time in the facility as bad, but she hadn't been in a cage.

"I was caged as well," Rose told her. "In the hold of Sazo's Class 5. And Fiona was held as a slave on a Garmman trader."

"So I had it relatively easy." She leaned back, looking between the two women.

"You were held longer than we were. And Sazo said Paxe, the Class 5 involved in your abduction from Earth, tried to kill you. That's why they brought you to Tecra. To keep you safe from him." Imogen tapped her fingers on her knee. "Paxe tried to kill me, too, at first. In the end, though, he was really sorry about it. He told the others about you, so they could look for you and rescue you."

"I wouldn't be here without Bane." Lucy glanced at the camera in the corner. "They'd have taken me in the square just before I met Dray, and no one would have been any the wiser."

"Well done, Bane." Rose stretched out on her couch.

"It was my pleasure," Bane said. "And also satisfying to block their every move."

Rose laughed. "I hear you threatened to blow up their statue."

"If it hadn't put Lucy in danger, I would have." There was no hint of remorse in Bane's tone.

"Even though you protected the city from cannon fire when

the Levron were shooting at you?" Lucy leaned forward on her elbows, surprised.

"I only chose to draw the Levron fire away from the city because they could just as easily have hit you as anyone else."

Lucy stood, suddenly blinking back tears again. "Thank you, Bane. Really. You risked yourself for me, and I want you to know how much I appreciate it."

He was silent a moment. "I would do it again without regret."

She couldn't respond, her throat was too tight, so she simply nodded and sat again.

Imogen must have gone to fetch grinabo, because she suddenly had a steaming cup thrust at her, and she took a grateful gulp.

"Aside from the hearing, what can I expect, though?" She set the cup down and worried the fabric of her pants, pinching it between her thumb and forefinger, letting it go, pinching it again. "Is there a way back home? What happens to me if there isn't?"

"Sazo destroyed all the maps to Earth so the Tecran couldn't go back there." Rose leaned forward, her expression serious. "There is a way he can retrieve them, but Imogen, Fiona and I have made the decision that there is no going back. We don't want anyone with bad intentions finding Earth, and there are still traitors among the Grih who supported the Tecran, as well as the Garmman and even a small clique in the Fitalian empire who have revealed ties to what was happening with the Class 5 project."

"So there is no group we can trust?"

"We can trust the Bukari, the Fitali and most especially the Grih, but there is always the chance of one or two corrupt individuals. We decided not to take the chance. Now we need to include you in the decision."

Lucy had already shed her tears, made her peace, so she gave a slow nod to Rose and then Imogen. "I agree with you."

They nodded back.

"The UC have paid each of us compensation for the loss of our former lives on Earth. None of us have to work again. But Fiona is now running a major way station, and Rose and Sazo accompany Dav on his exploration missions." Imogen tucked her feet under her on the couch. "I'm working as a singer. A music maker, the Grih call it. Camlar is stationed at UC headquarters on Bukari, and I live with him, and I'm slowly getting the Grih used to the idea of listening to music through visual comms. It was considered scandalous at first, they only ever considered listening to music live before. Although I've done two live performances as well."

"If you like singing and want to do it, the Grih will literally fall all over themselves to welcome you wherever you decide to settle," Rose said.

"The singing thing." Lucy lifted her hands, happy to move on to lighter topics. "What is with the singing thing?"

Rose and Imogen looked at each other for a moment, and then started to laugh.

# ABOUT THE AUTHOR

Michelle Diener is an award winning author of historical fiction, science fiction and fantasy romance.

Michelle was born in London and currently lives in Australia with her husband and children.

You can contact Michelle through her website or sign up to receive notification when she has a new book out on her New Release Notification page.

*Connect with Michelle*
www.michellediener.com

# ALSO BY MICHELLE DIENER

## SCIENCE FICTION NOVELS

*Verdant String series:*

Interference & Insurgency (Two Novellas of the Verdant String: Box set)

Breakaway

Breakeven

Trailblazer

High Flyer

Wave Rider

Enthraller

*Sky Raiders series:*

Intended (Prequel to Sky Raiders: Exclusive to VIP Newsletter Members)

Sky Raiders

Calling the Change

Shadow Warrior

*Class 5 series:*

Dark Horse

Dark Deeds

Dark Minds

Dark Matters

Dark Ambitions: A Class 5 Novella

Dark Class

Collision Course

---

## HISTORICAL FICTION NOVELS

*The Traffic Warden Mysteries*

Ticket Out

*Susanna Horenbout and John Parker series:*

In a Treacherous Court

Keeper of the King's Secrets

In Defense of the Queen

*Regency London series:*

The Emperor's Conspiracy

Banquet of Lies

A Dangerous Madness

---

## FANTASY NOVELS BY MICHELLE DIENER

*The Rising Wave series:*

The Rising Wave

The Turncoat King

The Threadbare Queen

Fate's Arrow

Truth's Blade

Mistress of the Wind

*The Dark Forest series:*

The Golden Apple

The Silver Pear

To receive notification when a new book is released, sign up at
www.michellediener.com.

# ACKNOWLEDGMENTS

Thanks to Creative Paramita for the wonderful cover. And to Edie, Justin and Jo, thank you for your eagle eyes.

www.ingramcontent.com/pod-product-compliance
Lightning Source LLC
Chambersburg PA
CBHW030528120726

47904CB00005B/1671